# Nosferatu
## A Symphony of Horror

# Nosferatu
## A Symphony of Horror

A NOVEL

Adapted By

# Jonathan Miller

MAPLE & QUILL PUBLISHERS LLC
JANESVILLE, USA

**Nosferatu: A Symphony of Horror**
Adapted by Jonathan Miller

This novel is an adaptation of the 1922 silent film *Nosferatu: A Symphony of Horror*, directed by F.W. Murnau and produced by Prana Film. As the original film is in the public domain, this work is a creative reinterpretation and homage to its story, themes, and legacy. The characters, settings, and plot have been expanded and reimagined to provide a deeper narrative experience.

The events and characters in this book are fictitious. Any similarity to actual persons, living or dead, is purely coincidental.

First Edition

January 2025

ISBN: 9798308386643

© 2025 Maple and Quill Publishers LLC

All rights reserved. No part of this book may be reproduced or transmitted in any form or by any means, electronic or mechanical, including photocopying, recording, or by any information storage and retrieval system, without permission in writing from the publisher, except for the inclusion of brief quotations in a review.

Published by Maple and Quill Publishers LLC
P.O. Box 421
Janesville, Wisconsin 53547

For information regarding this, or other Maple and Quill titles, contact Info@MapleAndQuill.com

Printed in the United States of America

For Rachel,

whose unwavering love and support illuminate even the darkest shadows.

For my children,

whose boundless curiosity and joy remind me that even in a world of fear, there is always light.

And for those who carry stories in their hearts,

this is for you—may you always find the courage to step into the shadows and discover what lies beyond

# Nosferatu
## A Symphony of Horror

# Author's Foreword
## The Haunting Legacy of Nosferatu

There are some films that transcend their time, leaving an indelible mark on the cultural psyche. Among them stands Nosferatu, a silent specter that emerged from the shadows of 1922 and has lingered in the minds of audiences ever since. Directed by F.W. Murnau and released during the golden age of German Expressionism, Nosferatu: A Symphony of Horror is not merely a film—it is an atmosphere, a feeling, a harrowing descent into the gothic unknown. Its legacy is not just as a story of a vampire but as a work of cinematic art that forever redefined what horror could mean.

Nearly a century after its creation, the film retains its haunting allure. Unlike the polished portrayals of vampires that would follow in later decades, Nosferatu is raw and primal, its central figure, Count Orlok, grotesque and alien. Where Dracula might seduce, Orlok terrifies. With his gaunt, rodent-like appearance, elongated fingers, and predatory gaze, Orlok does not merely drink blood—he embodies death itself. There is no romantic allure here, only the creeping inevitability of decay and despair.

But Nosferatu is more than its monster. It is a film that speaks to universal fears—the fear of the unknown, the fear of disease, and the fear of the darkness that lurks just beyond the edges of our understanding. It is a story of shadow and light, both literally and metaphorically, capturing the fragility of human life against forces far beyond its control. These fears, so vividly portrayed on the screen, remain as potent today as they were a century ago, ensuring that Nosferatu endures not only as a piece of cinema but as a cultural touchstone.

What makes Nosferatu truly remarkable is that it almost didn't survive. Born from controversy and nearly lost to history, the film's very existence is a testament to the resilience of art. Though it was an unauthorized adaptation of Bram Stoker's Dracula, leading to a legal battle that ordered all copies destroyed, Nosferatu defied annihilation. A handful of prints survived, scattered like ashes across Europe, and from these fragments, the film was resurrected, taking on a near-mythic quality.

For all its struggles, Nosferatu has achieved immortality, much like the creature it depicts. It is a work that has inspired countless filmmakers, from Alfred Hitchcock to Werner Herzog, and has become a cornerstone of both the horror genre and the broader language of cinema. Its shadow looms large over the cultural landscape, a reminder that some stories, no matter how fragile or fleeting, refuse to fade away.

F.W. Murnau's Nosferatu is a masterpiece of silent cinema, but its very nature as a visual medium imposes certain limitations. Silent films, constrained by runtime and the absence of spoken dialogue, must rely heavily on imagery and minimal intertitles to convey their story. While this approach creates a haunting, almost dreamlike quality, it leaves much of the narrative and its characters' inner lives unexplored. The film tells its tale through broad strokes, hinting at motivations and emotions rather than diving into them fully. For a modern audience accustomed to richly detailed novels, the opportunity to expand on these elements is irresistible.

When I first set out to adapt Nosferatu into a novel, it felt less like a choice and more like an obligation—an act of devotion to a work of art that has haunted me for years. The film is undeniably a masterpiece, a cornerstone of cinematic horror, but it is also a silent enigma. So much of its story is left unsaid, its characters' thoughts and fears buried beneath shadows. I couldn't help but wonder: what if we could hear their voices? What if we could step into their minds and feel their struggles, their dread, their courage? Writing this novel was my way of answering those questions.

Ultimately, expanding the narrative was about creating a deeper, richer world for the story to inhabit. The film Nosferatu leaves so much to the imagination—its silent format and minimalist storytelling invite the viewer to fill in the gaps. But as a writer, I wanted to step into those gaps and explore what lies within. What does the forest smell like as Hutter rides through it, the trees dark and foreboding? What does Ellen hear in the silence of her home as she waits for news of her husband? What thoughts run through Orlok's mind as he watches Wisborg from the shadows?

This novel is not just an adaptation; it is an expansion, a reimagining, a love letter to a film that has haunted audiences for nearly a century. It is my way of stepping into the shadows, not to banish them but to understand them. Because, after all, isn't that what horror is about? Not just facing our fears, but embracing them, exploring them, and finding the humanity hidden within the darkness. When adapting Nosferatu into a novel, one of my greatest priorities was to preserve the haunting, gothic atmosphere that makes the film so unforgettable. From its foreboding castle to its eerie shadows creeping across moonlit walls, Nosferatu is steeped in a sense of dread and beauty that is uniquely cinematic.

My challenge as a writer was to translate these visuals into prose—

capturing not just the look of the film but its feel, its essence, its oppressive weight. The novel needed to immerse readers fully in this world, allowing them to experience its darkness and decay in ways that only language can achieve.

Furthermore, one of the most enduring aspects of Nosferatu is its ability to evoke the fear of the unknown. Orlok himself embodies this fear—he is grotesque, unnatural, and otherworldly, a being who defies the rules of the natural world. His presence is unsettling not just because of what he does but because of what he represents: the incomprehensible, the alien, the shadow that lurks at the edge of human understanding.

In my retelling, I sought to expand on this theme by exploring how each character experiences the unknown in their own way. For Hutter, it is the gradual realization that the world is far more dangerous and mysterious than he ever imagined. His journey from the safety of Wisborg to the eerie isolation of Orlok's castle mirrors the human experience of venturing into uncharted territory, where familiar rules no longer apply.

In adapting to a novel format, it was my hope to preserve the gothic atmosphere of Nosferatu, and allowing immersion—drawing the reader so deeply into the world of the story that they feel its shadows on their skin and hear its silences echoing in their minds. The novel is not just a retelling of the film but an invitation to step into its world, to walk through its halls, to feel its dread. Every word, every description, is chosen with this goal in mind: to make the reader a participant in the story, not just an observer.

Writing this novel was an act of love—for the film, for the gothic tradition, and for the power of storytelling to transport us into places both terrifying and beautiful. In preserving the atmosphere of Nosferatu, I sought to honor the film's legacy while creating something new—a work that stands on its own while remaining true to the spirit of the original.

Above all, adapting Nosferatu into a novel was an act of

preservation. The film, nearly lost to history after the infamous copyright lawsuit, has survived against all odds, its shadow stretching across the decades. By reimagining it as a novel, I hope to ensure that its story continues to reach new audiences, inspiring fear and fascination for generations to come.

This adaptation is not just a retelling of Nosferatu—it is a tribute to the power of storytelling itself. The film's ability to evoke such profound emotion and terror with its minimalist tools is a testament to the enduring power of art. In bringing its story to the page, I sought to honor that legacy, creating a work that captures the spirit of the original while offering something new.

# Chapter 1
## A Peaceful Beginning

The town of Wisborg lay cradled between the arms of a dense forest and the winding silver ribbon of a restless river. Its narrow streets meandered beneath the shadow of steep-roofed houses, their dark wooden frames weathered by years of rain and wind. On the surface, the town appeared tranquil, its charm undisturbed by the creeping modernity that encroached on other places. Yet, there was an air of heaviness about it, a sense that the peace was fragile, as though some unseen force pressed against it, waiting for the right moment to shatter the illusion.

At the edge of this sleepy town stood a modest home, tucked away like a secret. The morning light spilled through its windows, cutting through the gloom of an overcast sky. Inside, Ellen Hutter stood by the kitchen window, her delicate hands clasping the edge of the wooden sill. Her dark hair fell loose over her shoulders, framing a pale, thoughtful face. Her gaze drifted beyond the garden, toward the river, where the mist hung like a spectral curtain over the water.

The room behind her was warm and inviting, filled with the scent of fresh bread and the faint smokiness of a lingering fire. It was a place of comfort, of safety, and yet Ellen felt a hollow weight in her chest. She could not name it, but it had lingered there for days, a quiet whisper of unease that she could neither dismiss nor understand.

Her husband, Thomas, appeared in the doorway, his youthful face brightened by a boyish grin. His auburn hair, unruly as ever, caught the faint light as he stepped into the room. He carried himself with an air of confidence, his movements brisk and sure. There was no shadow in his demeanor, no hint of the apprehension that gripped Ellen.

"Ellen, my love, why do you always look so lost in thought?" he asked, his voice warm as he approached her. "The morning is beautiful, isn't it?"

She turned to him, her lips forming a faint smile, though her eyes betrayed her inner turmoil.

"It is," she replied softly, her voice tinged with melancholy. "But the mist…it feels heavier than usual. As though it carries something with it."

Thomas chuckled, reaching out to brush a stray strand of hair from her face.

"You and your poetic thoughts," he said. "I think the mist is just the mist. Nothing more."

Ellen's smile faltered, her hands tightening on the windowsill.

"Perhaps," she said, though her tone was distant. She hesitated before adding, "Do you ever feel as though something is watching us? Something just beyond the edge of sight?"

Thomas tilted his head, his brow furrowing slightly.

"Watching us? Ellen, you've been reading too many of those old books. There's nothing here but the town, the river, and the forest. You're safe with me."

The certainty in his voice was meant to reassure her, but it only deepened her unease. She turned back to the window, her eyes scanning the trees that loomed like sentinels at the edge of the garden.

The mist seemed to cling to them, wrapping their trunks in an unnatural stillness.

"I know," she said finally, her voice barely above a whisper. "But sometimes, Thomas, I feel as though peace is a fragile thing. It can slip away so easily."

Thomas smiled gently, though her words seemed to linger in the air longer than they should have.

"I promise you, Ellen, nothing is going to change," he said, brushing a loose strand of her dark hair away from her face. "I must be off. Knock's expecting me, and I can't delay. You know how particular he is about time."

Ellen's gaze fell to the floor, her hands tightening in front of her. Herr Knock, Thomas's employer, was a man of peculiar reputation in Wisborg—a figure whispered about in cautious tones. He had a way of inspiring unease even in those who worked for him, though Thomas had always dismissed such talk as idle gossip. Now, as he prepared to meet with Knock for yet another assignment, Ellen couldn't shake the sense that this time would be different.

The morning light cast long shadows on the walls as Thomas kissed her forehead and grabbed his coat.

"I'll be back before you know it," he said, his voice warm and confident. Ellen nodded, but her heart felt heavy as she watched him leave. He paused at the doorway, glancing back with that same boyish grin she loved so much. Then he was gone, the sound of his boots fading into the quiet street.

On the outskirts of Wisborg, Herr Knock's office awaited—a small, unassuming building that housed its owner's eccentric energy. The townsfolk spoke in hushed tones of the strange dealings that took place there, the peculiar habits of the man who ran it. But to Thomas, it was simply his place of work, another stop on his path to a better life. And yet, as he walked toward it through the gathering mist, even he could not ignore the faint sense of foreboding that crept at the edges of his thoughts.

The office of Herr Knock was an unassuming building on the outskirts of Wisborg, a stone's throw from the busy market square. Its unremarkable façade belied the strange undercurrent of energy that seemed to flow from within, an energy that many in the town whispered about but few dared to investigate. The interior was dim and cluttered, its walls lined with shelves buckling under the weight of dusty tomes and ledgers. A faint, acrid smell lingered in the air, a mix of ink, damp paper, and something else—something metallic and faintly sour.

Knock sat hunched at his desk, his wiry frame silhouetted against the pale light of a small, grimy window. His long fingers moved with unsettling precision as he scratched out letters in spidery handwriting. His movements were sharp and deliberate, as though he were in the thrall of some unseen force. His head twitched occasionally, a quick, birdlike movement, and his lips muttered words that did not seem intended for anyone but himself.

"Ah, Hutter," Knock said suddenly, his voice cutting through the heavy silence without warning. He didn't look up from his writing. "Punctual, as always."

Thomas Hutter stepped into the room, his usual confidence faltering slightly in the presence of his eccentric employer. There was something about Knock that unsettled him, though he could never quite place it. Perhaps it was the man's pale, sunken cheeks or the way his eyes darted about the room like a predator scanning for prey. Whatever it was, Thomas had learned to ignore it. Knock was a shrewd businessman, and his knack for acquiring clients with deep pockets had made him an invaluable employer.

"You asked to see me, Herr Knock?" Thomas said, his voice steady despite his unease.

Knock's head snapped up, and a wide grin spread across his face, exposing uneven, yellowing teeth.

"Indeed, indeed. Come, sit. I have a most important assignment for you."

Thomas hesitated for a fraction of a second before moving to the chair opposite Knock's desk. He sat down, his hands resting on his knees as he waited for the man to speak. Knock leaned forward, his grin widening as he pushed a thick envelope across the desk toward Thomas.

"This," Knock said, tapping the envelope with a long, bony finger, "is a contract for a client of the highest caliber. A Count. A man of wealth and refinement. He seeks to purchase a property here in Wisborg."

Thomas raised an eyebrow, intrigued.

"A Count, you say? That's certainly unusual. Where is he from?"

Knock's grin twisted into something almost predatory. "The Carpathian Mountains. A place steeped in legend and mystery. Count Orlok is his name, and he has taken an interest in a secluded property by the river."

Thomas frowned slightly, the name striking an odd chord within him.

"Orlok," he repeated. "I can't say I've ever heard of him."

"Few have," Knock replied, his tone low and conspiratorial. "He is…reclusive. A man of peculiar tastes, you might say. But his wealth is undeniable, and his interest in Wisborg is genuine. He has requested you specifically to oversee the transaction."

"Me?" Thomas asked, surprised. "Why me?"

Knock chuckled, a sound that made the hairs on Thomas's arms stand on end. "You are young, charming, and resourceful. The perfect man for the job. And let us not forget the commission—oh, the commission! It will be more than worth your while."

Thomas leaned back in his chair, considering the offer. The prospect of traveling to the Carpathian Mountains intrigued him. It was a chance to see a part of the world he had only heard of in stories, to immerse himself in a place of wild beauty and ancient history. The financial incentive was equally appealing; with the money from the commission, he and Ellen could secure a brighter future.

"I'll do it," he said finally, his decision made.

"Excellent!" Knock exclaimed, clapping his hands together. He pushed the envelope closer to Thomas. "The details are all here. You'll leave tomorrow. The Count is expecting you."

Thomas took the envelope, his fingers brushing against the rough paper. He couldn't shake the feeling that the room had grown colder, the air heavier. Knock's grin remained fixed; his eyes gleaming with a strange light as he watched Thomas rise from the chair.

"One last thing," Knock said as Thomas turned to leave. "Be sure to make a good impression. The Count is…particular about his associates."

Thomas nodded, forcing a smile.

"I'll keep that in mind."

As Thomas stepped out into the crisp evening air, the weight that had settled over him in Knock's office began to lift. The town square was quiet, the market stalls abandoned for the night, but the familiar sights and sounds of Wisborg reassured him. He glanced back at the office, its dark windows staring out at the square like empty eyes. He shook his head, dismissing the unease that lingered in his chest.

That evening, as the light faded and the house grew dim, Ellen found herself drawn to the window. She stood there in silence, her gaze fixed on the forest as the last traces of daylight slipped away. The darkness seemed alive, shifting and moving at the edges of her vision. She blinked, and the sensation was gone, leaving her alone with her thoughts.

Thomas entered the room, carrying a stack of letters and papers. He set them on the table with a satisfied sigh.

"Knock has given me a new assignment," he announced, his tone carrying a note of excitement. "A wealthy client, someone with an interest in moving to Wisborg. It's a rare opportunity, Ellen. The commission could be substantial."

Ellen turned to him; her expression unreadable.

"Who is the client?" she asked.

Thomas hesitated, his brow furrowing.

"I'm not certain. He's from the Carpathian Mountains. Knock says he's eager to purchase a property here—a secluded one."

The name sent a chill through Ellen, though she could not explain why.

"The Carpathian Mountains?" she echoed. "That's a long way from here."

"Yes," Thomas replied, his grin returning. "And I'll be traveling there to meet him. Knock insists I handle the transaction personally. It's a rare chance, Ellen. Think of what it could mean for us."

Ellen's heart sank. She wanted to tell him not to go, to beg him to stay, but she knew he would dismiss her fears as irrational. She forced a smile instead.

"Be careful," she said. "The world is not always as safe as it seems."

Thomas laughed, wrapping her in a warm embrace.

"You worry too much," he said. "I'll be back before you know it. And when I return, we'll have a better life waiting for us."

Ellen rested her head against his chest, but her mind was far from at ease. In the silence of their embrace, she could feel the darkness pressing against the edges of their world, waiting to creep in.

The stars had emerged faintly over Wisborg, their light diffused by the mist that lingered in the night air. Inside the Hutter home, Ellen sat by the window in her nightgown, the fabric pooling like pale mist around her ankles. The room was quiet, save for the occasional crackle of the dying fire and the distant howl of a dog somewhere in the village. Her hands rested in her lap, clutching the locket Thomas had given her when they were first married—a small, simple token of his love.

Ellen had always been a sensitive soul. Where others saw the world in sharp lines and solid forms, she felt it as an ever-shifting tapestry of light and shadow. It was both a gift and a burden, this sensitivity. It allowed her to appreciate the subtleties of life—a bird's song at dawn, the way sunlight danced on water—but it also made her susceptible to the unseen currents that flowed beneath the surface of things.

Tonight, those currents felt stronger than ever.

She closed her eyes, letting the faint warmth of the fire touch her skin. Her breath came slow and shallow as she tried to calm the unease that had been growing within her. But as the quiet deepened, she felt herself slipping into a strange, dreamlike state, her thoughts drifting beyond her control.

In this half-dream, half-waking state, Ellen found herself standing at the edge of the forest that bordered Wisborg. The trees loomed taller than she remembered, their gnarled branches twisting into unnatural shapes. The mist clung to the ground like a living thing, curling around her feet and seeping into the folds of her gown.

Somewhere in the distance, a soft voice called her name. It was faint, almost indistinguishable from the rustling of the leaves, but it carried a weight that made her chest tighten. She turned toward the sound, her bare feet moving soundlessly over the mossy ground. The air grew colder as she walked, the mist thickening around her.

Then she saw him.

A figure stood just beyond the edge of the mist; his form shrouded in shadow. He was impossibly tall, his posture hunched as though burdened by some unseen weight. His face was obscured, but his eyes—oh, his eyes—glowed faintly in the darkness, like embers smoldering in the ashes of a dying fire.

Ellen froze, her body refusing to move as those eyes fixed on her. They were not the eyes of a man but something older, something far removed from the realm of humanity. They seemed to pierce through her, reading her soul with a cruel, detached hunger.

"Ellen…" the voice whispered again, though the figure's lips did not move.

Her heart thundered in her chest as she took a step back, the mist swirling around her legs like clutching hands. The figure began to move toward her, his steps slow and deliberate, and Ellen felt a scream rise in her throat—but it would not come.

The vision shattered.

Ellen jolted awake; her body drenched in cold sweat. The room was dark now, the fire reduced to faintly glowing embers. Her breath came in ragged gasps, her hands clutching the locket so tightly that the chain bit into her palm.

For a moment, she could not distinguish dream from reality. Her eyes darted to the window, half-expecting to see those glowing eyes staring back at her from the darkness. But there was nothing—only the faint rustling of the trees outside and the gentle creak of the house settling into the earth.

She rose from her chair on unsteady legs and moved to the bed where Thomas slept soundly, his breathing deep and even. She knelt beside him, her trembling hand brushing a strand of hair from his forehead. He looked so peaceful, so blissfully unaware of the storm that raged within her.

"Thomas," she whispered, her voice barely audible. "Something is coming. I can feel it."

He stirred slightly but did not wake. Ellen pressed a kiss to his temple, tears stinging her eyes as she climbed into bed beside him. She curled into his warmth, seeking comfort in the steady rhythm of his heartbeat, but her unease remained. The vision lingered in her mind; its details etched into her memory like a scar.

Somewhere, in the depths of her soul, Ellen knew that the figure in her dream was no mere phantom of her imagination. It was real, and it was coming.

The next morning, Ellen said nothing of the dream. She moved through her day with the same quiet grace as always, tending to her garden and exchanging polite words with the neighbors. But her melancholy had deepened, her smiles more fleeting, her gaze often drifting to the forest or the distant mountains.

Thomas, oblivious to her inner turmoil, remained focused on his preparations for the journey. He spoke excitedly of the mysterious Count Orlok and the potential fortune the transaction could bring them, his optimism a sharp contrast to Ellen's growing dread.

Ellen tried to shake the feeling, telling herself it was only a dream. But as the sun set and the shadows lengthened, she found herself standing by the window once more, her hands clutching the locket as her eyes searched the horizon.

The darkness felt closer tonight.

The morning sunlight struggled to pierce the veil of mist that blanketed Wisborg, giving the town an ethereal, dreamlike quality. Thomas Hutter stood in the small bedroom he shared with Ellen, packing his leather satchel with a sense of excitement he could barely contain. The details of his assignment still swirled in his mind—the enigmatic Count Orlok, the distant Carpathian Mountains, the promise of wealth and success.

For Thomas, it was an opportunity too grand to refuse. His life in Wisborg, though comfortable, had always felt too small for his ambitions. The prospect of venturing into the unknown, of seeing lands steeped in ancient lore and mystery, filled him with a boyish eagerness. Yet, as he folded his shirts and carefully packed his writing tools, he could not ignore Ellen's quiet presence in the corner of the room.

She sat in the small armchair by the window, her gaze fixed on the gray horizon. Her hands rested in her lap, clutching the locket he had given her on their wedding day. The faint lines of worry etched into her face pained him more than he cared to admit. He paused, watching her in silence for a moment, before crossing the room and kneeling beside her.

"Ellen," he said softly, taking her hands in his. "You've barely spoken since last night. What troubles you so?"

She turned to him, her eyes glistening with unshed tears.

"I don't know, Thomas," she admitted, her voice trembling. "It's just…something about this journey feels wrong. The Carpathian Mountains, this Count Orlok—it all seems so far away, so strange."

Thomas smiled gently, squeezing her hands.

"You worry too much, my love. This is an incredible opportunity for us. Think of what this commission could mean—new possibilities, a better future."

"But what if—" She hesitated, struggling to put her fears into words. "What if there's danger out there? What if something happens to you?"

"Danger?" Thomas laughed, though the sound was warm and reassuring rather than dismissive. "Ellen, you've been reading too many of those old stories. The world is not so perilous as you imagine. I'll be careful, I promise."

Ellen shook her head, her grip on his hands tightening. "It's not just the stories, Thomas. It's this feeling I have, this…heaviness. As though something dark is waiting for you out there."

He cupped her cheek, his thumb brushing away a stray tear. "I'll be fine, Ellen. I'll return before you know it. And when I do, we'll have everything we've ever dreamed of."

Her lips quivered, but she nodded, unable to argue further. She leaned into his touch, closing her eyes as she tried to ignore the cold knot of dread coiled in her chest.

By mid-morning, Thomas was ready to leave. His satchel was packed, his coat buttoned, and his boots laced tightly against the chill. Ellen walked with him to the edge of the town square, her hand resting lightly on his arm. The mist clung to the cobblestones, muffling the sounds of their footsteps and adding a surreal quality to their parting.

At the edge of the square, a carriage waited to take Thomas to the first leg of his journey. The driver, a dour man with a weathered face, stood by the horses, his hands tucked into his coat for warmth. Thomas turned to Ellen, his expression softening as he saw the worry etched into her features.

"Please, don't look so sad," he said, tilting her chin up to meet his gaze. "I'll write to you as soon as I reach the Count's castle. And I'll return before you even have time to miss me."

Ellen forced a smile, though it didn't reach her eyes.

"I'll hold you to that," she said, her voice barely above a whisper.

He leaned down, pressing a kiss to her forehead.

"Take care of yourself, Ellen. And don't let those dreams of yours frighten you. They're only dreams."

As he climbed into the carriage, she stepped back, her arms crossed over her chest as though to shield herself from the cold. The horses snorted and stamped their hooves, eager to be on their way. Thomas waved as the carriage began to move, his grin bright and confident.

Ellen watched him go, her heart aching with a mixture of love and fear. She stayed there long after the carriage disappeared into the mist, her mind replaying the dreams she had tried so hard to forget. The dark figure, the burning eyes, the voice that had whispered her name—they haunted her still, like shadows that refused to be banished by the light.

Finally, she turned and made her way back to the house, the locket clutched tightly in her hand. The silence of Wisborg enveloped her as she walked, the mist swirling around her like a living thing. Somewhere deep within her, she knew that Thomas's journey would change everything—and that the shadows he had dismissed so easily were far closer than either of them realized.

# Chapter 2
## Feelings of Absence

The house felt emptier without Thomas. Though he had been gone only a few hours, his absence cast long shadows over every room. Ellen moved through the quiet space like a ghost, her footsteps soft on the worn wooden floors. She tried to focus on her daily tasks—tidying the kitchen, tending to the small garden—but her thoughts were heavy, and her hands trembled as she worked.

The locket Thomas had given her hung around her neck, its weight a small comfort against the growing unease that churned in her chest. She clutched it often, her fingers tracing the familiar grooves of its surface as though it could anchor her to something solid, something real.

By midday, she abandoned the garden and retreated to the sitting room, the pale sunlight filtering through the lace curtains doing little to warm the space. She sat by the window, her eyes drawn once again to the forest that bordered the town. The trees seemed darker than usual; their branches tangled like the fingers of some unseen giant reaching toward the sky. The mist that clung to the ground never seemed to lift, even as the sun reached its peak.

Ellen felt it then—a strange, suffocating sensation, as though the air around her had grown heavier. Her breath caught in her throat, and for a moment, she was sure she saw something moving in the shadows of the trees. A flicker of motion, too quick to follow, yet unmistakably real.

She pressed her hand to her chest, willing her heart to slow. It's nothing, she told herself. Just the wind, or a bird, or your imagination playing tricks on you.

But the feeling would not leave her.

As the afternoon wore on, Ellen found herself drawn outside, her feet carrying her toward the edge of the garden almost without her consent. The cool air brushed against her skin, carrying with it the faint scent of damp earth and something metallic, something she could not quite place. She shivered, pulling her shawl tighter around her shoulders.

Standing at the edge of the garden, she stared into the forest, her eyes scanning the dense undergrowth for any sign of movement. The shadows seemed alive, shifting and twisting in ways that defied logic. She thought of her dreams, the dark figure with burning eyes, and the voice that had called her name.

"Thomas," she whispered, her voice trembling. "Why do I feel this way? Why does it feel like something is watching me?"

The wind picked up, rustling the leaves and sending a chill down her spine. For a brief moment, she thought she heard something in the distance—a low, guttural sound, almost like a whisper. It was faint, barely audible, but it froze her in place.

She clutched the locket tightly, her fingers trembling. The sound faded, leaving only the rustling of the trees and the distant cry of a bird. Ellen turned and hurried back to the house, her heart racing. The feeling of being watched lingered, a cold, oppressive weight that pressed against her chest.

That night, Ellen's sleep was restless. The fire in the hearth had long since died, leaving the room bathed in shadows. She tossed and turned beneath the heavy quilt; her mind plagued by images she could not control.

In her dream, she was standing in the forest again, the mist swirling around her feet. The trees loomed taller than they should have, their twisted branches clawing at the sky. The air was thick, suffocating, and the ground beneath her feet felt damp and unsteady.

"Ellen..." The voice came again, soft and insistent. It carried an unnatural weight, a force that seemed to press against her very soul.

She turned, and there he was—the figure from her earlier dreams. He stood just beyond the reach of the moonlight, his tall, skeletal frame shrouded in shadow. His eyes glowed faintly, twin points of red that burned into her. His face was pale, almost translucent, and his thin lips curled into a smile that was neither warm nor kind.

"Who are you?" she tried to ask, but her voice was lost in the thick air. Her lips moved, but no sound came. The figure stepped closer, and the shadows seemed to move with him, like a cloak of living darkness.

"Ellen..." the voice repeated, though the figure's mouth did not move. "You are already mine."

Her scream caught in her throat as the figure extended a long, clawed hand toward her. The air seemed to ripple around him, the mist rising in thick tendrils to wrap around her ankles, pulling her down into the cold, damp ground.

Ellen woke with a start, her chest heaving as she gasped for air. The room was dark, the only light coming from the pale glow of the moon through the window. She sat up, clutching the locket with trembling hands, her heart racing.

For a long moment, she sat there in silence, her breath shallow and uneven. She tried to tell herself it was just a dream, nothing more than her imagination running wild in Thomas's absence. But the details were too vivid, too real. She could still feel the damp cold of the ground beneath her feet, the oppressive weight of the air, the burning intensity of the figure's gaze.

The rest of the night passed in a haze of sleeplessness. Ellen sat by the window, staring out at the forest and clutching her locket like a talisman. The shadows seemed deeper than usual, their movements slower, more deliberate. She could not shake the feeling that something was out there, watching her, waiting.

When the first light of dawn crept over the horizon, Ellen let out a breath she hadn't realized she was holding. The new day brought no comfort, only the lingering dread of her dreams and the heavy silence of the empty house.

Ellen whispered a prayer, her voice trembling as she spoke.

"Please, Thomas," she said softly. "Come back to me."

But the house gave no reply, its silence as heavy as the mist outside.

The house felt even colder the next evening, though no draft disturbed the air. Ellen sat alone by the fire, its faint glow casting flickering shadows across the walls. She stared into the embers, her thoughts drifting to Thomas. She imagined him on the road, his face lit with excitement as he began his journey to the Carpathian Mountains. She wondered if he felt the same chill she did, a nameless unease that crept into her bones and refused to leave.

The locket around her neck was warm from her touch, the chain light but grounding. She traced its edges absentmindedly as the fire shrank into a dull orange glow. Her eyelids grew heavy, the day's exhaustion weighing on her. She moved to the small bed they had shared, its emptiness more striking now than ever. Wrapping the quilt tightly around herself, she closed her eyes, though her mind would not rest.

When sleep finally came, it did not bring peace.

She stood in a field of ash-gray mist that stretched endlessly in all directions. The air was thick, almost suffocating, and the ground beneath her feet felt damp and unstable. Around her, shadowed shapes loomed—trees, or the broken remains of them, their twisted branches clawing at the crimson-tinged sky above. A low wind whispered through the emptiness, carrying with it faint, indistinct voices.

"Thomas…" she called, her voice echoing unnaturally. The sound barely carried, swallowed almost instantly by the oppressive quiet. She took a hesitant step forward, her bare feet sinking slightly into the cold earth.

Ahead, a figure emerged from the mist. It was distant at first, a vague outline that seemed to waver and distort as though it were not truly part of the world around it. Ellen froze, her breath catching in her throat. The figure moved closer, its form growing clearer with every step it took.

It was a man—no, not a man. His body was too gaunt, his limbs elongated and unnatural. His head was bald, his skin as pale as moonlight. But it was his eyes that held her—two orbs of burning darkness, devoid of humanity yet filled with hunger. They fixed on her with an intensity that made her feel as though her very soul were being stripped bare.

She wanted to run, to turn and flee into the endless mist, but her legs refused to move. She stood rooted in place as the figure came closer. His face was sharp, skeletal, with a mouth that twisted into a grotesque smile. Long, clawed fingers extended toward her, each movement deliberate, as if savoring the moment.

"Ellen…" The voice was soft, a whisper that seemed to come from everywhere and nowhere. It was not the voice of Thomas, nor of any human. It was deeper, ancient, and it resonated inside her head like the toll of a distant bell.

The figure stopped just a few feet from her, his shadow stretching unnaturally long, reaching toward her like grasping hands. Ellen could feel the cold emanating from him, a chill that seeped into her skin and settled in her bones.

"You… are mine," the voice whispered again, though his lips did not move. The mist around her thickened, rising like tendrils to wrap around her ankles, pulling her down into the cold, damp ground. Her heart pounded, her breaths coming in short, desperate gasps as she struggled to free herself.

The figure's claws moved closer, their sharp points glinting faintly in the dull light. Ellen opened her mouth to scream, but no sound came. The mist rose higher, enveloping her, until all she could see were those burning eyes, piercing through the darkness.

Ellen woke with a start, her body drenched in sweat and her heart racing. The room was dark, the faint glow of the moon filtering through the curtains. She sat up, clutching the locket around her neck, its cool surface grounding her in the reality of the present.

Her breaths came in shallow gasps as she tried to calm herself, but the images of the dream lingered, vivid and oppressive. She could still feel the cold of the mist, the weight of the figure's gaze, the clawing sensation of being pulled into the earth.

She rose from the bed, her bare feet silent on the wooden floor as she moved to the window. She stared out at the forest, its dark silhouettes standing stark against the pale light of the moon. The shadows beneath the trees seemed deeper than before, darker and more alive. She pressed a hand to the glass, her breath fogging the surface as her trembling fingers tightened around the locket.

Somewhere, deep in the pit of her stomach, she felt it: the figure in her dream was not a figment of her imagination. It was real. And it was coming.

Ellen sank to her knees by the window, her head resting against the cold glass as silent tears slipped down her cheeks. She whispered Thomas's name into the dark, her voice shaking.

"Please... come back to me."

The shadows outside remained silent, but Ellen could not shake the feeling that they were watching, waiting.

# Chapter 3
## The Journey

The sun hung low in the sky, casting a warm, golden light across the rolling hills and meadows that stretched endlessly beyond the cobbled roads of Wisborg. Thomas Hutter sat comfortably in the carriage, his satchel resting on his lap, its weight a reminder of the task ahead. The rhythmic clatter of the horses' hooves on the packed dirt and the gentle creak of the wheels created a soothing cadence that matched the idyllic scenery passing by.

Fields of wildflowers swayed in the soft breeze, their vibrant hues painting the landscape in shades of gold, violet, and crimson. A scattering of quaint farmhouses dotted the horizon, their chimneys puffing faint trails of smoke that rose lazily into the sky. The air was crisp and carried the faint, earthy scent of freshly turned soil and blooming flowers. It was the kind of countryside that seemed untouched by time, a place where the troubles of the world felt distant and small.

Thomas leaned out of the carriage window, letting the cool breeze wash over his face. His spirits were high, buoyed by the sense of adventure that accompanied this journey. He had always dreamed of seeing more of the world beyond the quiet streets of Wisborg, and this trip to the Carpathian Mountains felt like the first step toward something grand. The stories he had read about the region—a land of jagged peaks, ancient forests, and crumbling castles—filled his mind with romantic notions of discovery.

The carriage passed through a small village nestled at the edge of a dense forest, its cobblestone streets bustling with activity. Merchants called out to passersby, their stalls laden with fresh produce, handwoven textiles, and intricate wood carvings. Children chased one another through the narrow alleys, their laughter carrying on the wind. Thomas waved to a group of farmers who tipped their hats in return, their faces weathered but kind.

"This is what life should be," Thomas thought to himself, a smile tugging at his lips. "Open skies, hard work, and the promise of something more just beyond the horizon."

As the hours passed and the sun began its slow descent, the landscape began to change. The rolling hills gave way to dense forests, their towering trees casting long shadows over the road. The warmth of the day faded, replaced by a cool, damp chill that seeped through Thomas's coat. The cheerful chirping of birds was replaced by the occasional rustle of leaves and the distant cry of a raven.

The carriage driver, a stoic man who had said little since their departure, seemed to grow uneasy. His eyes darted toward the treeline, his hands gripping the reins tightly. Thomas noticed the change in his demeanor but said nothing, his own excitement undimmed by the growing stillness of the forest.

The trees grew denser as they traveled deeper, their gnarled branches intertwining overhead to form a canopy that blocked out the fading light. The road narrowed, its edges lined with moss-covered stones and tangled roots that seemed to reach toward the carriage like skeletal fingers. Thomas felt a faint shiver crawl up his spine but dismissed it as the chill of the evening air.

As they rounded a bend, the driver slowed the horses and glanced over his shoulder.

"We'll stop at the next village for the night," he said, his voice low and steady. "The roads ahead aren't safe after dark."

"Not safe?" Thomas repeated, raising an eyebrow. "What do you mean?"

The driver didn't answer immediately. He flicked the reins, urging the horses forward.

"The mountains have their share of…stories," he said after a pause. "Best not to travel through them at night."

Thomas smiled, leaning back in his seat.

"Stories, you say? Superstitions, no doubt. I've heard them before—ghosts, spirits, that sort of thing. The kind of tales villagers tell to scare their children."

The driver's expression remained grim.

"Believe what you like, Herr Hutter. But I've seen enough to know there's truth in some of those tales."

Thomas was about to press him further, but the driver's sharp tone discouraged him. Instead, he turned his attention back to the road, the fading daylight painting the forest in shades of gray and shadow.

By the time they reached the village, the sun had disappeared entirely, leaving only the pale glow of the moon to light their way. The village was small, its cluster of timber-framed houses huddled close together as if for protection. The streets were quiet, the windows of the homes shuttered tightly against the night. A single lantern hung outside the inn, its flickering flame casting faint light over the weathered sign that swayed gently in the breeze.

The driver pulled the carriage to a stop and climbed down, his boots crunching against the gravel.

"We'll rest here," he said, his tone leaving no room for argument. "The horses need a break, and so do I."

Thomas stepped out of the carriage, stretching his legs and glancing around the village. It felt different from the cheerful hamlets they had passed earlier. There was no laughter here, no sound of conversation or life. The air was heavy, the stillness oppressive. He couldn't help but notice the way the driver glanced nervously over his shoulder as he led the horses to the stable.

The innkeeper, a stout man with a furrowed brow, greeted them at the door. His eyes lingered on Thomas for a moment, his expression unreadable.

"You'll want supper and a room, I imagine," he said, his voice gruff. "Come in, then. And mind the door—we don't leave it open after dark."

Thomas followed him inside, the warmth of the fire in the hearth a welcome reprieve from the chill outside. The room was dimly lit, its wooden walls adorned with faded tapestries and crude carvings. A handful of villagers sat at the long table, their heads bowed in quiet conversation. They fell silent as Thomas entered, their eyes darting toward him briefly before returning to their drinks.

Thomas sat near the fire, his mind still buzzing with thoughts of the journey ahead. As he sipped the mulled wine the innkeeper placed before him, he couldn't help but feel that the village itself was holding its breath, as if waiting for something to pass.

The driver caught his eye from across the room.

"Get some rest, Herr Hutter," he said, his voice low. "Tomorrow's road will take us deeper into the mountains."

Thomas nodded, though he couldn't shake the faint unease that lingered at the edges of his mind. As he climbed the creaking stairs to his room, he wondered briefly about the stories the driver had mentioned, the warnings left unspoken.

Outside, the forest stretched endlessly into the night, its shadows alive with possibilities.

The fire in the inn's hearth crackled softly, casting dancing shadows on the rough wooden walls. Thomas Hutter sat at a small table near the corner, sipping a cup of mulled wine. The warmth of the drink spread through him, chasing away the chill that had clung to him since entering the dense forests that surrounded the village. Yet, despite the fire and the wine, an unease lingered in the air, as though the very walls of the inn absorbed the anxieties of those who sheltered within them.

The innkeeper bustled about, his broad frame moving with quiet efficiency as he tended to the few patrons scattered throughout the room. Most were men with weathered faces, dressed in heavy coats and boots caked in mud. They spoke in hushed tones, their voices little more than murmurs, but their words ceased altogether when Thomas entered. Though they had since resumed their conversations, Thomas could still feel their glances, fleeting but sharp, as though assessing the stranger in their midst.

He set his cup down and leaned back in his chair, the crackling of the fire the only sound that filled the space around him. The innkeeper approached with a wooden platter of bread and roasted meat, setting it down with a gruff nod.

"You'll need a full belly for the road tomorrow," the innkeeper said, his voice low and rough, like stones grinding together. "The mountains take their toll on travelers."

Thomas smiled, nodding his thanks.

"It seems the mountains inspire a lot of caution in these parts."

The innkeeper glanced over his shoulder, his thick brow furrowing.

"They do," he said simply. He hesitated, as if weighing whether to say more, then added, "They've seen more than their share of strange things. Enough to keep wise men wary."

"What kind of strange things?" Thomas asked, leaning forward. His tone was light, curious, though there was a glimmer of amusement in his eyes.

The innkeeper shifted uneasily, his gaze flicking toward the other patrons before returning to Thomas.

"Old stories," he muttered. "Tales of shadows that move where no light should touch. Voices that call to travelers in the dead of night, leading them to places they're better off avoiding."

Thomas chuckled softly, though the sound rang hollow in the quiet room.

"It sounds like the kind of stories meant to keep children from wandering too far from home."

The innkeeper's expression darkened.

"Perhaps," he said, his voice dropping to a near whisper. "But some of us have seen things that can't be so easily dismissed. The mountains have their secrets, Herr Hutter, and they don't give them up lightly."

Thomas raised an eyebrow at the innkeeper's tone but said nothing. He tore a piece of bread from the loaf and ate in silence, his thoughts turning to the task ahead. The words of the villagers might have unsettled others, but he refused to let them dampen his spirits. He was here for business, not to be frightened by old legends.

As the evening wore on, the inn grew quieter, the few patrons filtering out one by one until only Thomas, the innkeeper, and a small group of older men remained. They sat near the fire, their faces lit by its flickering glow. Their conversation, once muted, grew louder, emboldened by the emptiness of the room and the ale in their cups.

One of the men, his face lined with deep creases and his hands rough with years of labor, turned toward Thomas.

"You're traveling to the mountains, aren't you?" he asked, his voice gruff but not unkind.

Thomas looked up from his meal, nodding.

"That's right. I have business with a client who lives there."

The man exchanged glances with his companions, his frown deepening.

"The Carpathians are no place for city folk. Especially not strangers."

Thomas smiled politely.

"I appreciate your concern, but I'm quite capable of handling myself."

The man shook his head.

"It's not a matter of capability," he said. "The mountains are...different. Things happen there that don't make sense to those who haven't lived near them. You'd do well to heed the warnings."

"Warnings?" Thomas prompted, his curiosity piqued despite himself.

The man leaned forward, his voice dropping to a conspiratorial whisper.

"There's an old legend," he began, his words slow and deliberate. "Of creatures that dwell in the mountains, hidden from the eyes of men. They're not human, not anymore. They feed on the living, drawing strength from blood. They're bound to the dark, to the soil, and they bring ruin wherever they go."

Thomas stared at the man, his expression unreadable. He had heard stories like this before—tales of vampires and other such creatures, woven into the folklore of nearly every culture. He had always dismissed them as superstitions, the imaginings of frightened people trying to explain the unknown.

"And you believe this?" he asked, his tone carefully neutral.

The man met his gaze, his eyes unflinching.

"I've seen things," he said simply. "And I know what I've seen."

One of the other men spoke up, his voice trembling.

"If you're going to the mountains, you should turn back. There's nothing there but death. And if you must go, for God's sake, don't stay out after dark."

Thomas leaned back in his chair, crossing his arms.

"I appreciate your concern, truly," he said. "But I'm not afraid of old stories. My business is important, and I have no intention of turning back."

The men fell silent, their warnings given and dismissed. The fire crackled softly, its light casting long shadows across the room.

That night, as Thomas lay in the small room above the inn, his thoughts drifted back to the villagers' words. Though he told himself they were nothing more than superstition, a faint unease stirred within him. He dismissed it quickly, closing his eyes and focusing instead on the promise of the future. The Carpathians awaited, and with them, the chance to secure his and Ellen's dreams.

Outside, the wind howled softly, carrying with it the faint, distant cry of something that was neither animal nor man.

The morning came cloaked in mist, the pale sun struggling to pierce the dense shroud that blanketed the village. Thomas rose early, eager to continue his journey into the Carpathian Mountains. The chill of the night still clung to the air, and the quiet streets seemed even more subdued than they had the day before. As he stepped into the common room of the inn, he found the innkeeper already awake, tending to the embers in the hearth.

"Breakfast is on the table," the innkeeper said without looking up, his voice low and rough from sleep.

Thomas thanked him and sat down at the long wooden table, helping himself to a piece of bread and a wedge of cheese. The room felt emptier in the morning light, the shadows less pronounced but no less oppressive. He ate quickly, eager to be on his way, but the creak of the door behind him gave him pause.

The old man from the night before entered, his face lined with concern. He walked with a slow, deliberate pace, his boots scuffing against the floorboards. Without a word, he sat down across from Thomas, folding his hands on the table.

"You'll be heading into the mountains today," the old man said, his voice softer than it had been the previous night.

"That's right," Thomas replied, tearing off another piece of bread. "I'm meeting a client—Count Orlok. He's interested in purchasing property in Wisborg."

The old man's expression darkened at the mention of the Count's name.

"Orlok," he murmured, as though testing the weight of the word. "I should've known."

Thomas raised an eyebrow, intrigued by the man's reaction.

"You know of him?"

The old man nodded slowly, his gaze distant.

"Not much is known about the Count," he admitted. "But the name... it's been whispered in these parts for generations. Always tied to strange happenings, to loss and misfortune."

Thomas leaned forward, his curiosity piqued.

"What kind of strange happenings?"

The old man hesitated, glancing toward the innkeeper, who stood silently by the hearth. When no interruption came, he continued, his voice low and cautious.

"There's a legend, older than anyone can remember, about creatures that dwell in the shadows of the Carpathians. They're called Nosferatu—creatures of the night, bound to the darkness that sustains them. They feed on the lifeblood of the living, and wherever they go, death follows."

Thomas suppressed a smile, though he couldn't entirely hide his amusement.

"You believe these legends?"

The old man's eyes met Thomas's, and there was no humor in them.

"You'd be wise not to dismiss them," he said. "The Nosferatu are not like the ghosts and spirits of children's tales. They are real, and they are dangerous. They walk among us, hidden in plain sight, until it's too late."

Thomas leaned back in his chair, crossing his arms.

"I appreciate your concern," he said carefully. "But I don't frighten easily. I've heard stories like this before—every region has its legends, its monsters. But they're just that: stories."

The old man sighed, shaking his head.

"Believe what you will," he said. "But I'll give you this advice: if you're going to the Count's castle, do not eat or drink anything he offers you. And never let him see your fear. The Nosferatu are drawn to it, like moths to a flame."

Thomas's smile faltered for a moment, the man's tone so grave that it pierced his skepticism. He nodded politely, though he could not suppress the faint unease that settled in the pit of his stomach.

"Thank you for the warning," he said. "I'll keep it in mind."

The old man stood, his expression weary but resigned.

"I hope you return safely, Herr Hutter. For your sake, and for the sake of those who wait for you."

The driver had readied the carriage by the time Thomas finished his meal. He climbed into the seat, his satchel resting beside him, and nodded to the driver to begin. The horses snorted, their breath visible in the crisp morning air, and the carriage lurched forward, leaving the quiet village behind.

As they traveled deeper into the forest, the road narrowed, winding between ancient trees whose gnarled branches seemed to reach out toward the carriage. The morning mist lingered, wrapping the forest in an otherworldly silence that was broken only by the creak of the wheels and the occasional call of a raven.

Thomas found himself replaying the old man's words in his mind, though he tried to dismiss them as fanciful superstition. Still, the way the man had spoken, the weight of his voice, left an impression that Thomas could not shake. He glanced at the treetops, their dark silhouettes swaying faintly in the breeze.

"Nosferatu," he murmured to himself, the word strange and unfamiliar on his tongue. It was absurd, of course—an invention of overactive imaginations. And yet, as the carriage climbed higher into the mountains, the shadows grew longer, and the chill in the air deepened.

Somewhere in the depths of the forest, Thomas thought he heard something—a faint rustling, a whisper of movement too deliberate to be the wind. He turned his head, but the road behind them was empty, the trees still and silent. He shook his head, smiling to himself.

"Just stories," he muttered. "Nothing more."

But the whispering trees seemed to disagree.

The carriage climbed higher into the mountains, the road narrowing with every passing mile. The dense forest that had surrounded them for much of the journey began to thin, giving way to jagged outcroppings of rock and steep cliffs that plunged into unseen depths below. The wind picked up, whistling through the narrow passes and carrying with it a bone-deep chill that no coat could ward off.

Thomas leaned out of the carriage window, gazing at the shifting landscape. The world around him felt increasingly foreign, as though he had crossed some unseen boundary into a realm untouched by time or reason. The sky above was a pale, lifeless gray, and the sun, though still visible, seemed muted and distant. The jagged peaks of the Carpathians loomed ahead, their snow-capped summits shrouded in mist.

The driver, who had been mostly silent throughout the journey, grew visibly uneasy as they ascended. His hands gripped the reins tightly, and his eyes darted toward the shadows that seemed to stretch longer with each turn of the road. Thomas noticed the man muttering under his breath, his words too low to discern but carrying an air of prayer or plea.

"Is everything all right?" Thomas asked, his tone light but curious.

The driver glanced back at him, his expression tight.

"These roads are not safe," he said. "Not this late in the day."

Thomas raised an eyebrow.

"The road seems sturdy enough."

"It's not the road," the driver muttered, his eyes fixed ahead. "It's the things that walk beside it."

Thomas chuckled softly, though the driver's unease was infectious. "Still thinking about those stories, are you?" he teased.

The driver didn't reply. He flicked the reins, urging the horses to move faster. The carriage jolted slightly as it rounded a sharp bend, and Thomas had to steady himself against the window frame. The sheer drop on one side of the road was dizzying, the mist swirling below like a sea of ghosts.

As the afternoon wore on, the forest reappeared, its ancient trees towering over the road like silent sentinels. Their twisted branches intertwined overhead, forming a canopy that blocked out what little light remained. The air grew colder, heavier, and the shadows beneath the trees seemed alive, shifting and stretching in ways that defied the wind.

Thomas couldn't help but feel as though he were being watched. It was a ridiculous thought, he told himself—nothing more than the result of the villagers' tales lingering in his mind. And yet, every so often, he caught himself glancing over his shoulder, his eyes scanning the darkened treeline for movement.

Once, he thought he saw something—a figure standing between the trees, impossibly tall and still. But when he blinked, it was gone, leaving only the swaying branches and the rustling of leaves.

"Did you see that?" he asked the driver, leaning forward.

The man shook his head, his knuckles white on the reins.

"I see nothing," he said curtly. "And neither should you."

Thomas sat back, frowning. The driver's response only heightened his sense of unease. He glanced at the treetops, their jagged silhouettes swaying against the pale sky, and felt a shiver run down his spine.

As the road wound deeper into the forest, the carriage passed a strange monument at the edge of a clearing. It was a tall, weathered stone carved with symbols that Thomas did not recognize. The markings were intricate, looping and twisting in patterns that seemed to shift when viewed from different angles. Moss clung to its base, and the air around it felt colder, as though the stone exuded an unnatural chill.

The horses reared slightly as they neared the monument, their eyes rolling and their breath coming in sharp, frightened bursts. The driver cursed under his breath, pulling hard on the reins to steady them.

"What is that?" Thomas asked, leaning out of the carriage to get a better look.

The driver shook his head, his face pale.

"An old marker," he said, his voice tight. "A warning, some say. Others say it's a boundary."

"A boundary for what?"

"For things better left undisturbed," the driver replied, flicking the reins to move the horses past the clearing as quickly as possible. "We shouldn't linger."

Thomas watched the stone until it disappeared behind them, its strange carvings etched into his mind. He wanted to dismiss it as a relic of some forgotten superstition, but he couldn't shake the feeling that the air around it had been different—thicker, colder, and heavy with an unspoken menace.

The sun was sinking behind the mountains by the time they reached the final stretch of the road. The fading light cast long shadows across the rocky terrain, and the wind howled through the narrow pass like a mournful wail. The driver grew increasingly agitated, urging the horses to move faster, his mutterings growing louder and more desperate.

"We're close," he said, his voice taut with tension. "But night comes quickly in these parts. Too quickly."

Thomas glanced at the sky, where the first stars were beginning to appear. The light was fading faster than he had expected, the gray clouds thickening and darkening with alarming speed. The road ahead seemed to dissolve into the growing gloom, its edges blurring as the shadows closed in.

A chill ran through him, deeper than the cold of the mountain air. He tightened his coat around him and leaned back in his seat, trying to push away the unease that gnawed at the edges of his thoughts. But as the carriage pressed on into the gathering darkness, he couldn't shake the feeling that the shadows were more than just shadows—and that something, somewhere, was watching.

# Chapter 4
## The Forest

The road twisted and turned as the carriage entered the forest's edge, where the trees grew so close together that their branches tangled like grasping fingers. The last light of the sun disappeared entirely, swallowed by the dense canopy overhead, leaving only the pale, cold glow of the rising moon to guide the way. Thomas pulled his coat tighter around him as a chill settled in the air, far colder than any he had felt before. It was not merely the temperature—it was a deep, penetrating cold that seemed to seep into his very bones.

The forest had a strange stillness about it. No birds sang, no animals rustled in the underbrush, and even the wind seemed to hold its breath. The only sounds were the steady clatter of the carriage wheels and the rhythmic stamping of the horses' hooves, though even those seemed muted, muffled by the oppressive silence that pressed in from all sides.

Thomas leaned out of the carriage window, peering into the darkness. The trees loomed like sentinels, their trunks knotted and twisted in grotesque shapes. In the faint moonlight, the bark seemed to shimmer, as though it were slick with some unnatural substance. The shadows between the trees stretched unnaturally long, shifting and curling at the edges of his vision.

"What sort of place is this?" he muttered under his breath.

The driver did not respond. His focus was fixed on the road ahead, his shoulders hunched and his hands gripping the reins so tightly that his knuckles were bone white. Thomas noticed that the man was muttering under his breath again, his words too soft to make out but filled with a desperate urgency.

"Driver," Thomas called, raising his voice slightly. "What's the matter?"

The man flinched at the sound, glancing over his shoulder with wide, frightened eyes.

"The forest is alive," he said in a hoarse whisper. "It doesn't like intruders."

Thomas frowned, leaning back in his seat. The man's fear was almost palpable, his movements jerky and anxious. It unnerved Thomas more than he cared to admit. He had dismissed the villagers' warnings as superstitions, but now, surrounded by this unnatural landscape, he felt a flicker of doubt.

The deeper they traveled into the forest, the stranger the atmosphere became. The air grew thicker, heavier, as though it were weighted with unseen forces. A faint sound began to rise from the shadows—a low, almost imperceptible whisper that seemed to come from everywhere and nowhere at once.

Thomas sat up straighter, his heart pounding. The sound was faint, just on the edge of hearing, but it was undeniably there. It was not the rustle of leaves or the creak of tree branches but something altogether different. It was soft, insistent, and carried a rhythm that was almost speech.

He glanced at the driver, who was visibly trembling now, his muttering growing louder as if trying to drown out the whispers.

"Do you hear that?" Thomas asked, his voice tinged with unease.

The driver didn't answer. He flicked the reins, urging the horses to move faster. The carriage jolted as it sped up, the wheels rattling against the uneven road. Thomas tightened his grip on the window frame, his gaze darting to the shadows that seemed to shift and writhe at the edges of the path.

The whispers grew louder, more distinct, though the words remained incomprehensible. They were not spoken in any language Thomas recognized, but their tone was unmistakable—hungry, searching, and filled with malice.

As they rounded a bend in the road, the horses suddenly reared, their terrified whinnies echoing through the forest. The driver cursed, struggling to keep them under control as they stamped and tossed their heads. Thomas leaned out of the carriage, his eyes scanning the darkness for whatever had startled them.

There, just beyond the reach of the moonlight, two glowing eyes stared back at him. They burned with an unnatural light, a sickly yellow hue that seemed to pierce through the shadows. The figure they belonged to was obscured, its form blending into the darkness, but the eyes were unmistakable—unblinking, predatory, and utterly devoid of humanity.

"What in God's name…" Thomas whispered, his breath catching in his throat.

The driver shouted something in his native tongue and cracked the reins, forcing the horses forward. The glowing eyes vanished into the shadows, but the sense of being watched remained. Thomas sat back in his seat, his heart racing and his hands trembling. For the first time since the journey began, he felt a flicker of true fear.

The road grew narrower, the trees pressing closer together as though trying to bar their passage. The carriage jolted and swayed as the wheels struck roots that seemed to rise out of the ground like grasping hands. The horses snorted and whinnied, their breath visible in the cold air, their panic palpable.

The whispers rose to a crescendo, joined now by faint, eerie laughter that seemed to echo from the depths of the forest. Thomas gripped the edge of his seat, his eyes darting from shadow to shadow as he tried to make sense of the chaos around him.

The driver shouted a warning, his voice sharp and panicked, and Thomas barely had time to brace himself as the carriage lurched violently to one side. A root had caught one of the wheels, nearly tipping the vehicle over. The horses reared again, their hooves striking the air as the driver fought to regain control.

"Keep going!" Thomas yelled, his own voice trembling now. "Don't stop!"

The driver didn't need to be told twice. With a crack of the reins, he pushed the horses onward, the carriage careening through the narrowing path. The forest seemed alive now, the trees bending and twisting as though reaching for them. The shadows danced and flickered, forming shapes that Thomas dared not look at too closely.

Just as the forest seemed ready to swallow them whole, the path widened, and a faint glow appeared in the distance. It was not the warm, golden light of a village but a cold, silvery luminescence that seemed to hover in the air like a will-o'-the-wisp. The whispers faded, replaced by an oppressive silence that was almost worse.

The driver pulled the carriage to a halt, his chest heaving as he caught his breath. He turned to Thomas, his face pale and drenched with sweat.

"We're here," he said, his voice barely audible. "This is as far as I go."

Thomas frowned, looking around. The path ahead stretched into the darkness, the glow growing fainter as it receded into the distance.

"What do you mean?" he asked. "We're not at the castle yet."

The driver shook his head.

"I won't go any further," he said. "You'll have to continue on foot."

Before Thomas could argue, the driver climbed down from the carriage, opened the door, and gestured for him to step out. The air was colder here, heavier, and Thomas felt an involuntary shiver run through him as his boots touched the ground.

In the distance, a faint sound reached his ears—the creak of wheels and the steady clatter of hooves. Another carriage was coming, though its outline was obscured by the mist. Thomas turned to the driver, but the man was already climbing back onto his seat, his expression grim.

"Good luck, Herr Hutter," the driver said, and with that, he turned the carriage around and disappeared into the forest, leaving Thomas alone on the darkened path.

The forest thickened as the light from Thomas's lantern faded into the mist, leaving him alone on the narrow, winding road. The stillness pressed in around him, broken only by the crunch of his boots on the frost-rimmed path. His breath hung in the cold air, curling in faint wisps as he glanced uneasily over his shoulder, half-expecting the forest to close behind him like a cage.

From somewhere in the distance, the faint sound of wheels on gravel reached his ears. It was slow at first, almost rhythmic, a hollow, deliberate cadence that grew louder with each passing moment. Thomas stopped in his tracks, the sound carrying through the oppressive silence like the echo of a tolling bell. He turned toward the noise, his heart quickening as a pale light began to pierce the gloom.

The sound grew sharper, more defined: the creak of wood, the faint snort of horses, and the metallic jingle of harnesses. Through the veil of mist, a dark shape emerged—a coach unlike any Thomas had ever seen. Its body was black as pitch, its surface faintly glistening as though damp with dew or something more sinister. The wheels, carved with intricate patterns, turned unnaturally smoothly, gliding over the uneven road without a sound. Even the horses that pulled it seemed unnatural—large and unnervingly still, their eyes gleaming faintly in the moonlight like polished stones.

But it was the driver that seized Thomas's breath. The figure atop the coach was hunched, cloaked in heavy black fabric that obscured every detail. Their face was hidden beneath a wide-brimmed hat, and their hands, gloved in leather, moved with mechanical precision as they gripped the reins. The stillness of their posture was unnerving, as though they were more statue than living being.

The coach came to a stop just a few feet from where Thomas stood. For a moment, neither man nor driver moved. The air between them grew heavy, and Thomas could hear the faint pounding of his heart in his ears. Then, slowly, the driver turned their head, their movements almost too fluid, and gestured toward the coach door with a gloved hand.

Thomas hesitated, a cold sweat breaking out on his brow. His instincts screamed at him to turn back, to retreat to the safety of the village and abandon this entire enterprise. But the thought of failure, of returning empty-handed, was too great to bear. He squared his shoulders and stepped closer, the faint crunch of gravel beneath his boots breaking the silence.

The door of the coach opened without warning, its hinges groaning like the opening of a crypt. The interior was dimly lit, a pale, flickering light casting faint shadows on the worn velvet seats. The cold emanating from within was almost physical, seeping into his skin as he stood at the threshold. He glanced at the driver again, searching for any sign of humanity in the shadowed figure, but found none. Their gloved hand gestured again, more insistent this time.

Thomas swallowed hard and stepped into the coach. The air inside was thick, carrying a metallic tang that stung his nostrils. The door slammed shut behind him with a force that made him jump, the sound reverberating unnaturally in the confined space. He placed his satchel on the seat beside him and tried to steady his breathing, but the eerie atmosphere refused to release its grip on him.

The coach lurched forward, its motion unnervingly smooth despite the rough terrain. Outside the small, heavily tinted windows, the forest passed by in a blur of darkness and mist. Thomas pressed his forehead against the glass, trying to catch a glimpse of the world beyond, but the view was murky and distorted, as though the glass itself refused to reveal what lay outside.

The interior of the coach felt alive, the flickering light casting strange, shifting shadows that danced across the walls. Thomas closed his eyes, willing himself to ignore the strange sensations creeping up his spine. He focused instead on the task ahead: his meeting with Count Orlok, the details of the property sale, and the promise of wealth and opportunity that had driven him this far.

Thomas tried to steady his breathing, focusing on the steady rhythm of the wheels and the faint clatter of the horses' hooves.

"Just stories," he whispered to himself, though the words offered little comfort. "It's only superstition."

But even as he spoke, his eyes darted toward the corners of the cabin, where the shadows seemed to stretch and curl in unnatural patterns. The light flickered again, its glow dimming momentarily before returning to its pale, steady shimmer.

He closed his eyes, leaning back against the seat. The weight of the journey was beginning to press down on him—not just the physical distance but the oppressive atmosphere that seemed to cling to him like a second skin. He thought of Ellen, her worried face as she had stood in the village square, her hand clutching the locket he had given her. He imagined her waiting by the window, watching the horizon for his return. The thought gave him some comfort, though it was fleeting.

The coach accelerated, and Thomas's eyes snapped open. Outside, the forest was darker than before, the shadows deeper and more impenetrable. The road had narrowed to a thin, winding path, flanked by jagged rocks and gnarled trees that leaned over the coach like silent sentinels.

He glanced toward the driver, visible only through a small opening near the front of the cabin. The figure remained perfectly still, their head tilted slightly forward as they guided the horses through the winding path. The stillness of the driver unnerved him more than he cared to admit. They moved only when absolutely necessary, their gestures slow and deliberate, as though they were conserving their energy for something far more sinister.

After what felt like hours, the road opened into a clearing, and the oppressive darkness of the forest gave way to an eerie, open expanse. The sky was visible now, though it was devoid of stars, the pale moonlight illuminating the scene in shades of silver and gray. Ahead, rising out of the mist like a jagged wound against the horizon, stood the castle.

Count Orlok's home loomed like a specter, its spires piercing the heavens and its walls crumbling with age. The windows were dark and empty, their shapes resembling hollow eyes that stared into the surrounding landscape. The air was colder here, sharper, and it carried a faint, sickly sweet scent that turned Thomas's stomach.

The coach slowed as it approached the castle gates, their heavy iron bars standing slightly ajar. The horses came to an unnaturally precise stop, their breaths steaming in the frigid air, and the driver climbed down from their seat with a fluid grace that sent another shiver down Thomas's spine.

The driver gestured toward the open door of the coach, their gloved hand extending toward the castle as if to say, This is your destination. Thomas hesitated, his instincts screaming at him to stay in the relative safety of the coach. But there was no turning back now—not when he was so close.

He stepped out into the clearing, the cold biting at his skin despite his heavy coat. The driver remained silent, their shadowed face turned toward him as he adjusted his satchel and straightened his posture. Without a word, they climbed back onto the coach, flicked the reins, and disappeared into the mist as suddenly as they had appeared.

Thomas stood alone at the base of the castle, his breath visible in the cold night air. The wind howled faintly through the open gates, carrying with it a sound that might have been the cry of a distant wolf—or something far more menacing. He took a deep breath, his fingers tightening around the strap of his satchel, and stepped forward.

The gates creaked as he pushed them open, their weight groaning in protest. Beyond them, the castle loomed larger, its darkened windows and jagged edges seeming to watch him as he made his way toward the entrance. His footsteps echoed on the stone path, each step bringing him closer to whatever waited within.

# Chapter 5
## Orlok's Castle

The gates swung open with a groan, the sound reverberating through the cold, heavy air like a warning bell. Thomas Hutter stood at the threshold, his breath visible in the pale moonlight. Before him loomed Count Orlok's castle, its jagged silhouette rising against the dark sky like a monument to some forgotten god. The structure was enormous, its walls blackened with age and decay, as though the very stone had absorbed centuries of shadow and sorrow.

The castle's towers twisted unnaturally, their spires piercing the heavens at crooked angles. Crumbling gargoyles clung to the edges of the battlements, their features eroded into grotesque mockeries of the human form. The windows, narrow slits in the towering walls, were dark and empty, like the hollow eyes of a corpse. A faint light flickered somewhere within, barely visible against the oppressive darkness that seemed to emanate from the castle itself.

The courtyard was littered with broken stone and overgrown weeds, the cobblestones cracked and uneven. The air carried a strange, metallic tang, mingled with the faint scent of damp earth and rot. Thomas hesitated, his eyes tracing the twisted architecture, his mind struggling to reconcile its strange beauty with its overwhelming sense of menace.

He adjusted his satchel and stepped forward, the sound of his boots crunching against the gravel unnaturally loud in the stillness. The castle seemed to watch him as he approached, its presence oppressive, its shadow stretching toward him like a living thing. His heart pounded in his chest, but he forced himself to keep moving, each step a battle against the instinct to turn and run.

The heavy wooden doors of the castle stood slightly ajar, their surface carved with intricate designs that seemed to writhe and shift in the flickering moonlight. Thomas pushed them open, the hinges creaking in protest, and stepped into the entrance hall.

The air inside was colder than the night outside, and the silence was so complete that it seemed to press against his ears. The room was vast, its ceiling disappearing into the shadows above. The walls were adorned with faded tapestries, their once-vivid colors dulled by time and neglect. Stone pillars rose like skeletal fingers, their surfaces etched with runes and symbols that Thomas did not recognize.

A grand staircase dominated the far end of the hall, its steps worn smooth by countless feet. A dim light flickered at the top, casting long shadows that danced across the walls. The faint sound of wind echoed through the corridors, though there were no open windows to explain its presence.

As Thomas took another step forward, the sound of his boots echoed through the hall, breaking the oppressive silence. He paused, glancing around, his unease growing with every passing moment. The castle felt alive, as though it were a living, breathing entity, and he was an intruder in its heart.

"Welcome, Herr Hutter."

The voice came from the shadows, low and deliberate, with a strange accent that sent a shiver down Thomas's spine. He turned sharply, his eyes searching the darkness at the top of the staircase. For a moment, there was nothing—only the flickering light and the deep, impenetrable shadows.

Then a figure emerged, moving with a grace that seemed at odds with its gaunt, skeletal frame. Count Orlok descended the staircase slowly, his long, bony fingers trailing along the banister. His figure was tall, almost unnaturally so, and his movements were fluid, like a predator stalking its prey. His face came into view as he stepped into the light, and Thomas felt his breath catch in his throat.

The Count's skin was pale, almost translucent, stretched tightly over sharp cheekbones and a pointed chin. His eyes were deep-set and dark, their gaze piercing and unrelenting. His nose was thin and hooked, and his lips, unnaturally red against his pallid complexion, curved into a smile that revealed teeth far too long and sharp. His head was completely bald, the skin gleaming faintly in the dim light, and his ears, pointed and angular, added to his otherworldly appearance.

"You have traveled far," Orlok said, his voice a low murmur that seemed to resonate in the stillness. "And you are welcome here, in my humble home."

Thomas forced himself to smile, though his mouth felt dry, his words caught in his throat.

"Thank you, Count Orlok," he managed, his voice trembling slightly. "It's an honor to meet you."

Orlok reached the bottom of the staircase and extended a hand. Thomas hesitated for the briefest moment before taking it, surprised by the Count's grip. His fingers were cold as ice, their texture almost leathery, and his touch lingered a moment too long.

"You must be tired," Orlok said, his gaze never leaving Thomas's face. "Come. Allow me to show you to your quarters. We will speak more at dinner."

Thomas nodded, his pulse pounding in his ears as Orlok turned and began to lead him deeper into the castle. The flickering light cast the Count's shadow across the walls, stretching and twisting unnaturally as they moved. Thomas followed, his steps hesitant, his unease growing with every passing moment.

The corridors of the castle seemed endless, twisting and turning in a labyrinth of shadow and stone. Thomas followed Count Orlok in silence, his footsteps echoing faintly behind the Count's soundless movements. The air grew colder as they ventured deeper into the castle, the dim light from the sconces along the walls casting long, flickering shadows. It was as if the castle itself was alive, its walls breathing and whispering in a language too ancient to understand.

Thomas's eyes darted around the hallway, taking in the strange and unsettling details. The walls were lined with faded portraits, their subjects depicted with faces that seemed just slightly wrong—eyes too large, mouths too small, and expressions that hinted at some hidden malice. The stone floors were uneven, as though they had shifted over centuries, and the faint smell of dampness and decay lingered in the air.

Count Orlok moved with an unnatural grace, his long figure almost gliding rather than walking. He did not speak as he led Thomas to a large sitting room near the castle's heart. The room was sparsely furnished, its grandness muted by age and neglect. A long table stood in the center, its surface marred by deep scratches, and a fire crackled weakly in a hearth on the far wall, providing the only source of warmth in the otherwise cold chamber.

"Please," Orlok said, gesturing toward a chair by the fire. "Make yourself comfortable."

Thomas nodded and moved to the chair, setting his satchel down beside him. He lowered himself into the seat, the worn upholstery creaking beneath his weight. Orlok did not sit but remained standing, his tall frame casting a long shadow that seemed to stretch unnaturally far across the room.

Now that they were face-to-face, Thomas could not help but study the Count more closely. There was something deeply wrong about him, something that stirred a primal sense of unease. His skin, pale and almost translucent, seemed to glow faintly in the firelight. His eyes, dark and unblinking, held a strange intensity that made Thomas feel as though he were being dissected, his thoughts laid bare.

Orlok's hands were perhaps the most unsettling feature of all. They were long and bony, the fingers unnaturally thin and ending in sharp, claw-like nails. When he moved, his hands seemed to linger in the air, their movements deliberate and almost hypnotic. Thomas forced himself to look away, focusing instead on the fire, though even its flickering warmth could not chase the chill that clung to his skin.

"It is not often that I receive visitors," Orlok said, his voice low and measured. "You must forgive the state of my home. It has seen many years, and time has not been kind."

"It's... magnificent," Thomas said, though the words felt hollow as he spoke them. "Truly unlike anything I've ever seen."

Orlok tilted his head, his thin lips curving into a faint smile that did not reach his eyes.

"You are kind to say so, Herr Hutter. I have lived here for a very long time, and it has become... comfortable to me."

Thomas shifted in his seat, uneasy under the weight of Orlok's gaze.

"It must be quite isolated," he said, trying to fill the silence. "The nearest village is hours away."

"Isolation suits me," Orlok replied, his tone sharp but not unkind. "I find solace in the quiet. It allows me to focus on the things that matter most."

Orlok's eyes narrowed slightly, and his smile widened just enough to show the tips of his unnervingly long teeth.

"I am very much looking forward to my new property in Wisborg," he said, his voice taking on an almost reverent tone. "Tell me, Herr Hutter, what is the town like? Is it lively? Full of... spirited people?"

Thomas hesitated, unsure how to respond. There was something in Orlok's tone that made the question feel far more significant than it should have been.

"Wisborg is a quiet town," he said carefully. "Peaceful, for the most part. The people are hard-working and welcoming."

"Welcoming," Orlok repeated, the word lingering on his tongue as though tasting it. "How delightful. And you, Herr Hutter—you are married, yes?"

Thomas blinked, surprised by the abrupt shift in the conversation.

"Yes," he said slowly. "My wife, Ellen. She's waiting for me in Wisborg."

Orlok's smile widened further, his teeth gleaming faintly in the firelight.

"Ellen," he said, as though savoring the name. "A lovely name. And I am certain she is… quite lovely as well."

Thomas felt a flicker of discomfort at Orlok's words, though he forced himself to keep his expression neutral.

"She is," he said simply. "Ellen is everything to me."

Orlok tilted his head again, his dark eyes studying Thomas intently.

"You are fortunate, Herr Hutter. A wife's devotion is a rare and precious thing. I envy you."

The words were polite, but there was something in the way Orlok said them that made Thomas's skin crawl. He looked down at his hands, unsure of how to respond, and the silence stretched between them like a taut wire.

"You must be tired from your journey," Orlok said after a moment, breaking the silence. "But I insist you join me for dinner before you retire. A meal shared is a bond formed, after all."

Thomas hesitated, but Orlok's gaze left no room for refusal.

"Of course," he said, his voice steady despite the unease gnawing at him. "Thank you."

"Excellent," Orlok said, clapping his hands together softly. "I shall have everything prepared. In the meantime, please, make yourself at home."

With that, Orlok turned and left the room, his long shadow trailing behind him as he disappeared into the dark corridor. Thomas exhaled, realizing he had been holding his breath. The warmth of the fire did little to ease the cold that lingered in the room, and he found himself glancing toward the doorway, half-expecting Orlok to reappear at any moment.

As he sat alone in the silence, Thomas couldn't shake the feeling that his first meeting with the Count had been more than a simple exchange of pleasantries. There was a weight to Orlok's words, a hidden intent that Thomas could not yet understand. He glanced at the flickering fire, his thoughts drifting to Ellen and the safety of Wisborg. For the first time, he wondered if he had made a terrible mistake.

The dining hall was a cavernous room filled with shadows that seemed to stretch endlessly across the cold stone walls. A single candelabra sat at the center of the long, dark table, its thin, flickering flames barely illuminating the chamber. The table was set with ornate silverware and a single polished goblet, its surface gleaming faintly in the dim light. The rest of the room remained in near-total darkness, the faint glow of the candles revealing hints of faded tapestries and crumbling stone.

Thomas Hutter stood at the threshold, his boots echoing softly on the uneven floor as he hesitated. The sheer emptiness of the space seemed almost oppressive, the silence broken only by the distant sound of the wind howling through the castle's high towers.

"Come, Herr Hutter," came Count Orlok's voice, soft but commanding. It seemed to carry from everywhere at once, bouncing off the walls in an unnatural way. Orlok stood at the far end of the table, his tall frame partially obscured by the flickering shadows. His pale, gaunt face caught the light of the candles, his dark eyes fixed on Thomas with an intensity that sent a shiver down his spine.

Thomas forced himself to move forward, his steps measured and careful. As he approached the table, Orlok gestured toward the chair opposite him.

"Please, sit," he said, his thin lips curling into a faint smile. "You must be hungry after your long journey."

Thomas hesitated only for a moment before taking the offered seat. The chair creaked under his weight, the sound unnaturally loud in the silence. Orlok remained standing for a moment, his hands resting on the back of his own chair, his eyes never leaving Thomas. Then, with a slow and deliberate motion, he sat down, his long fingers steepled in front of him.

The clatter of a door echoed somewhere behind them, and a pale, silent servant appeared, carrying a silver tray. Thomas hadn't seen anyone else in the castle until now, and the sudden appearance of the servant startled him. The figure moved with an unsettling precision, their face expressionless as they placed the tray on the table. Without a word, they poured a deep red liquid into the goblet before retreating back into the shadows, their footsteps disappearing into the gloom.

Thomas glanced at the goblet, his stomach twisting. The liquid inside caught the candlelight, its deep crimson hue unnervingly like blood. He tried to push the thought away, telling himself it was simply wine, though the metallic tang in the air made him doubt his own reasoning.

"Drink," Orlok said, his voice soft but insistent. "It will warm you."

Thomas hesitated, then lifted the goblet to his lips. The wine was bitter and heavy, its taste lingering unpleasantly on his tongue. He forced himself to swallow, setting the goblet down quickly and wiping his mouth with the back of his hand.

Orlok's smile widened, his sharp teeth glinting in the dim light.

"Good," he murmured. "A strong wine for a strong man."

Thomas shifted uncomfortably in his seat, his unease growing with every passing moment.

"I appreciate your hospitality, Count Orlok," he said, trying to keep his voice steady. "You've been very kind to receive me on such short notice."

"It is my pleasure," Orlok replied, his tone silky. "I have been eager to meet you, Herr Hutter. Your reputation precedes you."

Thomas raised an eyebrow, surprised.

"I didn't realize I had much of a reputation."

"Oh, but you do," Orlok said, leaning forward slightly. "A man of ambition, seeking to secure a better future for himself and his wife. Such determination is admirable. Rare, even."

Thomas's throat tightened at the mention of Ellen, though he forced a polite smile.

"Ellen is my reason for everything," he said carefully. "She's the one who inspires me to take these risks."

"Ellen," Orlok said, drawing out the name as though savoring it. "A name that carries light and warmth. Tell me, Herr Hutter, is she as radiant as her name suggests?"

Thomas felt a flicker of irritation beneath his unease.

"She is," he said, his voice firm. "And she's waiting for me in Wisborg."

Orlok tilted his head, his smile lingering.

"How fortunate you are to have such devotion waiting for you."

Orlok's gaze drifted toward the candelabra, the flickering light casting deep shadows across his angular face. For a moment, he seemed lost in thought, his expression unreadable. Then he spoke, his voice quieter now, almost wistful.

"The Carpathians are a land of ancient histories, Herr Hutter," he said. "A place where time moves differently, where the past and present intertwine. Do you feel it? The weight of this place? The shadows of those who came before us?"

Thomas glanced around the room, his unease deepening. There was something in Orlok's words that resonated, though he couldn't explain why. The castle did feel heavy, as though it were imbued with the memories of countless lives that had passed through its walls.

"It's... unlike anywhere I've been," Thomas admitted, his voice hesitant.

Orlok's dark eyes gleamed.

"Yes," he said softly. "Few truly understand what it means to walk in the shadow of eternity. But you will, Herr Hutter. In time, you will."

The cryptic nature of Orlok's words sent a chill through Thomas, and he shifted uncomfortably in his chair. He tried to change the subject, steering the conversation back to the business that had brought him here.

"The property in Wisborg," he began. "I've brought the necessary documents for you to review. I think you'll find it a fine choice—a spacious home with a commanding view of the town."

Orlok's smile widened, his teeth glinting faintly.

"I have no doubt it will suit my needs perfectly," he said. "Wisborg has... everything I require."

There was something in the way he said it, a strange emphasis that made Thomas's skin crawl. He forced himself to nod, reaching for his goblet again, if only to have something to do with his hands.

As the meal drew to a close, Orlok rose from his chair, his movements fluid and deliberate. "You must be tired, Herr Hutter," he said, gesturing toward the door. "Allow me to show you to your quarters. You will find everything you need to be most comfortable during your stay."

Thomas stood as well, his legs feeling heavier than they should.

"Thank you, Count Orlok," he said, his voice tinged with weariness. "You've been very generous."

Orlok's smile returned, sharp and knowing.

"It is my pleasure," he said softly. "You are my guest, after all."

With that, Orlok led him from the dining hall, his tall shadow stretching down the corridor as they disappeared into the depths of the castle. The oppressive silence returned, and Thomas felt the weight of the castle pressing down on him once more. He could not explain it, but something about Orlok's hospitality felt less like kindness and more like a trap—one he had willingly walked into.

# Chapter 6
## Lovely Throat

The room Thomas had been given was a modest chamber near the castle's upper levels, far removed from the grandiosity of the dining hall or the eerie vastness of the entrance. It was sparsely furnished, with a single bed draped in faded linens, a small writing desk, and a wardrobe that leaned slightly as though weary of its centuries of use. A narrow window allowed a sliver of moonlight to pierce the oppressive darkness, its view obscured by the thick mist that clung to the castle's exterior.

Thomas placed his satchel on the desk, his hands trembling slightly as he worked to unbuckle its straps. The strange dinner with Count Orlok lingered in his mind, each cryptic word and unsettling glance replaying itself in his thoughts. He shook his head, attempting to dismiss his unease. It was the castle, he told himself—the strange architecture, the isolation. It was enough to unsettle anyone, but it didn't mean anything sinister.

He withdrew the documents he had prepared for Orlok, neatly stacked and tied with a ribbon. As he did, the corner of something familiar peeked out from beneath the papers—a small, worn photograph. He paused, a faint smile crossing his lips as he carefully pulled it free.

The photograph was of Ellen, her soft features illuminated in the faint light of the room. She stood by the window of their home in Wisborg, her gaze distant, her expression a mix of quiet melancholy and strength. Thomas ran a thumb over the edge of the photo, the memory of her standing there vivid in his mind. He could almost hear her voice, soft and steady, calling his name.

Lost in thought, he didn't notice the faint creak of the door as it opened behind him.

"Ah, Herr Hutter," came Orlok's voice, low and deliberate.

Thomas startled, turning quickly to see the Count standing in the doorway. Orlok's tall frame was half-shrouded in shadow, his dark eyes gleaming faintly in the dim light. His movements were unnervingly silent, his arrival unnoticed until he chose to speak.

"Forgive my intrusion," Orlok said, stepping into the room with slow, deliberate strides. "I wished to ensure you were comfortable."

Thomas forced a smile, quickly tucking the photograph back into his satchel.

"Thank you, Count Orlok," he said, his voice steadier than he felt. "The room is quite sufficient."

Orlok's gaze lingered on the satchel for a moment, his smile widening ever so slightly.

"You carry many treasures with you, Herr Hutter," he said, his tone almost playful. "What was it you were holding just now? A keepsake, perhaps?"

Thomas hesitated, but the intensity of Orlok's stare left him little choice. Slowly, he pulled the photograph out again, holding it up for the Count to see.

"It's... my wife," he said, his voice soft. "Ellen."

Orlok stepped closer, his long, bony fingers clasped tightly in front of him. His eyes locked onto the photograph with an intensity that made Thomas uneasy, as though he were studying it far too closely.

"Ellen," Orlok murmured, his voice almost a whisper. "A beautiful name."

Thomas nodded, his discomfort growing.

"She's waiting for me in Wisborg," he said, his words quick and clipped. "I brought this to remind me of her while I'm away."

Orlok tilted his head, his dark eyes narrowing slightly.

"She has a delicate beauty," he said, his voice carrying an unsettling edge. "A rare purity. And such a lovely… throat."

Thomas froze, the words hanging in the air like a blade. Orlok's gaze flicked to him, his thin lips curling into a smile that was far from reassuring.

"You are fortunate, Herr Hutter," he continued, his tone soft but chilling. "To possess such a treasure."

Thomas shifted uncomfortably under Orlok's unrelenting gaze, the photograph of Ellen still trembling slightly in his hand. The Count's words, spoken with a strange reverence, seemed to linger in the air longer than they should have, heavy with a meaning Thomas could not—or would not—comprehend.

"Yes," Thomas said finally, his voice stiff as he carefully returned the photograph to his satchel, tucking it safely beneath the documents. "She's everything to me."

Orlok didn't reply immediately. He remained standing, his gaunt frame silhouetted against the pale glow of the moonlight streaming through the narrow window. His elongated fingers twitched faintly, as though resisting the urge to reach for the satchel. His eyes, deep and piercing, seemed to glimmer as he spoke.

"Love is a curious thing," Orlok murmured, his voice almost a purr. "It binds us, yes, but it also exposes us. To love so deeply, to care so fully for another—it is both a gift and a curse. Don't you think, Herr Hutter?"

Thomas frowned, unsure of how to respond. He forced a polite smile, though the unease stirring in his gut was growing harder to ignore.

"I don't see it as a curse," he said. "Ellen gives me purpose. She's the reason I'm here—to secure a better future for us."

Orlok tilted his head, the faint smile on his pale lips widening to reveal the edges of his unnaturally sharp teeth.

"A noble sentiment," he said, his tone laced with something that sounded almost like mockery. "But tell me, Herr Hutter—what would you do if someone tried to take her from you?"

The question struck Thomas like a blow. He straightened in his seat, his eyes narrowing slightly as he met Orlok's gaze.

"No one will take her from me," he said firmly, his voice tinged with defiance.

Orlok's smile did not falter, though his expression darkened subtly, his eyes narrowing with an intensity that made Thomas's skin crawl.

"How fortunate she is," Orlok said softly. "To have someone so devoted to her. Such loyalty is… rare."

The silence that followed was thick and oppressive, broken only by the faint rustling of the wind against the castle walls. Thomas swallowed hard, his throat dry, and shifted in his chair. He felt as though the Count's words were a trap, carefully laid, though he couldn't quite discern their purpose.

Orlok moved toward the window, his tall, skeletal frame casting a long shadow across the room. He stared out into the misty darkness, his back to Thomas, and spoke in a tone that was both wistful and menacing.

"There is a beauty in fragility, is there not?" he said. "The delicate curve of a neck, the faint pulse of life beneath the surface. It is fleeting, ephemeral. A reminder that all things—no matter how precious—can be lost."

Thomas stiffened, his discomfort sharpening into something closer to fear.

"I suppose," he said cautiously, unsure of how to respond. "But I'd rather focus on preserving what I have than dwelling on what might be lost."

Orlok turned his head slightly, just enough for Thomas to see the glint of his dark eyes.

"Spoken like a man who has never tasted true loss," he said, his voice almost pitying. "But forgive me, Herr Hutter. I did not mean to trouble you with such musings."

Thomas forced a weak smile, eager to steer the conversation to safer ground.

"I appreciate your concern, Count Orlok," he said. "But I assure you, Ellen and I are quite happy. We've built a good life together, and this opportunity to work with you will only make it better."

Orlok stepped away from the window, moving closer to Thomas with a grace that was both fluid and unnatural. He placed one long-fingered hand on the back of Thomas's chair, leaning down just enough to make his presence oppressive.

"And what a life it must be," he murmured, his voice low and velvety. "To know that such beauty and devotion await you in Wisborg. It must be... intoxicating."

Thomas swallowed hard, his hands gripping the edge of the desk. The Count's words, though spoken with a veneer of politeness, carried an undercurrent of something darker—something predatory. He felt as though Orlok were probing him, testing the boundaries of his resolve.

"I should rest," Thomas said abruptly, rising to his feet. "It's been a long journey, and I'll need my energy for tomorrow."

Orlok straightened, his expression unreadable.

"Of course," he said smoothly, stepping back. "I would not dream of keeping you from your rest. But remember, Herr Hutter—if you should require anything, you need only ask."

Thomas nodded stiffly, gathering his satchel and moving toward the door. Orlok watched him, his eyes gleaming faintly in the dim light, and for a moment, Thomas felt as though he were being hunted. He forced himself to step into the hallway, closing the door firmly behind him.

Thomas's footsteps echoed softly in the empty corridor as he made his way back to his room. The air was colder now, the chill seeping into his skin despite the thick walls of the castle. He couldn't shake the feeling that Orlok's words, his questions about Ellen, had been more than idle curiosity.

When he reached his room, he locked the door behind him and leaned against it, exhaling heavily. The photograph of Ellen was still tucked safely in his satchel, but the memory of Orlok's gaze as he looked at it lingered in Thomas's mind like a shadow that refused to be banished.

As he lay in the narrow bed, staring at the dark ceiling above, the Count's voice echoed in his thoughts: "What would you do if someone tried to take her from you?" The words gnawed at him, planting seeds of doubt and fear that grew with every passing moment.

Sleep came slowly that night, and when it did, it was restless and filled with strange, haunting dreams of shadows and whispered threats.

Thomas awoke to the pale, gray light of dawn filtering through the narrow window of his chamber. The mist that clung to the castle the night before had not lifted, instead thickening to obscure the view entirely. The cold air of the room bit at his skin as he sat up in the creaking bed, his body stiff and his mind clouded from a restless night of broken sleep. The fragments of dreams—or nightmares—lingered at the edges of his thoughts, fleeting images of dark figures and whispered warnings that dissolved as soon as he tried to recall them.

He rubbed his eyes and forced himself to his feet, moving to the window to peer out into the bleak morning. The castle grounds below were as silent and desolate as they had been the previous evening, the barren courtyard framed by the jagged silhouettes of the surrounding mountains. He shivered, pulling his coat tighter around himself. The oppressive weight of the place seemed to settle heavier on his shoulders with each passing hour.

Thomas's thoughts drifted to the events of the previous night: Count Orlok's unsettling words, his fixation on Ellen, and the strange intensity in his gaze when he spoke of her. The memory made Thomas's skin crawl, though he quickly shook his head, trying to banish the feeling. It was just the Count's way, he told himself—eccentric, perhaps overly curious. There was no real harm in his questions. No reason to dwell on them.

Still, a faint unease lingered, gnawing at the edges of his mind.

Thomas busied himself by unpacking his belongings, hoping that a sense of routine might steady his nerves. He laid out the documents for Orlok's review on the small writing desk, smoothing the pages carefully and double-checking that everything was in order. The photograph of Ellen lay tucked safely inside his satchel, its corners just visible beneath a layer of papers.

He paused, his hand hovering over the photograph. For a moment, he considered leaving it out, keeping it close to remind himself of her warmth and strength. But the memory of Orlok's gaze as he looked at the photograph gave him pause. The Count's strange fascination with Ellen, his words about her beauty and fragility, felt intrusive and wrong.

With a sigh, Thomas pushed the photograph deeper into the satchel and closed the flap, as though hiding it might shield her from Orlok's unsettling attention.

"It's nothing," he muttered to himself, his voice sounding hollow in the empty room. "Just a harmless eccentricity."

But even as he said the words, they felt like a lie.

The hours passed slowly. Thomas tried to immerse himself in his work, reviewing the details of the property Orlok intended to purchase and preparing his notes for their next meeting. Yet the oppressive silence of the castle seemed to creep into his thoughts, making it difficult to focus. The weight of the ancient walls, the faint creaks and groans of the structure, and the ever-present chill conspired to unsettle him further.

He found himself glancing toward the door frequently, half-expecting it to creak open and reveal the Count's gaunt figure. Though he was alone, he couldn't shake the sensation of being watched. The shadows in the corners of the room seemed to shift when he wasn't looking directly at them, and the faintest whispers echoed at the edge of his hearing, too indistinct to make out but impossible to ignore.

Thomas pushed back from the desk, rubbing his temples.

"Get a hold of yourself," he muttered. "It's just an old castle. Drafty, creaky, and nothing more."

But the words felt unconvincing, even to him.

By late afternoon, Thomas decided he needed to clear his head. He left his room and wandered the halls of the castle, hoping that movement might ease the tension that had settled over him. The corridors were vast and winding, their walls adorned with faded tapestries and portraits of long-dead figures whose eyes seemed to follow him as he passed. The floor was cold beneath his boots, the sound of his footsteps echoing endlessly through the empty halls.

Thomas tried to think of Ellen, of her laughter and the warmth of her presence. He imagined her waiting for him in Wisborg, the light in her eyes when he returned with news of his success. The thought brought him a measure of comfort, though it was fleeting. Even the memory of her seemed dimmed by the oppressive atmosphere of the castle.

As he turned a corner, he caught sight of one of the servants—the same pale, silent figure who had served them during dinner. They moved quickly and without sound, their head bowed and their steps deliberate. Thomas called out, intending to ask where Orlok might be, but the servant did not respond. They disappeared around the next corner without so much as a glance in his direction.

Thomas hesitated, staring after them, a faint chill creeping up his spine.

"Just superstitions," he murmured to himself again, trying to shake off the unease. "It's all in my head."

By the time he returned to his room, the pale light of the day was already fading, the long shadows of dusk creeping across the walls. Thomas sat heavily in his chair, staring at the documents spread before him without truly seeing them. He thought again of the villagers' warnings, the old man in the inn who had spoken of the Nosferatu and the dangers of the Carpathians. He had dismissed them all as nonsense, the fears of people bound by superstition and old tales.

But now, sitting alone in the heart of Orlok's castle, he wasn't so sure.

"No," he said aloud, his voice firm. "It's just a house. And he's just a man."

The words rang hollow in the silence, but Thomas clung to them nonetheless. He had a job to do, and he wouldn't allow himself to be swayed by irrational fears. Ellen was waiting for him, and he would return to her soon. Whatever unease he felt now would fade, left behind with the castle and its strange master.

He rose and lit the small lamp on the desk, the warm glow pushing back the encroaching darkness. The light steadied him, grounding him in the present. He sat down again, determined to focus on his work and ignore the shadows that seemed to shift and whisper at the edges of his vision.

But even as he worked, a faint unease lingered—a sense that something was watching, waiting, just beyond the reach of the light.

# Chapter 7
## Whispering Shadows

Thomas Hutter sat at the small desk in his chamber, staring at the flickering candle before him. The flame danced and sputtered in the cold, damp air of the castle, its light too feeble to chase away the encroaching shadows that filled the room. He had been trying to focus on the papers spread before him—documents detailing the property sale in Wisborg that had brought him to this godforsaken place—but his thoughts wandered again and again to the strange events of the previous night.

The Count's words, his fixation on Ellen, and the unnerving way he had studied her photograph lingered in Thomas's mind like a dark cloud. Orlok's presence had been oppressive, his movements deliberate and precise, as though every step and gesture were part of some inscrutable ritual. Thomas had tried to rationalize his unease, blaming the unfamiliarity of the castle and the isolation of the Carpathian wilderness. But deep down, he knew there was something more—something profoundly unnatural—about Orlok.

The cold in the room deepened, seeping into Thomas's bones despite the fire he had lit in the small hearth. The shadows cast by the weak flames seemed to stretch and twist unnaturally, flickering in ways that defied the movements of the light. He rubbed his hands together for warmth, his fingers trembling slightly as he picked up the pen and attempted once more to immerse himself in his work.

The scratching of the pen against the paper was the only sound in the room, but it was soon joined by something else—something faint and distant. Thomas paused, holding his breath as he strained to listen. It was a soft noise, almost imperceptible at first, like the faintest rustling of fabric or the whisper of dry leaves caught in the wind. It seemed to come from the far corner of the room, where the shadows gathered thickest.

He set the pen down and rose from his chair, his heart pounding as he moved cautiously toward the corner. The sound ceased as he approached, leaving only the oppressive silence of the castle. He stared into the darkness, his imagination conjuring shapes that he knew couldn't be there—twisted forms that seemed to shift and writhe just beyond the edge of visibility.

Shaking his head, Thomas stepped back, forcing a nervous laugh.

"You're imagining things," he muttered to himself, the sound of his own voice startlingly loud in the stillness. "This place is getting to you, that's all."

But as he turned to return to his desk, a sudden creak froze him in place. It was soft, almost tentative, but unmistakable—the sound of a floorboard shifting under the weight of something moving. His breath caught in his throat as he turned toward the door, half-expecting to see the gaunt figure of Count Orlok standing there.

The door was closed, the latch unmoved. The room was empty.

He stood motionless for several moments, his pulse racing as he scanned the room. The shadows seemed to press closer now, the faint rustling sound returning, though its source remained hidden. With a deliberate effort, he forced himself to sit back down, gripping the edge of the desk as though anchoring himself to reality.

As the hours dragged on, the atmosphere in the castle grew heavier. The faint, inexplicable noises persisted—soft creaks, distant whispers, and the occasional rustle that seemed to come from within the walls themselves. The candle on Thomas's desk burned lower, its light flickering weakly as though struggling against some unseen force. The air grew colder still, carrying with it a faint metallic tang that stung his nostrils and left an unpleasant taste in his mouth.

He glanced toward the window, hoping the sight of the courtyard would calm his nerves, but the view offered little comfort. The mist that clung to the castle grounds had thickened, swirling like a living thing as it wrapped itself around the jagged spires and crumbling battlements. The moon hung low in the sky, its pale light casting an eerie glow over the scene.

For a moment, Thomas thought he saw movement in the courtyard—a dark figure gliding through the mist, its outline indistinct and fluid. He leaned closer to the window, his breath fogging the glass as he strained to see. But whatever he had glimpsed was gone, leaving only the shifting mist and the oppressive silence.

Thomas pulled away from the window, his hands trembling as he rubbed them together for warmth. The unease that had been gnawing at him since his arrival was growing stronger, a sense of dread that seemed to seep into every corner of the castle. He tried to tell himself it was the isolation, the unfamiliar surroundings, the weight of the villagers' superstitions lingering in his mind. But the rational explanations felt hollow, unable to dispel the oppressive fear that gripped him.

As the night wore on, Thomas found himself unable to concentrate on his work. The documents remained untouched on the desk, their words blurring together in the dim light. He paced the room, his footsteps echoing softly against the stone floor, his thoughts racing.

He thought of Ellen, her quiet strength and unwavering devotion. He imagined her sitting by the window in their home, watching the horizon for his return. The memory brought a fleeting sense of comfort, but it was quickly overshadowed by the image of Orlok, his dark eyes fixed on her photograph, his voice lingering on the word throat with a strange and unsettling emphasis.

A faint tapping sound broke his reverie, coming from somewhere beyond the walls of his chamber. It was rhythmic and deliberate, growing louder with each passing moment. Thomas froze, his pulse pounding as he turned toward the source of the noise. The tapping ceased abruptly, leaving a silence that was somehow worse.

He moved to the door and pressed his ear against it, listening intently. The corridor beyond was silent, but the oppressive feeling of being watched was stronger than ever. His hand hovered over the latch, but he couldn't bring himself to open it. The thought of stepping into the cold, dark hallway filled him with an almost primal fear.

Instead, he turned back to the desk and sat down heavily, burying his face in his hands. The weight of the castle, its ancient walls steeped in shadow and secrets, pressed down on him like a physical force. He tried to shake off the feeling, telling himself it was all in his mind, but the fear refused to dissipate.

The candle burned lower, its flame guttering as the night deepened. Thomas's head nodded forward, exhaustion finally beginning to claim him. But just as sleep began to take hold, a faint whisper broke the silence, soft and indistinct, like the rustling of dry leaves.

He sat bolt upright, his heart hammering in his chest. The whisper grew louder, though the words were still impossible to make out. It seemed to come from all around him, as though the walls themselves were speaking. The shadows flickered and shifted, their movements unnatural, defying the light of the dying candle.

Thomas stared into the darkness, his hands gripping the edge of the desk so tightly that his knuckles turned white. His breath came in shallow gasps, the cold air stinging his lungs. The whispering grew softer, receding into the corners of the room, but the sense of dread remained, a heavy, suffocating presence that refused to let him go.

He reached for the candle, his fingers trembling as he adjusted the wick to coax more light from the failing flame. The flickering glow steadied slightly, pushing back the shadows, but the oppressive atmosphere of the room remained.

Thomas sat back in his chair, his mind racing with thoughts he could not control. The castle, the Count, the strange noises and shifting shadows—it all felt like the pieces of a puzzle he couldn't yet assemble. But one thing was certain: something was deeply, profoundly wrong.

As the first faint light of dawn crept through the window, Thomas finally allowed himself to exhale. But even in the pale morning light, the fear lingered, a shadow that refused to be banished.

The chill of the castle's night lingered in Thomas Hutter's bones as he rose from the desk. Sleep had refused to claim him, driven away by the strange sounds and shifting shadows that haunted the corridors of Count Orlok's ancient fortress. He paced the room restlessly, glancing often toward the heavy wooden door, as though expecting it to swing open and reveal the Count's gaunt figure standing in the threshold.

The castle felt alive, a breathing, malevolent entity. The whispers that had kept him on edge all night had grown softer, almost imperceptible, but they remained, faint tendrils of sound that crept beneath the door and curled around his thoughts. Thomas couldn't shake the feeling that he was being watched, though every time he peered into the gloom, he found nothing but the cold, unyielding stone of the walls.

His gaze fell on the small lamp flickering faintly on the desk. The flame danced as though in defiance of the oppressive darkness that seemed eager to smother it. He reached for the lamp, lifting it cautiously as he made his way to the door. His heart pounded as he opened it, the faint creak of the hinges splitting the silence like a knife.

The corridor beyond was empty, stretching into shadows that

seemed to devour the light of his lamp. The cold air hit him like a wave, carrying with it a faint, metallic tang that made his stomach churn. He hesitated, glancing back at the relative safety of his room, but something compelled him to step into the hallway. Perhaps it was curiosity, or perhaps it was the faint sound he had heard moments earlier—the unmistakable scrape of stone against stone, like a heavy lid being moved.

Thomas moved cautiously, his steps deliberate and silent as he followed the faint echoes through the twisting halls of the castle. The architecture seemed to shift around him, the corridors narrowing and bending in ways that made it impossible to determine their true layout. He passed through arched doorways and beneath crumbling lintels, his lamp casting flickering shadows that danced across the walls like specters.

The sound grew louder as he descended a winding staircase, each step colder than the last. The air here was thick and damp, carrying with it the unmistakable scent of earth and decay. It clung to him like a shroud, making each breath an effort. He tightened his grip on the lamp, his knuckles white as he pressed forward.

At the base of the stairs, he found himself in a long, low-ceilinged corridor lined with heavy wooden doors. The stone walls were damp with condensation, and the floor beneath his boots was uneven, slick with moisture. The whispers had faded, replaced by an oppressive silence that made his ears ache.

He moved toward the faint glow of light at the far end of the corridor, his pulse quickening with each step. As he drew closer, the metallic scent in the air grew stronger, almost choking in its intensity. The light flickered faintly, casting strange, jagged shadows on the walls. Thomas hesitated, his instincts screaming at him to turn back, but he forced himself forward, driven by a need to understand the strange occurrences that plagued the castle.

The corridor opened into a wide, vaulted chamber that smelled of damp soil and rotting wood. The light came from a single candle perched on a crude stone table, its flickering flame casting long, shifting shadows across the room. Thomas's eyes were drawn immediately to the object at the center of the chamber—a large wooden coffin, its lid resting slightly ajar.

He froze, his breath catching in his throat. The coffin was old and battered, its surface stained with dark streaks that looked suspiciously like blood. Dirt clung to its edges, spilling onto the stone floor in clumps that reeked of decay. The sight of it sent a shiver through Thomas, his rational mind struggling to reconcile what he saw with what he believed.

As he watched, the lid of the coffin shifted, scraping softly against the wood. Thomas stepped back, his pulse pounding in his ears, his lamp trembling in his hand. The shadows seemed to gather around the coffin, thickening and twisting as though drawn to it. He wanted to run, to flee back to his room and lock the door, but his legs refused to move.

The lid slid further, revealing the interior of the coffin. At first, Thomas saw only the dark soil that lined its base, its surface damp and glistening in the dim light. But then, slowly, a pale hand emerged from the shadows within—a hand with long, bony fingers and sharp, claw-like nails. The sight of it sent a bolt of terror through Thomas, his breath escaping in a faint gasp.

The hand gripped the edge of the coffin, pulling its owner into view. Count Orlok rose from the dark recesses of the coffin like a specter, his tall, gaunt frame unfolding with unnatural grace. His pale face was expressionless, his dark eyes open and unblinking as they stared into the shadows of the chamber. His movements were fluid, almost mechanical, as though his body were guided by strings invisible to the human eye.

Thomas stumbled backward, his lamp casting erratic beams of light as he struggled to keep hold of it. Orlok's gaze shifted, his dark eyes locking onto Thomas with an intensity that made his blood run cold. For a moment, the Count remained still, his expression unreadable, before a faint, unsettling smile curled across his thin lips.

Thomas's instincts took over, and he turned and fled, his boots pounding against the stone floor as he ran back the way he had come. The shadows seemed to chase him, twisting and writhing at the edges of his vision, their movements unnatural and menacing. The air grew colder as he ascended the staircase, his lungs burning with each desperate breath.

When he reached the safety of his chamber, he slammed the door shut and bolted it, his hands shaking as he leaned against the heavy wood. His heart thundered in his chest, his mind racing to process what he had just seen. Count Orlok was no ordinary man—of that, he was certain. But what he was, Thomas could not yet say.

He collapsed onto the bed, his body trembling, his thoughts consumed by the image of the Count rising from the coffin. The whispered warnings of the villagers echoed in his mind, their words now carrying a weight he could no longer ignore. He knew he couldn't stay in the castle much longer, but he also knew he couldn't leave without understanding the truth.

As the first faint light of dawn seeped through the narrow window, Thomas lay awake, his eyes fixed on the ceiling. The shadows in the room seemed to retreat with the rising sun, but the fear remained, a cold, unrelenting presence that refused to leave him.

The first light of dawn crept into Thomas's chamber, weak and pale, filtering through the narrow, grime-streaked window. The oppressive darkness of the night had begun to lift, but its weight lingered in Thomas's chest, an unshakable sense of dread that clung to him like a second skin. He sat at the edge of the bed, his hands trembling as he stared at the door he had locked so hastily just hours before.

His mind raced with fragments of the night's events: the darkened cellar, the coffin, and Count Orlok's pale, monstrous form emerging from the shadows like something born of nightmare. It had been real. He knew it had been real. No amount of rationalizing could explain away the sight of Orlok's bony hand gripping the edge of the coffin, his unblinking eyes piercing the darkness.

And yet, part of him still clung to disbelief, to the hope that what he had witnessed was some trick of the mind, some hallucination brought on by the castle's eerie atmosphere and his growing exhaustion. He rubbed his face with his hands, trying to steady his breathing. But the memory of Orlok's unnatural movements, the way his body unfolded with inhuman grace, was burned into his mind.

Thomas stood abruptly, pacing the small chamber. He couldn't leave—not yet. Whatever was happening in the castle, whatever Orlok truly was, it was tied to Wisborg. The Count's obsession with Ellen, his purchase of the property, and the strange warnings Thomas had ignored in the village all pointed to something far more sinister than he had anticipated.

He stopped at the desk, his hands gripping its edge as he stared down at the scattered papers. The photograph of Ellen lay tucked beneath them, hidden from view. He hesitated for a moment before pulling it free, his fingers brushing lightly over her familiar face. The warmth of her memory steadied him, if only briefly.

"I have to understand," he muttered to himself, his voice low and resolute. "I have to know what I'm dealing with. For her. For Wisborg."

Thomas turned to the window, his gaze sweeping over the mist-shrouded courtyard below. The castle looked no less menacing in the light of day, its jagged spires and crumbling walls casting long shadows over the desolate landscape. He thought of the cellar, of the dark, suffocating air and the faint stench of decay. He thought of Orlok, rising from the coffin like some unholy specter, and a chill ran through him.

But fear alone wasn't enough to stop him. If anything, it drove him forward, pushing him toward the truth he desperately needed to uncover. He could not leave the castle without answers. If Orlok intended to bring harm to Ellen, to Wisborg, then Thomas had to stop him—somehow.

He paced the room again, his mind racing with possibilities. The castle was vast and labyrinthine, its corridors winding and disorienting, but he was certain he could find the cellar again. He had to see it in the light of day, to confirm that what he had witnessed wasn't some fevered dream. He needed to understand the Count's true nature, no matter how terrifying the answer might be.

Thomas moved quickly, gathering what little he had brought with him. His satchel was already packed, save for the documents he intended to leave behind for Orlok. He slipped the photograph of Ellen into an inner pocket of his coat, keeping it close to his heart. It was a small comfort, a reminder of what he was fighting for.

He pulled on his boots and coat, fastening the buttons with trembling hands. The lamp on the desk had burned low, its light faint but steady. He refilled it with oil from a small flask he had brought with him, careful not to spill a single drop. The thought of descending into the castle's depths without its light was unthinkable.

As he worked, the faint sounds of the castle began to reach his ears—the creak of wood, the groan of distant stone, and the faint rustle of something moving in the walls. The noises had been there all along, he realized, but he had grown so accustomed to them that they had faded into the background. Now, every sound seemed sharper, more deliberate, as though the castle itself were alive and watching him.

He slung the satchel over his shoulder, gripping the lamp tightly as he moved toward the door. He paused, his hand hovering over the latch. A part of him wanted to turn back, to lock the door and wait for the sun to rise higher in the sky. But he knew he couldn't. Every moment he delayed was a moment lost, a moment closer to whatever terrible plan Orlok was preparing to enact.

With a deep breath, Thomas unlocked the door and stepped into the corridor.

The hallways of the castle were no less oppressive in the daylight. The narrow windows let in only the faintest slivers of sunlight, their glass thick and warped, distorting the view of the outside world. The air was cold and heavy, carrying with it the faint metallic tang that had become so familiar. Thomas moved cautiously, the light of his lamp casting long, flickering shadows on the stone walls.

He retraced his steps from the night before, his memory guiding him through the twisting corridors and down the spiraling staircase. The castle seemed quieter now, though the silence was no less unsettling. Each step echoed faintly, the sound swallowed quickly by the oppressive stillness.

When he reached the bottom of the stairs, he hesitated. The corridor leading to the cellar stretched out before him, its walls damp with condensation. The faint stench of decay lingered in the air, stronger now than it had been the night before. Thomas tightened his grip on the lamp, steeling himself as he moved forward.

The door to the cellar was ajar, its heavy wood warped and splintered with age. He pushed it open cautiously, the hinges creaking softly in protest. The chamber beyond was much as he remembered it—low and cramped, its walls lined with crumbling stone. The coffin sat in the center of the room, its lid closed, its surface streaked with dirt and dark stains.

Thomas stepped inside, the air growing colder with each passing moment. He approached the coffin slowly, his breath visible in the faint light of the lamp. The soil around its base was undisturbed, its dark, damp surface glistening faintly. The memories of the previous night flooded back—Orlok rising from the shadows, his skeletal hands gripping the edge of the coffin—and Thomas felt his resolve waver.

But he pressed on, determined to uncover the truth. He knelt beside the coffin, his hand trembling as he reached for the edge of the lid.

The whispers that had haunted him throughout the night seemed to grow louder, their soft, incomprehensible voices filling the chamber. He froze, his pulse pounding in his ears.

And then, from somewhere deep within the castle, a sound broke the silence—a low, guttural creak, like the groan of an ancient door swinging open. Thomas stood abruptly, his heart racing. The sound echoed through the corridors, growing fainter but no less ominous.

He turned back to the coffin, his courage faltering. Whatever lay within could wait. For now, he needed answers—and he needed to find them before the night returned.

# Chapter 8
## Coffins of Soil

The air in the castle had turned oppressively cold, and the silence that once hung heavily over its ancient corridors now seemed to carry a sinister energy. The echoes of Thomas's footsteps on the uneven stone floor reverberated through the passageway as he descended deeper into the bowels of Count Orlok's fortress. He was drawn forward not by courage but by a morbid curiosity that overpowered his mounting fear.

For hours—or so it felt—Thomas had wandered the halls in search of answers. His restlessness had become unbearable after the events of the previous night. The image of Count Orlok rising from his coffin with inhuman grace replayed in his mind, over and over again, until it was burned into his thoughts like a cruel brand. He had tried to convince himself it was a trick of the light or the product of his frayed nerves, but no rationalization could hold against what he had seen with his own eyes.

Now, that same unsettling curiosity drove him forward, guiding his reluctant steps deeper into the shadows. The air was damp and carried an earthy scent, mingled with the faint metallic tang he had noticed throughout the castle. It stung his nostrils and left an acrid taste on his tongue, but he pressed on. Something in the depths of this place held the answers he sought, even if those answers were ones he wasn't ready to confront.

Thomas turned a corner and came to an arched doorway partially hidden by hanging drapes of frayed black fabric. Beyond the threshold, a faint glow emanated from the chamber ahead, flickering like a distant flame. He paused, his breath shallow and his heart pounding in his chest. The smell of damp soil grew stronger here, mingled with a stench he couldn't quite place—a smell both ancient and decayed.

With hesitant steps, he crossed the threshold into the room.

The chamber was vast and dimly lit, its arched ceiling disappearing into shadow. At its center stood a row of large wooden coffins, their surfaces battered and stained. The lids of some were propped open, revealing dark, damp soil inside. A single lantern burned on a low stone table nearby, its faint light casting long, grotesque shadows across the walls. The flickering glow illuminated the crumbling masonry, the uneven floor littered with dirt and the remnants of broken crates.

And there, moving silently among the coffins, was Count Orlok.

Thomas froze, his body stiffening as a chill ran down his spine. The Count's tall, gaunt figure was bent over one of the open coffins, his long, skeletal hands scooping handfuls of dark soil from a burlap sack. He worked with slow, deliberate movements, his fingers spreading the dirt evenly across the coffin's interior as though performing a sacred ritual. His pale face, illuminated by the flickering lantern, was eerily serene, his dark eyes fixed intently on his task.

Thomas ducked into the shadows, pressing himself against the damp stone wall as he watched. His heart thundered in his chest, and he forced himself to steady his breathing, his eyes never leaving the Count's figure. He could hear the faint rustle of the soil, the soft creak of the wooden coffin as Orlok shifted it slightly, and the almost imperceptible sound of his breathing—if it could even be called that.

The coffins themselves were unremarkable at first glance, their surfaces weathered and cracked with age. But as Thomas's eyes adjusted to the dim light, he began to notice details that sent a shiver through him. Dark stains marked the wood—stains that could only be blood. The soil inside was not ordinary earth; it glistened faintly in the lantern's glow, as though imbued with some unnatural substance.

Thomas recalled the whispered warnings of the villagers he had dismissed so easily before. The Nosferatu, they had said, carried the earth of their homeland with them wherever they went. It was a source of their power, their connection to the darkness that sustained them. And here it was, laid out before him—proof of the ancient legends he had scoffed at only days ago.

Orlok straightened, his gaunt frame towering over the coffin as he surveyed his work. The soil was smooth and even, its surface undisturbed. He reached for the lid and lifted it with ease, setting it atop the coffin and pressing it into place. The sound of the wood scraping against wood was sharp and grating, echoing through the chamber.

Thomas's breath caught as Orlok turned, his movements unnervingly fluid. The Count approached another coffin, his hands brushing against its surface as though greeting an old friend. He worked with the same methodical care, his long fingers trailing through the soil before scooping it from another sack.

The scene before Thomas was almost too much to bear. Each movement, each sound, carried with it a terrible finality. He knew now, with grim certainty, that the coffins were being prepared for transport. Orlok was not merely filling them with soil for storage; he was preparing to leave the castle, to carry his curse to Wisborg.

The realization hit Thomas like a blow, and he staggered back, his hand clutching the damp wall for support. Orlok's words from the night before rang in his ears: "Wisborg has everything I require." He had thought it an idle remark, a polite comment made in the course of business, but now he understood its true meaning. The Count's obsession with Ellen, his purchase of the property, and his nocturnal habits all pointed to the same horrifying truth.

He tightened his grip on the lamp, the faint light flickering as his hand trembled. He wanted to run, to flee from the chamber and the terrible reality of what he had witnessed. But something held him in place—a morbid fascination, perhaps, or the faint hope that he could find some way to stop Orlok before it was too late.

The Count's movements slowed, and he straightened again, his dark eyes scanning the row of coffins as though ensuring each was perfect. He turned toward the far side of the room, where a heavy cart sat waiting, its wooden frame caked with mud. One by one, he lifted the coffins with ease, placing them onto the cart with a precision that seemed almost mechanical. The sound of wood meeting wood echoed through the chamber, each impact a grim reminder of the fate awaiting Wisborg.

Thomas remained in the shadows, his heart pounding as he watched Orlok finish his grim preparations. The Count paused beside the cart, his bony hands resting on the edges of the nearest coffin. He stood there for a moment, motionless, his pale face illuminated by the faint lantern light. Thomas felt as though the Count was listening, sensing something unseen in the room. He pressed himself further into the shadows, his breath held as he waited for Orlok to move.

At last, the Count turned, his gaunt frame disappearing into the gloom as he pushed the cart toward a narrow passage at the far end of the chamber. The sound of the wheels creaking against the uneven floor faded slowly, leaving behind an oppressive silence that seemed to seep into Thomas's very soul.

He exhaled shakily, his grip on the lamp loosening as he leaned against the wall. The weight of what he had seen settled over him, heavy and suffocating. Orlok was preparing to leave the castle, to bring his unholy presence to Wisborg. And Thomas, trapped in this cursed place, was powerless to stop him.

But even as despair threatened to consume him, a spark of determination flared in Thomas's chest. He couldn't allow Orlok to reach Wisborg unchallenged. He had to find a way to escape, to warn the town, to protect Ellen.

With trembling hands, he turned and began the long ascent back to his chamber, the shadows of the castle pressing close around him.

The air in the castle seemed heavier than ever, as though the ancient stones themselves were holding their breath. Thomas had retreated to his chamber after witnessing Count Orlok's macabre preparations in the cellar. But he couldn't stay there. Every nerve in his body screamed at him to leave, to flee from this cursed place, but he knew that his escape would not come easily. Orlok was not merely a man; he was something far older, far darker, and his presence loomed over the castle like a thundercloud.

The faint echoes of wheels creaking and footsteps reverberated through the hallways. Thomas pressed his ear to the door, listening intently. The sound was faint but unmistakable. Orlok was moving the coffins—the vessels of his plague—out of the castle.

Thomas opened the door a crack, peering into the dim corridor. The lantern he had carried earlier was extinguished, and the weak light of dawn barely penetrated the gloom. He slipped into the hallway, his steps silent as he followed the sounds. The faint creak of wood and the muffled thud of heavy coffins being loaded guided him like a beacon, pulling him deeper into the labyrinthine passages of the castle.

The trail of sounds led Thomas to a crumbling archway that opened onto the castle courtyard. The mist that had clung to the grounds all night still lingered, curling and twisting like living tendrils. The pale light of dawn filtered through the fog, casting an eerie glow over the scene.

At the center of the courtyard stood a cart, its frame groaning under the weight of its grim cargo. The coffins Thomas had seen in the cellar were stacked neatly atop it, their dark wood gleaming faintly in the weak light. The cart was harnessed to a team of gaunt, spectral horses, their pale coats glistening with sweat as they stamped and snorted in the cold air.

Count Orlok moved with deliberate efficiency, his tall frame unnervingly fluid as he secured the final coffin in place. His hands, long and skeletal, worked with unnatural precision, each movement calculated and smooth. He paused for a moment, standing beside the cart, his dark eyes scanning the misty courtyard as though sensing an unseen presence.

Thomas pressed himself against the cold stone wall of the archway, his breath shallow as he watched. He dared not move, his every instinct screaming at him to stay hidden. Orlok's pale face was expressionless, his gaze unblinking as he surveyed the courtyard. The stillness of the moment was suffocating, and Thomas felt as though even the faintest breath would draw the Count's attention.

At last, Orlok moved again, climbing onto the cart with a grace that defied his gaunt, angular frame. He took the reins in his hands, his fingers curling around the worn leather with a strength that seemed at odds with his emaciated appearance. The horses stirred, their movements almost as unnatural as Orlok's, and the cart began to creak forward.

Thomas watched as the cart rolled toward the castle's massive gates, their iron bars already pulled open to reveal the misty expanse of the Carpathian wilderness beyond. The sound of the wheels grinding against the uneven cobblestones was slow and deliberate, each turn a grim reminder of what was being carried within the coffins.

Orlok sat atop the cart, his silhouette stark against the pale fog. He seemed almost statuesque, his stillness unnerving. His dark eyes never wavered from the path ahead, as though he were locked onto some distant destination only he could see.

As the cart passed through the gates, the mist seemed to part for it, curling and swirling like smoke in its wake. Thomas felt a sudden surge of panic as the realization struck him—Orlok was leaving. He was carrying his coffins, his soil, and his dark intentions toward Wisborg. The people there, Ellen, would have no warning of the horror approaching them.

Thomas took a step forward, his instinct to stop the cart overpowering his fear. But as he moved, Orlok's head tilted slightly, his gaze snapping toward the archway. Even from the distance, Thomas could feel the weight of the Count's stare. It pinned him in place, cold and piercing, as though it had reached out and gripped his very soul.

Orlok's lips curled into the faintest of smiles, a cruel and knowing expression that sent a shiver down Thomas's spine. Without a word, the Count turned his gaze back to the path ahead, the cart disappearing into the mist as the gates closed behind it with a heavy, final clang.

The sound of the gates closing echoed through the courtyard, leaving behind a silence so profound it seemed to press against Thomas's ears. He stood frozen in place, his breath coming in shallow gasps as he stared at the spot where the cart had vanished. Orlok was gone, and with him, the grim cargo destined for Wisborg.

Thomas turned back toward the castle, his mind racing. He needed to warn the town, to reach Ellen before it was too late. But as he moved toward the open archway, his steps faltered. The path leading back into the castle now felt more like a trap than a refuge. The weight of the castle's presence pressed down on him, the shadows within its walls seeming to grow darker and more oppressive in Orlok's absence.

He made his way back through the corridors, his heart sinking with every step. When he reached the grand staircase that led to the upper levels, he tried the nearest door—only to find it locked. Panic set in as he tried another door, and then another, each one refusing to budge.

The castle had sealed him in.

Thomas leaned against the cold stone wall, his chest heaving as the reality of his situation sank in. Orlok was gone, free to spread his plague in Wisborg, and Thomas was left behind, trapped in this fortress of shadows and silence. The thought of Ellen, waiting for him with no idea of the danger approaching, filled him with a desperate resolve.

He had to escape. Somehow, he had to find a way out of the castle and return to Wisborg before it was too late. But as he glanced down the darkened corridor, the weight of the castle's ancient presence pressing against him, he couldn't help but feel as though the castle itself was conspiring to keep him here.

And somewhere deep in its shadowy halls, Thomas could still feel the faint echo of Orlok's piercing gaze, as though the Count's presence lingered, watching him even from afar.

The silence in the castle was now absolute, thick and oppressive as if the very stones were holding their breath. Count Orlok's departure had left a void, a sinister absence that Thomas felt in the marrow of his bones. He stood in the hallway, the dim light of his lantern flickering weakly against the encroaching shadows. His breath came in shallow gasps as his mind raced, piecing together the grim reality that had eluded him until now.

Orlok was no man. He had suspected it before, but now the truth loomed over him, undeniable and monstrous. The coffins filled with soil, Orlok's nocturnal behavior, his obsession with Ellen—these were not the eccentricities of a reclusive nobleman. They were the hallmarks of something far darker, something rooted in the whispered legends of the Nosferatu.

Thomas moved slowly, his legs trembling beneath him as he retraced his steps through the winding corridors. His thoughts swirled like a storm, fragments of memory and realization crashing together. The villagers' warnings, dismissed so easily at the time, now echoed in his mind with chilling clarity. Beware the Nosferatu. They bring death and plague wherever they go.

He reached his chamber and locked the door behind him, his hands shaking as he set the lantern on the small desk. The weak light illuminated the room's sparse furnishings, but it did little to chase away the dread that clung to him. He sank into the chair, his head in his hands, as the weight of his discovery pressed down on him like a physical burden.

The coffins, lined with the soil of Orlok's homeland, were not merely vessels for transportation. They were the Count's sanctuaries, his connection to the dark power that sustained him. Thomas could still see the glistening soil in his mind's eye, the faint metallic tang of it lingering in his nostrils. Orlok's careful preparation of the coffins had been almost reverent, a ritual as ancient as the legends themselves.

And now, those coffins were on their way to Wisborg.

Thomas thought of Ellen, her serene face in the photograph tucked safely in his coat pocket. She had always been sensitive to the unspoken, attuned to the invisible threads that connected the living and the unseen. Her warnings, her quiet melancholy before his departure, now felt like prophetic echoes. She had sensed something—perhaps even before he had left—something dark and foreboding.

The image of Orlok rising from his coffin flashed through his mind again, unbidden. The unnatural grace, the hollow stillness in his eyes—it was the stuff of nightmares, and yet it was real. Orlok was a creature of the night, bound by no mortal constraints, and his journey to Wisborg would bring ruin if Thomas could not find a way to stop him.

Panic clawed at Thomas's chest as he considered the implications of Orlok's arrival in Wisborg. The coffins of soil were not merely for his comfort; they were weapons. With them, Orlok would bring death and disease to the town, just as the villagers had warned. The plague would spread like wildfire, and no one would be safe—not the villagers, not Ellen.

Thomas stood abruptly, his chair scraping loudly against the stone floor. He paced the room, his thoughts churning. He had to escape, to warn the people of Wisborg before it was too late. But the castle was a labyrinth, and its doors seemed to close of their own accord, as though the very structure conspired to keep him prisoner.

The photograph of Ellen burned in his mind, her image a beacon that pulled him from the depths of despair. She had to be warned. Whatever the cost, whatever the risk, Thomas had to reach her. The alternative was unthinkable.

Thomas's mind turned back to Orlok's fixation on Ellen, the way he had lingered on her name, her photograph, her "lovely throat." The Count's interest in her was not idle curiosity; it was hunger. Thomas could see it now with horrifying clarity—Ellen was more than a distant fascination to Orlok. She was a target, a prize.

Orlok's departure had been methodical, his preparations meticulous. Everything about him spoke of patience and precision, the traits of a predator who understood the importance of the hunt. Thomas could almost feel the Count's shadow stretching toward Wisborg, reaching for Ellen with long, skeletal fingers.

And he was powerless to stop it. Or so it seemed.

Thomas clenched his fists, his nails digging into his palms as a surge of determination swept over him. He could not allow fear to paralyze him. Ellen needed him, and the people of Wisborg needed him. There had to be a way to escape this cursed castle, to reach the town before Orlok's plague could take root.

He moved to the small desk, pulling open the drawer and rummaging through its contents. His fingers brushed against a small, rusted blade—likely forgotten by some unfortunate soul who had once occupied this room. It wasn't much, but it was better than nothing. He tucked it into his coat pocket, its weight a small comfort.

He turned to the door, his resolve hardening. Orlok might have left, but the castle still held its secrets. If there was a way out, Thomas would find it. He had no other choice.

As he stepped into the hallway, the shadows seemed to close in around him, their whispers faint but persistent. The castle was alive, its ancient walls pulsing with malevolence. But Thomas would not be deterred. He would find a way to escape, to reach Wisborg, and to stop Orlok before it was too late.

The weight of his fear did not lessen, but it was joined now by something stronger—a desperate hope, fragile but unyielding. For Ellen, for Wisborg, for the people who had no idea of the horror that was about to descend upon them, Thomas would fight. No matter the cost.

# Chapter 9
## A Prisoner Within

The silence of the castle pressed against Thomas like a living thing, growing heavier with each step he took. He moved cautiously through the shadowy corridor, his lantern trembling in his hand as its faint glow illuminated the jagged stones beneath his feet. The oppressive atmosphere of Count Orlok's fortress weighed on him like an invisible chain, dragging at his limbs and whispering doubts into his mind. Every instinct told him to stop, to turn back, but the thought of Orlok's coffins, his sinister intentions, and Ellen's face burned in his memory, driving him forward.

Thomas had made up his mind: he had to escape. He could no longer afford to hesitate, to rationalize the bizarre occurrences of the past days. The truth of Orlok's nature was undeniable now, and the Count's journey to Wisborg carried with it the promise of death. But the castle seemed alive, an ancient predator unwilling to release its prey, its corridors twisting and closing around him as though to mock his resolve.

The faint metallic tang of the air grew sharper as Thomas descended a spiraling staircase, its cold stone steps slick with moisture. The lantern's flickering light cast jagged shadows that writhed along the walls, the shapes almost humanoid in their grotesque contortions. He tried to steady his breath, but each exhalation emerged as a shallow gasp, the chill of the air clawing at his throat.

He reached the bottom of the staircase and paused, pressing himself against the wall as he scanned the dim corridor ahead. The silence was profound, the kind of silence that seemed to absorb sound rather than merely lack it. He couldn't shake the feeling that the walls themselves were listening, that the castle was aware of his every movement.

As Thomas stepped cautiously into the corridor, he became aware of a faint sound in the distance—a low creak, like the groan of ancient wood under strain. His pulse quickened as he moved toward the noise, each step deliberate and measured. The air grew colder still, the faint scent of damp earth mingling with a sharper, almost metallic odor that set his teeth on edge.

Rounding a corner, he came face-to-face with a heavy iron gate that blocked the passage. The bars were thick and rusted, their surface pitted and worn with age. The lock was massive, an ornate mechanism that looked more like a relic than a functional device. Thomas's heart sank as he approached the gate, running his hands over its icy surface. He tugged at it experimentally, but it refused to budge. The metal was unyielding, as though fused into the very stone of the castle itself.

A surge of frustration boiled within him, but he forced it down, knowing that panic would do him no good. He turned back to search for another route, his lantern casting erratic beams of light as he swept it across the corridor. To his left, partially obscured by a pile of crumbled masonry, was a narrow opening—a small tunnel that seemed to lead downward.

Thomas hesitated, peering into the dark recesses of the passage. It was barely wide enough to accommodate him, and the thought of squeezing through such a confined space made his stomach churn. But there was no other way forward. With a deep breath, he crouched low and slipped into the tunnel, his body brushing against the damp walls as he moved.

The tunnel was suffocating, the air thick with the smell of wet stone and rot. Thomas had to hunch awkwardly as he navigated the cramped space, the lantern held close to his chest to avoid hitting the ceiling. His footsteps echoed faintly in the narrow confines, each sound amplified to an almost deafening degree.

As he moved deeper, the tunnel seemed to close in around him, the walls narrowing until his shoulders scraped against the rough stone. The air grew colder, the chill sinking into his bones and making his movements sluggish. His breath came in shallow gasps, fogging the glass of the lantern as he pressed forward.

A faint sound reached his ears—soft at first, but growing steadily louder. It was a low, rhythmic whisper, like the rustling of dry leaves caught in a breeze. Thomas froze, his heart pounding as he strained to listen. The sound seemed to come from all around him, reverberating through the stone like an unseen presence. He turned sharply, his lantern swinging to illuminate the darkness behind him, but there was nothing—only the cold, unyielding walls and the faint rustle of the air.

He pressed on, his steps quickening despite the cramped space. The whispers grew louder, their tone shifting to something more insistent, more urgent. He couldn't make out the words, but the sound carried a weight that made his skin crawl, as though the voices were speaking directly to him.

Without warning, the lantern's flame sputtered violently, its light dimming to a faint glow. Thomas's breath caught in his throat as the shadows around him seemed to come alive, shifting and writhing in the dim light. He stumbled, his foot catching on a loose stone, and fell hard against the wall. The lantern slipped from his grasp, clattering to the ground and extinguishing itself.

Darkness swallowed him.

Thomas scrambled to his feet, his hands searching desperately for the lantern. The whispers surged, their tone rising to a frenzied pitch, and the air around him seemed to pulse with a malevolent energy. He felt a sudden, sharp pain across his back, as though unseen claws had raked across his flesh. He cried out, stumbling forward, his hand finding the cold metal of the lantern.

Fumbling in the dark, he managed to relight the flame, its weak glow pushing back the shadows just enough to reveal the passage ahead. The whispers receded, but the oppressive weight of the air remained, pressing against him like an unseen force. Blood trickled down his back, warm against his cold skin, but he couldn't stop to assess the injury. He had to keep moving.

The tunnel finally opened into a larger chamber, its high ceiling disappearing into darkness. Thomas leaned against the wall, gasping for breath as the lantern's light revealed a crumbling archway at the far end of the room. The heavy iron gate beyond it was slightly ajar, its hinges groaning softly in the cold air.

Thomas staggered toward the archway, his legs trembling beneath him. The faint sound of water dripping onto stone echoed through the chamber, punctuating the oppressive silence. As he passed through the archway, the whispers returned, faint and mournful, as though the castle itself were lamenting his escape.

The air beyond the gate was colder still, carrying with it the scent of the forest and the promise of freedom. But as Thomas stepped through, the oppressive weight of the castle seemed to reach for him one last time, a low, guttural creak echoing through the chamber behind him. He turned, his lantern illuminating the dark recesses of the room, but there was nothing—only the cold, empty stone.

And yet, Thomas couldn't shake the feeling that the castle was watching him, its ancient walls alive with malice.

He pressed on, the open forest beckoning him toward freedom, though the shadows seemed to cling to his heels.

The forest beyond the castle stretched out before Thomas in a blur of gray mist and skeletal trees. The cold air hit him like a slap, stinging his face and filling his lungs with a sharp, biting chill. For a moment, he simply stood there, his legs trembling beneath him, his chest heaving as he struggled to catch his breath. The oppressive weight of the castle had lifted, but only slightly. Its dark silhouette loomed behind him, its jagged spires clawing at the pale sky like fingers desperate to hold him back.

Thomas reached up and touched his back, wincing as his fingers brushed against the torn fabric of his coat and the warm, sticky blood beneath. The unseen attack in the tunnel had left its mark, but there was no time to assess the damage. He had escaped the castle, but he was far from safe. The Count was already on his way to Wisborg, and every moment Thomas lingered here brought Orlok closer to his goal—and closer to Ellen.

The first steps were the hardest. Thomas's legs felt like lead, his body battered and weak from the ordeal of the past days. The wounds on his back throbbed with every movement, and the cold air seemed to seep into his very bones, draining what little strength he had left. But he forced himself to move, his hands gripping the gnarled trunks of the trees for support as he stumbled forward.

The forest was a labyrinth of twisted branches and uneven terrain. The ground beneath him was slick with mud and scattered with jagged rocks that threatened to trip him at every step. The mist curled around him like a living thing, clinging to his clothes and obscuring his vision. Every sound—the rustle of leaves, the snap of a distant branch—made him start, his eyes darting to the shadows as he imagined Orlok's skeletal form emerging from the gloom.

Thomas pushed the thought from his mind. Orlok was ahead of him, not behind. The Count had no reason to linger in the castle now, not when his coffins of soil were already en route to Wisborg. But the castle itself… Thomas could still feel its presence, a dark, unrelenting force that seemed to cling to him even here, in the open wilderness.

Hours passed, though they felt like days. The sun remained hidden behind a thick layer of clouds, offering no warmth or guidance. Thomas's feet were numb, his boots soaked through with mud and water. His hands, scratched and bloodied from the rough bark of the trees, shook uncontrollably as he pressed forward. The thought of stopping, of collapsing beneath the twisted branches and letting exhaustion take him, grew more tempting with each passing moment.

But then Ellen's face would rise in his mind, her serene smile and the quiet strength in her eyes. He thought of her waiting for him, unaware of the danger creeping toward her. The image filled him with a desperation that overpowered his fatigue, driving him onward despite the protests of his body.

The forest began to change as the day wore on. The trees grew sparser, their skeletal branches giving way to stretches of barren, rocky terrain. The mist thinned slightly, revealing glimpses of distant hills and valleys. But the path was no clearer, and Thomas had no sense of direction. He could only trust his instincts and hope that he was moving toward Wisborg rather than farther into the wilderness.

At last, Thomas could go no farther. His legs buckled beneath him, and he fell to the ground, his body sinking into the cold, damp earth. The world spun around him, the gray sky and dark trees blending into a chaotic blur. He tried to push himself up, but his arms gave out, and he collapsed again, his cheek pressing against the icy ground.

For a long moment, he lay there, his breath coming in shallow gasps, his vision dimming. The thought of giving up, of letting the cold claim him, felt almost like a relief. He had tried. He had escaped the castle. But the journey ahead seemed impossible, and his body was failing him.

A faint sound broke through the haze of his thoughts—the distant toll of a bell. His eyes fluttered open, and he strained to listen. The sound was faint and far away, carried on the wind, but it was unmistakable. A church bell.

Thomas forced himself to his hands and knees, his body trembling with the effort. The bell meant civilization. It meant people, shelter, and perhaps even a way to send a warning to Wisborg. He clung to the sound like a lifeline, his desperation giving him the strength to push himself upright.

The bell rang again, clearer this time, and Thomas stumbled toward it, his steps uneven and halting. The terrain grew steeper, the rocks beneath his feet shifting dangerously as he climbed. He slipped and fell more than once, his hands and knees scraping against the unforgiving ground, but he refused to stop.

The faint outline of a village appeared on the horizon, its rooftops barely visible through the thinning mist. The sight filled Thomas with a surge of hope, though it was tempered by the grim knowledge that this was only the beginning. The village was not Wisborg—it was too small, too remote. But it was a start.

Thomas staggered into the outskirts of the village as the last light of day faded into twilight. The streets were narrow and empty, the few houses he passed shuttered and dark. He banged on the door of the nearest building, his fist weak against the heavy wood. The sound echoed faintly, but there was no answer. He tried again, his voice hoarse as he called out, but the door remained closed.

At last, a light appeared in one of the windows, and the door creaked open to reveal an elderly man, his face lined with age and suspicion. He stared at Thomas for a long moment, his expression unreadable, before stepping aside to let him in.

Thomas collapsed onto the nearest chair, his breath coming in ragged gasps as the warmth of the room began to thaw his frozen limbs. He tried to speak, to explain, but his voice failed him. The old man pressed a cup of steaming liquid into his hands, and Thomas drank greedily, the heat spreading through his body and chasing away the worst of the chill.

When he finally found his voice, it was low and trembling.

"Please," he said. "I need to get to Wisborg. There's… there's danger. Terrible danger."

The old man frowned, his suspicion deepening.

"Wisborg?" he said, his voice rough and accented. "It's far from here. Two days, maybe three."

Thomas's heart sank at the words. Two days. He didn't have two days. But he pushed the despair aside, forcing himself to focus. He had escaped the castle. He had found help. Now, he just needed to keep moving.

"Can you help me?" he asked, his voice barely above a whisper. "I must get there. I have to warn them."

The old man stared at him for a long moment before nodding slowly.

"Rest tonight," he said. "We'll see about getting you on your way in the morning."

Thomas nodded, the weight of exhaustion finally overcoming him. As he sank into a fitful sleep, Ellen's face lingered in his thoughts, a fragile beacon of hope that refused to be extinguished.

Thomas awoke to the dim light of dawn spilling through the warped glass of the small window in the stranger's home. His body ached in ways he had never imagined possible. Every muscle screamed with protest as he shifted in the creaking chair, and the deep wounds on his back throbbed with a dull, persistent pain. He took a shaky breath, steadying himself against the table, and for a moment, he allowed himself to feel relief. He was alive. He was out of the castle.

But the weight of his mission returned as quickly as it had lifted. Count Orlok was ahead of him now, carrying his coffins of soil—and whatever terrible curse they contained—toward Wisborg. The people there were completely unaware of the threat approaching their quiet town, and Ellen… Thomas's chest tightened at the thought of her. Ellen was in danger, her name and image etched into Orlok's mind with an obsession that made Thomas's stomach churn. He could feel the urgency thrumming in his veins, pushing him forward despite his battered body.

The elderly man who had taken him in emerged from a back room, a walking stick tapping softly against the wooden floor. His weathered face was calm but distant, his brow furrowed as though weighed down by his own burdens. He carried a steaming mug of tea, setting it in front of Thomas with a faint nod.

"You look worse this morning than when you came in last night," the man said gruffly, his voice rasping with age. "Whatever trouble you've found yourself in, it must be serious."

Thomas wrapped his trembling hands around the mug, the warmth spreading through his chilled fingers.

"It's not just me," he said, his voice hoarse. "It's… it's Wisborg. There's something coming—something terrible."

The man raised an eyebrow, his expression skeptical but not unkind.

"And you're the one who's going to stop it?"

Thomas hesitated, his hands tightening around the mug.

"I have to try," he said quietly. "If I don't, no one else will."

The man sighed, leaning heavily on his walking stick.

"Wisborg's a long way from here. Even if you had a horse, you'd be lucky to make it in two days."

"I don't have two days," Thomas said, his voice rising slightly. "The Count… he's already on his way. If I don't warn them, it'll be too late."

The man studied him for a long moment, his dark eyes sharp and calculating. Finally, he nodded, though his expression remained grim.

"There's a farmer on the edge of the village. He keeps a cart and mule. It's slow, but it'll get you there faster than your feet."

Thomas felt a surge of hope, fragile but real. He pushed himself to his feet, ignoring the wave of dizziness that followed.

"Thank you," he said, his voice earnest. "Thank you for helping me."

The man waved him off with a gruff snort.

"Thank me when you've made it to Wisborg alive. And when this 'Count' of yours hasn't gotten there first."

The cart was as rough and battered as the old man had warned, its wooden wheels groaning with every turn as the mule trudged along the narrow dirt road. Thomas sat hunched in the back, his hands gripping the edges of the cart as it jostled and bumped over rocks and uneven ground. The cold wind bit at his face, carrying with it the faint scent of damp earth and pine.

The hours dragged on, the landscape shifting from the dense, skeletal forest to rolling hills and fields shrouded in a thin layer of mist. Thomas's thoughts raced as he stared at the horizon, his mind filled with images of Orlok and his terrible cargo. He could see the coffins stacked on the Count's cart, their dark wood glistening faintly in the moonlight. He could see Orlok himself, his gaunt figure perched atop the cart like a vulture, his dark eyes fixed on some distant, terrible destination.

But more than anything, Thomas saw Ellen. He saw her sitting by the window in their home, her hands folded in her lap, her expression distant and troubled. He could almost hear her voice, soft and melodic, calling his name as she turned to look at him. The thought filled him with equal parts determination and dread. He had to reach her. He had to warn her. But would he be in time?

The cart lurched suddenly, jolting him from his thoughts. He gripped the sides tightly, his heart pounding as the mule slowed to a halt. The driver—a grizzled farmer with a weathered face and sharp eyes—turned in his seat, his expression unreadable.

"This is as far as I go," the man said, his voice low. "The rest of the road gets rough, and I've no interest in getting my mule killed for some fool's errand."

Thomas nodded, though his chest tightened with anxiety. He climbed down from the cart, wincing as his feet hit the ground. The journey ahead would be on foot, and his body felt like it might give out at any moment. But there was no choice. He thanked the farmer and turned toward the road, his steps unsteady but determined.

The road to Wisborg stretched out before him, winding through hills and valleys that seemed endless. Thomas forced himself to keep moving, his breath ragged and his limbs heavy with exhaustion. Every step felt like a battle, but he couldn't stop. The image of Ellen, her safety threatened by the dark shadow of Orlok, spurred him forward.

The sun began to dip below the horizon, casting long shadows across the landscape. The mist thickened, curling around him like a living thing, and the cold deepened. Thomas's thoughts grew fragmented, his focus slipping as his body screamed for rest. But the urgency in his chest, the gnawing fear of what awaited in Wisborg, kept him going.

As the first stars appeared in the darkening sky, Thomas stumbled upon a small stream. He knelt beside it, his hands shaking as he cupped the cold water and drank deeply. The icy liquid burned his throat, but it cleared his mind, sharpening his thoughts. He gazed at his reflection in the rippling water, his face pale and hollow, his eyes shadowed with fatigue. He barely recognized himself.

"This isn't about me," he whispered, his voice trembling. "It's about her. About them. I can't stop now."

He pushed himself to his feet, his resolve hardening. The journey ahead was long, and Orlok was surely drawing closer to Wisborg with every passing moment. But Thomas would not stop. He would reach Ellen, even if it cost him everything.

# Chapter 10
## The Ship

The mist clung to the docks like a living shroud, curling around the skeletal masts of anchored ships and swallowing the faint glow of lanterns hung from their bows. The air was damp and cold, thick with the acrid stench of salt, rotting wood, and the faintly sweet reek of decaying fish. Beneath the dim light of the crescent moon, the port of Varna felt more like a realm of the dead than a bustling waypoint for trade and travel.

Count Orlok's arrival seemed to amplify the unnatural stillness. His gaunt silhouette loomed atop the cart as it rattled over the uneven cobblestones, the wheels groaning under the weight of the heavy, ominous cargo—six massive wooden coffins filled with soil. The horses pulling the cart moved with an eerie silence, their skeletal frames glistening with sweat despite the cool night air. Their eyes gleamed faintly, reflecting the pale moonlight, as though some unnatural force compelled them forward.

Dockhands paused in their tasks as the cart approached, their conversations trailing off into hushed murmurs. The sight of Orlok—his impossibly tall, emaciated frame draped in a dark coat that seemed to absorb the surrounding light—sent a ripple of unease through the gathered men. They exchanged uneasy glances, muttering superstitions under their breath, but none dared to meet the Count's piercing gaze.

The cart came to a halt before the *Empusa*, a schooner destined for Wisborg. The ship sat low in the water, its sturdy hull scarred from countless voyages. Its captain, a grizzled man with a face like weathered oak, emerged from the shadows, his sea-worn hands gripping the collar of his heavy coat. His sharp eyes scanned the coffins and the spectral figure atop the cart with a mixture of suspicion and dread.

"Are you the captain of this vessel?" Orlok's voice sliced through the cold air, low and deliberate, carrying an unnatural weight that made the dockworkers flinch. The Count did not bother with pleasantries or introductions; his tone was one of command, not inquiry.

The captain stepped forward, his boots scraping against the damp stone. He was a man unaccustomed to intimidation, yet he found himself faltering beneath Orlok's unblinking gaze.

"Aye," he said after a moment, his voice rough. "Captain Larsen. And who might you be?"

Orlok tilted his head slightly, the motion almost serpentine.

"My name is of no importance. What matters is that your ship will take me to Wisborg."

Larsen's frown deepened, his gaze flicking to the coffins.

"That your cargo?" he asked gruffly.

"It is," Orlok replied. "They are precious to me. They must remain sealed for the entirety of the journey. You and your men are not to touch them under any circumstances."

The captain's lips pressed into a thin line. He had carried strange cargo before—smuggled goods, exotic animals, even coffins bound for foreign graves—but there was something about this man, and these coffins, that set his nerves on edge. Still, he was not one to refuse payment, especially in the lean months before winter.

"Fine," Larsen said, though the unease in his voice was plain. "But it'll cost you extra for the trouble."

Orlok's thin lips curled into the faintest semblance of a smile, though it carried no warmth.

"Payment will not be an issue."

With a nod, the Count stepped down from the cart, his movements unnaturally smooth, as though he were gliding rather than walking. He gestured toward the coffins with one skeletal hand, and the dockworkers reluctantly approached, their steps hesitant.

The dockworkers began unloading the coffins, their murmurs growing louder as they drew closer to the ominous cargo. The wood of the coffins was dark and weathered, marked with deep scratches and stains that looked disturbingly like dried blood. Each coffin was bound with thick iron clasps and sealed with wax, as though its contents were too dangerous to be exposed to the world.

One of the younger men hesitated as he grasped the edge of a coffin, his face pale.

"What's in these?" he asked, his voice trembling.

"Not your concern," Orlok said sharply, his tone brooking no argument. His dark eyes bored into the young man, who quickly averted his gaze and resumed his work.

The first coffin was lifted onto the gangplank, the wood creaking under its weight. The sailors aboard the *Empusa* watched from the deck, their faces shadowed but tense. They muttered among themselves, their unease growing with each coffin that was carried aboard. By the time the final coffin was loaded into the hold, the atmosphere on the dock had grown unbearably tense, the air thick with a sense of foreboding.

Orlok stepped onto the gangplank, his figure cutting a stark silhouette against the pale glow of the lanterns. The sailors shrank back as he passed, their hands tightening on the ropes and rails as though seeking some anchor against the overwhelming presence of the man— or thing—now aboard their vessel.

The hold of the *Empusa* was dim and musty, its wooden walls stained with salt and age. The coffins were arranged in a neat row along the far wall, their iron clasps glinting faintly in the lantern light. Orlok stood before them, his gaunt frame motionless as he surveyed the arrangement.

The air seemed to grow colder in his presence, the lantern's flame flickering as though struggling to stay alight. Orlok reached out, his long fingers brushing against the lid of the nearest coffin. He whispered something—soft and guttural, in a language no living man could recognize—and for a moment, the faint scent of damp earth and decay grew stronger.

Satisfied, Orlok turned and ascended the narrow staircase leading back to the deck. The sailors avoided his gaze as he emerged into the night, their eyes fixed on their tasks as they prepared to set sail. The Count made his way to a secluded corner of the ship, his presence looming like a shadow that refused to be dispersed.

The captain approached cautiously, his expression guarded.

"We sail with the tide," he said gruffly. "It'll be a few hours yet."

Orlok inclined his head, his dark eyes glinting in the faint moonlight.

"Do as you must, Captain. But remember—my cargo is not to be disturbed."

With that, he turned away, his coat billowing slightly in the cold sea breeze. The captain watched him for a moment longer, then muttered something under his breath and returned to the helm.

When the tide finally turned, the *Empusa* slipped silently from the harbor, its sails catching the faint wind that carried it out to sea. The fog clung to the ship like a veil, swallowing it as it drifted farther from the shore. The sound of the waves lapping against the hull was the only noise, a soft and relentless rhythm that seemed almost mournful.

On the docks, the last of the dockworkers watched the ship

disappear into the mist, their unease lingering even as the night grew quiet. They would not speak of the Count or his coffins, not openly. But in the dim corners of the taverns and the flickering light of their homes, they would whisper of the man who had come and gone like a shadow, leaving behind a chill that could not be shaken.

And aboard the *Empusa*, hidden among the coffins of soil, Count Orlok waited, his dark eyes unblinking as he stared into the endless expanse of the sea.

The *Empusa* creaked and groaned as it sailed through the endless expanse of gray sea. The mist hung thick around the ship, a suffocating veil that obscured the horizon and swallowed the cries of the gulls. The crew moved about their tasks with a quiet efficiency, but there was an undercurrent of unease that permeated the air. The coffins in the hold, their strange weight and foreboding presence, were the subject of hushed whispers and sideways glances.

It began subtly, a series of small, unsettling events that gnawed at the edges of reason. The lanterns in the hold flickered unpredictably, their flames dimming and flaring without cause. The ship's rats, usually bold and numerous, vanished overnight, leaving the decks eerily silent. And then there was the cold—a deep, bone-chilling cold that seemed to radiate from the lower decks, seeping into every corner of the vessel no matter how brightly the sun shone.

The first disappearance was the kind of thing sailors might dismiss, attributing it to the dangers of life at sea. The boatswain, a wiry man with a crude sense of humor, had been assigned the night watch over the cargo hold. He was the first to voice his discomfort about the coffins, muttering to anyone who would listen that they "reeked of death." Still, he did his duty, his grumbling echoing through the hold as he paced back and forth, lantern in hand.

When morning came, the boatswain was gone.

The crew found his lantern lying near the hatch to the hold, its glass cracked and the flame extinguished. The metal was cold to the touch, as though it had been sitting there for hours. There was no sign of the man himself—no footprints, no discarded tools, nothing to suggest where he might have gone.

The captain scowled as he examined the scene, his jaw clenched.

"He must've fallen overboard," he muttered, though his voice lacked conviction. The crew exchanged uneasy glances but said nothing. It wasn't the first time a man had been lost at sea, and they had work to do.

But the silence that followed the boatswain's disappearance was heavy, a creeping dread that settled over the ship like a second fog.

On the second night, the young cabin boy was assigned to replace the boatswain on watch. Barely more than a child, he was eager to prove himself, though the fear in his wide eyes was impossible to miss. He stood guard outside the hold, clutching his lantern tightly as he tried to ignore the oppressive stillness around him.

The hours dragged on, the only sounds the rhythmic creak of the ship's timbers and the distant crash of waves. The boy kept his eyes fixed on the hatch, his grip on the lantern tightening every time the light flickered.

Somewhere in the shadows, something shifted.

The boy turned sharply, his heart pounding as he peered into the darkness.

"Who's there?" he called, his voice trembling. The shadows did not answer. He raised the lantern higher, its faint glow barely penetrating the gloom. The cold around him grew sharper, the air heavy with an unnatural stillness that seemed to press against his chest.

And then, out of the corner of his eye, he saw movement. A figure—tall, gaunt, and impossibly still—emerged from the darkness, its pale face barely illuminated by the flickering light. The boy's breath caught in his throat as the figure stepped closer, its dark eyes locking onto his with an intensity that froze him in place.

The lantern fell from his grasp, shattering against the wooden floor, and the darkness swallowed him.

By dawn, the boy was gone.

The crew gathered on the deck that morning, their faces pale and their voices low. Two men gone in as many nights, with no explanation. The captain tried to maintain order, barking orders and dismissing the crew's fears as "idle superstitions," but even he could not hide the unease in his eyes.

"There's something in the hold," one of the sailors whispered, his voice trembling. "Something that shouldn't be there."

"Nonsense," the captain snapped, though his hand lingered on the hilt of his cutlass. "There's nothing in that hold but wood and soil. You're all letting your imaginations get the better of you."

But the whispers continued, growing louder as the day wore on. The crew avoided the lower decks entirely, refusing to go near the hatch even under direct orders. The air around the hold seemed colder than the rest of the ship, and the faint smell of damp earth lingered, stronger now than it had been before.

By the third night, the crew was on edge, their nerves fraying under the weight of fear. The captain assigned two men to guard the hold together, hoping that strength in numbers would quell the growing panic. The men agreed reluctantly, their faces pale as they took up their positions.

The night was quiet, the fog clinging to the ship like a suffocating blanket. The two men sat side by side, their lanterns casting overlapping circles of light on the deck. They spoke in low voices, their words hesitant and broken, as though afraid to acknowledge the oppressive silence around them.

Hours passed without incident, and the men began to relax, their fear giving way to exhaustion. One of them leaned against the wall, his eyes drifting shut despite his best efforts to stay awake. The other remained alert, his gaze fixed on the hatch as his fingers drummed nervously against the hilt of his knife.

## Nosferatu

The faint sound of footsteps broke the silence.

The man sat up straight, his heart racing as he looked toward the shadows.

"Who's there?" he called, his voice cracking. There was no answer. He nudged his companion awake, whispering urgently, but the other man groaned and turned away, muttering something incoherent.

The footsteps grew louder, their rhythm slow and deliberate. The light from the lanterns flickered violently, casting jagged shadows across the deck. The man's grip on his knife tightened as the shadows seemed to move, twisting and shifting as though alive.

And then, the hatch to the hold creaked open.

The man froze, his breath caught in his throat as a figure emerged from the darkness below. It was Orlok, his gaunt frame impossibly tall, his pale face illuminated by the faint light. His dark eyes locked onto the man, and a thin, humorless smile curled across his lips.

The man screamed, but the sound was cut short.

By morning, neither guard remained.

The *Empusa* drifted through the endless fog like a phantom, its sails slack against the still air and its once-bustling deck now eerily silent. The crew, once lively with the chatter and gruff camaraderie of sailors, had dwindled to nothing. Only the faint creak of wood and the rhythmic slap of waves against the hull broke the oppressive stillness.

Captain Larsen stood at the helm, his face pale and gaunt, his weathered hands gripping the wheel with a desperation born of fear. He was alone now, the last living soul aboard the vessel. His crew had vanished, one by one, claimed by whatever malevolent force had taken root within his ship. He had tried to maintain order, to dismiss the strange occurrences as mere superstition, but now, standing beneath the gray sky with the weight of the ship's curse pressing down on him, he could no longer deny the truth.

Something was on board with him. Something ancient and unspeakably evil.

The empty corridors of the *Empusa* seemed to stretch endlessly, their shadows deep and impenetrable. Larsen had ventured below deck only once since the final disappearance, driven by a grim determination to confront whatever horror lay within the ship's hold. He had descended the narrow staircase with his lantern held high, the weak flame casting flickering light over the damp, salt-stained walls.

The coffins were still there, arranged in a neat row along the far wall. Their dark wood gleamed faintly in the lantern light, the iron clasps that sealed them untouched. The air in the hold was cold—unnaturally so—and carried a faint, sickly-sweet odor that made Larsen's stomach churn. The lantern's flame sputtered as he approached, the shadows around him shifting and twisting as though alive.

He had stopped only a few feet away, unable to bring himself closer. The coffins seemed to hum with an unseen energy, their presence suffocating in its intensity. The captain had stood there for what felt like hours, his hand gripping the hilt of his cutlass, his breath coming in shallow gasps. Then, as though compelled by an unseen force, he had turned and fled, the sound of his footsteps echoing through the empty corridors.

Now, standing alone on the deck, Larsen could feel the weight of the ship pressing down on him, its ancient timbers groaning beneath his feet. The fog clung to the vessel like a shroud, thick and impenetrable, obscuring the horizon and cutting him off from the rest of the world. The ship had become a tomb, and he its final occupant.

Larsen had not seen Orlok since the Count had boarded the *Empusa*, but he could feel his presence. It was in the cold that seeped into his bones, in the oppressive silence that seemed to smother every sound. At night, the captain would hear faint whispers carried on the wind, their incomprehensible words filling his mind with a creeping dread. Shadows moved where they shouldn't, twisting and writhing at the edges of his vision, and no amount of light seemed to dispel them.

## Nosferatu

On the rare occasions he dared to sleep, his dreams were filled with visions of pale, skeletal hands reaching for him, of dark eyes that pierced through his soul. He would wake in a cold sweat, the taste of damp earth lingering on his tongue and the scent of decay filling his nostrils.

He knew Orlok was watching him, waiting. The Count's patience was infinite, his hunger insatiable. Larsen had tried to reason with himself, to tell himself that it was all in his mind, but deep down he knew the truth. Orlok was biding his time, and when the moment came, the captain would join his crew in whatever dark abyss had claimed them.

Desperation drove Larsen to his logbook, its pages already filled with the grim details of the journey. He wrote feverishly, his pen scratching against the paper as he documented the disappearances, the strange occurrences, and his growing fear. His handwriting grew more erratic with each entry, the words slanting across the page as his thoughts spiraled into incoherence.

*"Third day: Boatswain gone. No sign of a struggle. Crew uneasy but manageable."*

*"Fifth day: Cabin boy disappeared. Found his lantern near the hold. No blood, no signs. Fear spreading."*

*"Sixth day: Two guards stationed. Both missing by morning. I am alone now. The hold... something in the hold. The coffins. God help me, the coffins..."*

He paused, his hand trembling as he dipped the pen into the inkwell. The lantern on the desk flickered violently, casting jagged shadows across the cabin. The air around him felt heavy, as though the ship itself were pressing down on him, suffocating him. He clenched his jaw and forced himself to continue writing.

*"If this log is found, let it serve as a warning. The Count... Orlok... he is not human. He is Nosferatu, a creature of the night. His coffins are vessels of death. Burn the ship. Burn everything."*

Larsen set the pen down and leaned back in his chair, his chest heaving as he stared at the final words. He could feel the weight of them, the grim finality of what he had written. He was sealing his own fate, but it was all he could do. Someone had to know. Someone had to stop Orlok.

The *Empusa* drifted closer to Wisborg, its sails tattered and its decks silent. From the shore, it would appear as any other vessel, its approach heralded by the distant tolling of the ship's bell and the faint sound of the waves. But aboard the ship, the silence was absolute, broken only by the groan of the timbers and the faint rustle of the wind.

Larsen stood at the helm, his eyes fixed on the horizon. The fog had begun to lift, revealing the faint outline of the town in the distance. Wisborg. It was so close now, but the sight brought him no relief. He knew that Orlok's journey was nearly complete, and that the people of Wisborg had no idea of the darkness that was about to descend upon them.

As the ship drew nearer to the dock, Larsen felt a sudden, suffocating chill. He turned slowly, his hand reaching for his cutlass, but the deck behind him was empty. And yet, he could feel it—an invisible presence, cold and unrelenting, creeping closer with every passing moment.

The shadows seemed to deepen, swallowing the faint light of the lanterns. Larsen's breath came in shallow gasps as he gripped the wheel, his knuckles white. He knew, without turning, that Orlok was there, watching him. The Count's dark eyes bored into him, piercing through the fog and the darkness and the fragile barrier of sanity that remained.

## Nosferatu

The *Empusa* drifted into the harbor, its journey complete. And aboard the ghost vessel, hidden among the coffins of soil, Count Orlok waited.

# Chapter 11
## Dreams of Shadows

The wind rattled the shutters of the Hutter home, its mournful howls threading through the cracks in the windowpanes. Outside, the town of Wisborg slumbered beneath a blanket of darkness, its cobblestone streets bathed in the faint silver glow of the waning moon. But inside Ellen's bedroom, sleep brought little relief. Her dreams had turned into a battleground, vivid and strange, filled with whispers of shadows and the ominous specter of danger.

That night, as the clock in the hall struck midnight with a hollow chime, Ellen's body lay still beneath the heavy quilt, but her mind was anything but at rest.

Ellen found herself standing in the garden behind her home. The world was awash in golden light, the late afternoon sun warming her skin and casting long, playful shadows across the flowers Thomas had so lovingly planted. She knelt in the soil, her hands brushing over the petals of a cluster of daisies, their bright faces turned toward the sun. She smiled softly, the peace of the moment sinking into her bones.

But then, as if a veil had been pulled from the sky, the light dimmed. The warmth on her skin evaporated, replaced by a chill that crawled down her spine. The daisies in her hands began to wither, their white petals curling inward, turning brittle and gray. Around her, the garden seemed to decay in an instant. The vibrant greens of the foliage turned to ash, and the fragrant blooms rotted before her eyes, their perfume replaced by the acrid stench of decay.

Ellen stood, the hem of her dress brushing against the blackened soil, her chest tightening as she gazed around the lifeless garden. A shadow appeared at the edge of her vision, stretching across the ground like an encroaching tide. She turned, her breath catching as the figure stepped into view.

He was tall, impossibly so, his elongated frame draped in a black cloak that seemed to drink in the dim light. His face was a mask of death—pallid and drawn, with sunken cheeks and dark, hollow eyes that glimmered with an unnatural intensity. His head tilted slightly as he gazed at her, his long, skeletal fingers curling at his sides.

Though he said nothing, Ellen felt the weight of his presence press down on her like a physical force. She wanted to move, to run, but her limbs refused to obey. She was frozen in place, her heart pounding against her ribs as his shadow reached for her, stretching across the dead garden like a living thing.

And then, she saw Thomas.

The scene shifted abruptly, and Ellen found herself standing on the edge of a jagged cliff. Below her, the sea churned violently, its dark waves crashing against the rocks with a deafening roar. The air was thick with salt, and the wind tugged at her hair and dress as though trying to pull her into the abyss.

Thomas stood on the opposite edge of the cliff, separated from her by a great, yawning chasm. His face was pale and gaunt, streaked with dirt and blood, his clothes torn and battered as if he had been through some terrible ordeal. He reached out to her, his eyes wide with desperation, his lips moving as he called her name.

But the wind carried his voice away, leaving her straining to hear words that would not come. She tried to call back to him, but her voice caught in her throat, her cries swallowed by the roaring sea.

Behind her, the shadow moved again.

She didn't have to turn to know it was there. She could feel it—an icy presence that crawled up her spine, sending shivers through her entire body. The shadow stretched toward Thomas, dark tendrils unfurling like fingers reaching for him. He tried to move away, but the chasm between them grew wider, the distance insurmountable.

"Thomas!" she finally screamed, her voice breaking with anguish as the shadow engulfed him. His figure dissolved into the darkness, leaving her alone on the cliff's edge, the wind and waves howling in her ears.

Ellen jolted awake, a sharp cry escaping her lips as she sat upright in bed. Her chest heaved as she gasped for breath, her heart pounding so loudly she could hear it in her ears. Her hands clutched at the quilt, the fabric bunched tightly in her fists as though it could anchor her to reality.

The room was dark, the only light coming from the faint glow of the moon filtering through the curtains. For a moment, she thought she could still feel the cold touch of the shadow on her skin, an unnatural chill that made her shiver despite the warmth of the bed. She pressed her trembling hands to her face, her breathing uneven as she tried to shake the images from her mind.

But the dream lingered, its details sharp and vivid in her memory. She could still see Thomas's face, his eyes wide with fear, his voice silenced by the distance that had stretched between them. And the shadow—that terrible, looming figure with its piercing gaze and skeletal hands—felt as real as if it had been standing in the room with her.

Ellen swung her legs over the side of the bed, her bare feet touching the cold wooden floor. She crossed the room to the window, pushing the curtains aside to gaze out at the darkened streets of Wisborg. The town was quiet, the houses dark and still, but Ellen felt no comfort in its familiar sights. The sense of foreboding that had plagued her since Thomas's departure had grown stronger, solidifying into a weight that pressed against her chest.

She touched the glass with her fingertips, her reflection pale and ghostly in the faint light. Somewhere out there, Thomas was in danger—she was certain of it. And though she didn't understand how or why, she knew that the shadow from her dreams was connected to him, to the strange journey he had undertaken, and to the growing sense of dread that gripped her heart.

Ellen stayed at the window for hours, watching as the moon sank below the horizon and the first light of dawn began to creep over the rooftops. Her body ached with exhaustion, but sleep was a luxury she could no longer afford. The shadow from her dreams was no mere figment of her imagination—it was real, and it was coming for her.

The days that followed brought no respite for Ellen. Though the waking world carried on with its familiar rhythms—the murmur of the market square, the toll of the church bell, the distant clatter of hooves on cobblestones—Ellen felt as though she were drifting farther and farther from it all. The world around her seemed dulled, its colors faded and its sounds muffled, while a strange and oppressive presence grew stronger in the recesses of her mind.

The figure from her dreams, the shadowy specter with the hollow eyes, was no longer confined to the hours she spent asleep. His presence lingered, a cold weight at the edge of her awareness, pressing against her thoughts like a slow, creeping fog. She would feel him in the still moments, in the spaces between breaths, when the air seemed too heavy to fill her lungs. At first, she dismissed it as lingering unease from her nightmares, but as the sensation grew more distinct, she realized that it was something far more sinister.

Ellen was not imagining him.

Her connection to the shadowy figure—Count Orlok, though she did not yet know his name—grew stronger with each passing day. It was as though an invisible thread had been strung between them, a tether that pulled at her with increasing force. She would wake in the middle of the night, drenched in sweat, her heart racing and her body trembling, unable to recall what had woken her but certain that he had been there. The faintest flicker of a presence in the room, the briefest chill that lingered on her skin—these were the only traces he left behind.

The toll on her body was undeniable. Her once-bright eyes grew shadowed, rimmed with dark circles that spoke of sleepless nights. Her skin, once warm and flushed with health, turned pale and waxen. Every step she took seemed heavier, her movements slowed as though she were wading through an unseen tide. Frau Schröder, her kind neighbor, often visited with fresh bread or a pot of soup, her concern evident in the tight lines around her mouth.

"You're not eating, child," Frau Schröder said one afternoon, her voice firm but tinged with worry. She reached across the table to place a hand on Ellen's arm. "And you've barely touched your tea. If you don't start taking care of yourself, you'll waste away."

Ellen forced a weak smile, her hands trembling as she lifted the teacup to her lips. The hot liquid tasted bitter on her tongue, and she set it down almost immediately.

"I'm fine," she murmured, though the words rang hollow even to her own ears. "Just tired."

Frau Schröder's eyes narrowed, but she said nothing more. After a moment, she patted Ellen's arm and rose to leave, her skirts rustling softly as she made her way to the door.

"Rest, Ellen," she said before departing. "Whatever troubles you, it will pass."

But Ellen knew better. This wasn't something that could be soothed with rest or chased away with Frau Schröder's comforting presence. The shadow was real, and it was growing stronger.

## Nosferatu

One evening, as the sun dipped below the horizon and the long shadows of dusk crept into the room, Ellen stood by the window, staring out at the darkened streets of Wisborg. Her reflection in the glass was pale and spectral, her hollow eyes staring back at her like those of a stranger. She felt the chill of the evening air seeping through the panes, but she didn't move to fetch a shawl. The cold had become familiar to her now, as much a part of her existence as the beating of her heart.

As she gazed into the fading light, a sudden wave of dizziness washed over her. She gripped the windowsill, her knuckles white, as the room seemed to shift and blur around her. Her vision darkened, and for a moment, she thought she might faint.

And then she saw him.

The figure from her dreams—tall, gaunt, and impossibly still—stood at the edge of her vision, his hollow eyes fixed on her with an intensity that made her blood run cold. He wasn't in the room, not exactly, but she could feel his presence pressing against her, invading her thoughts. His lips moved, though no sound emerged, and yet she could hear him, his voice low and guttural, echoing in the corners of her mind.

"Ellen," he whispered, her name a dark caress that made her shudder. "You cannot escape me."

She clutched at her chest, her breath coming in short, shallow gasps as the vision faded. The room returned to focus around her, the oppressive presence receding but not vanishing entirely. She stumbled to a chair, her trembling hands gripping the armrests as she tried to steady herself.

The vision left Ellen drained, her body weak and her mind heavy with the weight of what she had seen. She tried to convince herself that it was just a trick of the light, a hallucination born of exhaustion and grief. But deep down, she knew the truth. The shadow—Orlok—had reached across whatever distance separated them and touched her soul. The connection between them was no accident; it was deliberate, a tether that he had forged to bind her to him.

As the days wore on, the strain of the connection began to take its toll. Ellen could barely eat, her appetite stolen by the constant nausea that gripped her. Her limbs felt heavy, her movements sluggish and awkward. Even the simplest tasks became a struggle, and she found herself collapsing into bed long before nightfall, though sleep brought no relief.

Her dreams grew darker, filled with images of Orlok's pale, hollow face and the unsettling gleam of his eyes. She saw his hands reaching for her, his long fingers brushing against her skin with a cold that burned like frostbite. She saw Thomas, trapped in a shadowy maze of corridors, his voice calling out to her as the walls closed in around him.

By the time the first frost settled over Wisborg, Ellen had become a ghost of herself, her once-bright spirit dimmed to a flicker. She could feel Orlok's presence growing stronger, his shadow stretching ever closer, and she knew that it was only a matter of time before he arrived.

Ellen was no longer afraid for herself. Her thoughts turned to Thomas, to the people of Wisborg, to the quiet town that had no idea of the darkness creeping toward it. She felt powerless against the connection that bound her to Orlok, but she resolved to fight it for as long as she could.

For now, she would endure. But deep down, she feared that when Orlok finally arrived, she would not have the strength to resist him.

Ellen sat at the edge of her bed, the pale light of the moon filtering through the sheer curtains and spilling onto the wooden floor. Her hands rested limply in her lap, her fingers cold to the touch despite the fire crackling faintly in the hearth. She could hear the rhythmic ticking of the clock in the hall, each passing second marked by the steady march of time, yet it felt as though the hours themselves were dissolving into nothingness. Days and nights had begun to blur together, the world outside her home losing its shape and meaning as the oppressive weight of dread settled fully upon her.

The connection to the shadow, to Orlok, had grown more potent, and with it came a darkness that she could neither name nor understand. She felt it in her bones, a deep, aching cold that no blanket or fire could chase away. Her chest tightened as she looked out the window, her gaze fixed on the inky black horizon. Somewhere out there, he was coming. She could feel it as surely as she felt her own heartbeat.

The feeling was no longer confined to the hours of night. During the day, Ellen would catch glimpses of something moving at the edges of her vision—a shadow that disappeared the moment she turned her head. The house itself seemed darker, the sunlight muted and pale, as though afraid to fully enter the space. The once-familiar sounds of the market square, the chatter of neighbors, and the toll of the church bell seemed distant, muffled as though heard through thick glass.

The oppressive presence made her every movement feel labored. Simple tasks—brushing her hair, pouring tea, even climbing the stairs—felt as though she were moving underwater, her body weighed down by an invisible force. She avoided looking at her reflection in the mirror, not because of vanity but because she could no longer recognize the woman who stared back at her. Her face was pale, her eyes sunken and rimmed with shadows, her expression hollow. She looked like a ghost of herself, and sometimes, in the moments between waking and sleeping, she wondered if that's what she had become.

One evening, Ellen sat by the window, her hands wrapped around a steaming cup of tea that had long since gone cold. She stared out at the gathering darkness, her eyes scanning the streets of Wisborg with a restless intensity. She didn't know what she was searching for, but the pull in her chest grew stronger with every passing moment. It was as though the shadow—Orlok—was calling to her, drawing her gaze outward to meet him halfway.

The thought both terrified and intrigued her. She had never felt so profoundly connected to anyone, and yet the connection was not born of love or comfort but of something primal and unknowable. It was as though Orlok's will had reached across the distance and entangled itself with her own, threading through her thoughts and dreams like a spider weaving a web.

She couldn't explain it, but she felt as though she already knew him. The thought chilled her to the core.

The visions came unbidden now, not only in her dreams but in fleeting flashes during the day. She would close her eyes for a moment and see the *Empusa*, its tattered sails straining against the wind as it drifted through a sea of mist. She saw Orlok standing at the bow, his dark cloak billowing around him like smoke, his unblinking eyes fixed on the horizon. She saw the coffins in the hold, their dark wood glistening with damp earth, each one a vessel of death. And she saw herself, standing in her own home, the shadow stretching toward her as though it had already claimed her as its own.

The weight of these visions left Ellen weak and trembling, her resolve fraying with each passing hour. She tried to speak of them once, to Frau Schröder during one of the woman's routine visits, but the words had died in her throat. What could she say? That she was being haunted by a figure from her dreams? That she could feel the approach of something ancient and malevolent, something that defied reason? Frau Schröder would only dismiss her fears as the imaginings of a young wife longing for her husband's return.

Even so, Ellen tried to find solace in small tasks. She cleaned the house in slow, deliberate movements, each action a fragile attempt to reassert control over her unraveling world. She tended the flowers in the garden, though they seemed to wilt under her touch. She forced herself to eat, though each bite turned to ash in her mouth. None of it helped. The sense of dread followed her everywhere, a shadow she could not escape.

One night, as Ellen sat by the window, her mind heavy with

exhaustion, she felt it. A shift in the air, a subtle but undeniable change that made her shiver despite the warmth of the fire. She leaned forward, her eyes narrowing as she peered into the darkness beyond the garden. The night seemed darker than usual, the shadows deeper and more pronounced, as though something was moving within them.

Her breath caught in her throat as a flicker of movement drew her gaze to the horizon. She saw nothing concrete, only the faintest impression of something vast and looming, but it was enough to send a wave of icy fear coursing through her. She pressed a hand to the glass, her fingers trembling as she tried to steady herself.

"He's coming," she whispered, her voice barely audible. "He's coming for me."

The realization settled over her like a shroud. Orlok was drawing nearer with every passing moment, his shadow stretching across the distance that separated them. She could feel him now, closer than ever before, his presence wrapping around her like a suffocating fog.

And yet, mixed with the fear, there was something else—a faint, inexplicable pull, like a whisper at the back of her mind urging her to surrender to the darkness. She shook her head violently, pushing the thought away, but the feeling lingered, insidious and persistent.

Ellen turned from the window, her heart pounding in her chest. She knew now that there was no escaping what was coming. The shadow would soon reach her doorstep, and she would have to face it—alone.

# Chapter 12

## The Ghost Ship

The harbor at Wisborg was quiet in the pale light of dawn. Wisps of mist curled over the still waters, their delicate tendrils catching the faint glow of the rising sun. The early hours were always peaceful here, broken only by the soft lapping of the waves against the stone docks and the occasional cry of a gull overhead. Fishermen moved about with slow precision, unhurried as they prepared their nets for the day. Merchants arranged their wares under canvas awnings, the scents of fresh bread and salted fish mingling in the crisp air. Life, for the moment, felt undisturbed.

But as the mist thickened and the breeze shifted, carrying with it the faintest trace of something sour and metallic, an unnatural silence fell over the harbor. The fishermen paused in their work, their gazes drawn to the horizon, where a dark shape emerged from the dense fog.

At first, it was barely more than a shadow, a smudge against the pale sky. But as the minutes passed, the shadow grew sharper, revealing itself as the silhouette of a ship—a schooner with sagging sails and a hull darkened with grime. It moved slowly, drifting more than sailing, the wind failing to stir its torn canvas. The men on the docks exchanged uneasy glances, their conversations faltering. There was something wrong with this vessel, though none could articulate exactly what.

The *Empusa* crept closer, its arrival heralded by the low groan of its timbers and the faint, rhythmic slap of water against its bow. It moved as if under its own power, untouched by the wind or tide, a silent specter gliding toward the shore. No voices called from the deck, no figures moved among the rigging or along the rails. The ship was utterly still, save for the slow, erratic sway of its mast.

The harbormaster, a stout man with a sharp eye and an even sharper tongue, stepped out of his office, drawn by the sudden quiet that had fallen over the docks. His boots clattered against the worn stone as he approached the edge of the pier, his hands resting on his hips. He squinted into the fog, his frown deepening as the ship loomed closer.

"What in the devil…?" he muttered, his voice low but carrying in the stillness.

The *Empusa* drifted into view, its hull streaked with salt and grime, its once-proud figurehead battered and splintered. The sails hung in tattered shreds, fluttering weakly in the faint breeze, and the ropes swayed limply as if abandoned. The ship looked like it had been dragged from the depths of the sea, a ghostly remnant of its former self.

The harbormaster motioned for a handful of dockworkers to join him, though they hesitated, their movements slow and reluctant.

"Come on," he barked, his tone harsher than usual. "Let's see what's what."

The men exchanged nervous glances but followed, their boots echoing hollowly on the wooden gangplank as they stepped aboard the silent vessel. The air seemed to change as they crossed the threshold, growing colder and heavier, carrying with it a faint but unmistakable stench. It was the smell of decay—cloying and sickly sweet, like rotting wood and damp earth mingled with something far darker.

The deck was empty, the ropes slack and the sails unmanned. The harbormaster and his men moved cautiously, their boots creaking against the warped planks. They called out, their voices sharp and hollow in the silence, but no answer came. The ship seemed devoid of life, a hollow shell adrift on the tide.

As they moved toward the aft of the vessel, one of the workers stopped suddenly, his face pale as he pointed toward a dark smear on the deck. "Blood," he whispered, his voice barely audible.

The harbormaster crouched to examine the stain, his expression hardening. It was blood, dried and blackened, as though it had been there for days. The trail led toward the hatch that descended into the lower decks, disappearing into the shadowed opening.

"Stay here," the harbormaster ordered, his voice steady despite the unease that gnawed at him. He drew a lantern from his belt and lit it, the flame flickering weakly as though struggling against an invisible wind. The workers muttered among themselves but obeyed, their eyes darting nervously toward the hatch as the harbormaster descended alone.

The air below deck was stifling, thick with the smell of mildew and damp wood. The harbormaster's lantern cast long, flickering shadows on the narrow walls, the faint light illuminating patches of peeling paint and water-stained beams. His footsteps echoed hollowly as he made his way toward the captain's cabin, his heart pounding against his ribs.

When he reached the door, he hesitated, his hand hovering over the latch. A faint noise came from within—so faint he almost missed it—a soft, rhythmic creaking, like the groan of wood under strain. He steeled himself and pushed the door open, the hinges screeching in protest.

The cabin was small and cluttered, its walls lined with shelves buckling under the weight of damp books and scattered maps. The lantern's glow fell on the desk in the center of the room, where the captain sat slumped over, his head resting on the open pages of his logbook. His shoulders were hunched, his coat wrinkled and stained, and his white-knuckled hands gripped the edges of the desk as though clinging to it for dear life.

"Captain?" the harbormaster called, his voice tight.

The figure didn't move.

The harbormaster stepped closer, the lantern shaking in his grasp. The smell of decay was stronger here, almost overwhelming, and as he drew near, he saw why. The captain's face, half-turned toward him, was pale and bloodless, his eyes wide and staring. His lips were parted in a silent scream, frozen in an expression of terror so profound that it made the harbormaster's skin crawl.

The harbormaster stumbled back, his heart racing as he turned and fled the cabin. He didn't stop until he was back on the deck, where the workers stood huddled together, their faces etched with unease.

"This ship..." he began, his voice hoarse. "There's something wrong. No one touches anything until we sort this out."

As he spoke, the faint sound of rustling caught his ear. He turned sharply, his lantern swinging to illuminate the far end of the deck. From the shadows emerged a swarm of black, writhing shapes—rats. Dozens of them, their eyes gleaming in the lantern light, their bodies spilling onto the deck like a tide.

The workers cried out, scrambling back as the rats surged forward, scattering in every direction. The harbormaster swore under his breath, his hand tightening around the lantern's handle as he watched the vermin pour over the gangplank and onto the dock.

And in the shadows of the ship's hold, beneath the weight of its ominous cargo, Count Orlok stirred.

The morning bustle of Wisborg's harbor had turned to a stunned silence, broken only by the whispers of dockworkers and the occasional creak of the *Empusa* as it rocked gently against the pier. News of the ship's arrival spread quickly through the town, drawing a small crowd of onlookers who gathered at a cautious distance, their expressions marked by equal parts curiosity and unease.

The harbormaster, his face pale and drawn, stood at the edge of the dock, issuing sharp orders to his men.

"No one goes near the ship unless I say so," he barked, though his voice carried a tremor. He had seen enough in the captain's cabin to know that this was no ordinary vessel, and the eerie silence that clung to it had unnerved even the most hardened workers.

Yet despite his warnings, there was a sense of inevitability as the townsfolk pressed closer, their murmurs growing louder as rumors began to circulate.

A handful of the braver—or perhaps more foolish—men from the crowd volunteered to join the harbormaster in inspecting the ship further. Armed with lanterns and lengths of rope, they moved hesitantly up the gangplank, their footsteps echoing on the damp wood. The harbormaster led the way, his jaw set in grim determination, though his hand trembled slightly as it rested on the hilt of his knife.

The deck, still silent and empty, seemed almost to breathe beneath their boots, the wood groaning faintly as though protesting their presence. The group paused at the hatch leading below deck, their lanterns casting long shadows over the darkened opening. The air here was thicker, heavier, carrying the unmistakable stench of death.

The harbormaster hesitated for a moment before descending the stairs, his steps slow and deliberate. The others followed reluctantly, their lanterns swaying as they moved deeper into the bowels of the ship. The narrow corridor that greeted them was lined with warped timbers and stained beams, the dampness of the sea having seeped into every corner.

"Careful," the harbormaster muttered, his voice low and tense. "Keep your eyes open."

They found the captain in the same position as before, slumped over his desk with his face frozen in a grimace of terror. One of the men let out a low curse, crossing himself as he stepped back from the grisly sight. The harbormaster took a deep breath and gestured toward the logbook, still open beneath the captain's lifeless hands.

"Grab it," he said, his voice tight. "We'll need to know what happened here."

One of the younger men, his face pale but determined, stepped forward and reached for the book. His fingers brushed against the captain's hand, and he recoiled with a shudder. The flesh was cold and stiff, the grip of death unmistakable. He pulled the log free, careful not to disturb the body further, and handed it to the harbormaster.

"Let's keep moving," the harbormaster said, his tone brooking no argument. He turned toward the hold, his lantern casting its faint light over the darkened path ahead.

The hold of the *Empusa* was even darker and colder than the cabin, the damp air thick with the smell of earth and rot. The men hesitated at the threshold, their lanterns barely piercing the gloom. The harbormaster moved forward cautiously, his breath visible in the frigid air, and gestured for the others to follow.

The sight that greeted them made their blood run cold. Lined neatly along one wall of the hold were six massive coffins, their dark wood glistening with moisture. The iron clasps that sealed them were rusted and pitted, and faint traces of dirt clung to the edges. The coffins seemed to radiate a sense of unease, their presence suffocating in its intensity.

"What in God's name...?" one of the men whispered, his voice trembling. He crossed himself again, his eyes wide as he stared at the macabre cargo.

The harbormaster approached the nearest coffin, his lantern held high. The light revealed scratches on the wood—deep, jagged marks that looked almost like claw marks. He reached out, his fingers brushing against the surface, and recoiled at the chill that seemed to seep from the wood.

"They're filled with dirt," he said, his voice flat. "But why...?"

"Dirt?" another man asked, incredulous. "What kind of cargo is this?"

The harbormaster didn't answer. He stepped back from the coffin, his gaze lingering on the scratches, and turned to the others.

"We're sealing the hold," he said firmly. "No one touches these. Not until we figure out what we're dealing with."

As the group made their way back to the deck, the oppressive atmosphere of the ship seemed to press down on them, growing heavier with each step. The shadows seemed to shift and writhe in the corners of their vision, and the faint creak of the timbers sounded almost like whispers.

By the time they emerged into the sunlight, their faces were pale, their expressions grim. The crowd on the dock pressed closer, their questions rising in a cacophony of anxious voices.

"What did you find?"

"Is it true the ship's cursed?"

"Why were there no crew?"

The harbormaster raised his hands, silencing them with a sharp gesture.

"There's nothing to worry about," he lied, his voice firm despite the doubt gnawing at him. "The ship's cargo will be secured and investigated. For now, go home. There's no need for panic."

The townsfolk murmured their discontent but began to disperse, though many cast nervous glances back at the *Empusa* as they left. The harbormaster watched them go, his jaw clenched. He knew he couldn't keep the truth hidden for long. Whatever had happened aboard the ship, it was unlike anything he had ever encountered.

As the crowd thinned, the harbormaster turned back to the vessel. He could still feel the oppressive presence that clung to it, a shadow that seemed to stretch out over the town like a dark cloud. Whatever curse the ship carried, it had already begun to take root.

And in the shadows of the hold, the coffins remained

undisturbed—waiting.

The *Empusa* loomed at the dock like a dark omen, its tattered sails swaying faintly in the morning breeze. Though the harbormaster and his men had sealed the hold and ordered everyone away, the sense of foreboding around the ship had already begun to infect the town. Rumors of its eerie silence and the grim discoveries aboard spread quickly through Wisborg, carried in whispers that grew more sinister with each telling.

But as the sun began to set, casting the harbor in long, jagged shadows, the true horror that the *Empusa* carried revealed itself.

It began quietly. A dockworker, lingering near the ship to secure a loose line, heard the faint sound of scratching from within the hull. He paused, his brow furrowing as he tilted his head to listen. The sound was faint at first, a soft rustling like leaves stirred by the wind. But as he stood there, it grew louder, more insistent—a relentless skittering that seemed to come from every corner of the ship.

Before he could react, a black shape darted out of the shadows near the gangplank. It was a rat, its small body sleek and filthy, its beady eyes glinting in the fading light. The man recoiled, muttering a curse under his breath. But then another followed. And another. And another.

The worker's shout of alarm echoed through the harbor as the swarm erupted from the ship.

Dozens of rats poured out from the hold, their black bodies writhing and churning like a living tide. They spilled over the gangplank and onto the dock, their sharp claws scraping against the wood as they scattered in every direction. The sound of their movement was deafening—a cacophony of squeals and skittering limbs that seemed to vibrate through the air.

The dockworker stumbled back, his eyes wide with terror as the vermin swarmed past him. Some climbed the ropes hanging from the ship, their tiny bodies disappearing into the rigging. Others darted into the cracks and crevices of the dock itself, their movements frantic and erratic. But most headed for the town, their dark forms vanishing into the narrow streets and alleys.

The rats moved like a plague, their numbers growing with every passing moment. By the time they reached the market square, their presence was impossible to ignore. Shopkeepers and merchants screamed as the swarm descended upon their stalls, knocking over crates and scattering wares in their frenzy. The vermin darted between feet and climbed onto tables, their sharp teeth tearing into sacks of grain and hunks of bread.

Ellen watched from her window as the chaos unfolded, her hands pressed tightly against the glass. She had heard the commotion from the harbor—the shouts of the dockworkers, the eerie screeches of the rats—and now she could see the effects spreading like ripples through the town. People fled in every direction, their faces pale with fear as they tried to escape the swarm.

The rats were everywhere, their black bodies weaving through the crowd like shadows given life. Children screamed as the vermin darted toward them, their parents snatching them up and running for the safety of their homes. Vendors abandoned their stalls, their goods left to be ravaged by the relentless tide.

Ellen felt a chill run down her spine as she watched the scene below. This was no ordinary infestation. The rats seemed driven by a singular purpose, their movements too coordinated, too unnatural. And though she could not see him, she could feel his presence—the shadow that lingered at the edges of her mind, growing stronger with each passing moment.

As the rats spread through Wisborg, so too did the sickness. By morning, the first cases of the plague were reported. People awoke with fevers and chills, their skin marked with dark lesions that spread rapidly. The town's physician, a stooped old man with a sharp mind and steady hands, was overwhelmed by the sheer number of cases. He worked tirelessly, moving from house to house with his bag of tinctures and poultices, but his efforts were futile. The sickness defied all remedies, spreading with a speed and ferocity that left him baffled.

The plague claimed its first victim within hours—a young merchant who had been bitten on the hand as he tried to chase a rat from his stall. His death was swift and agonizing, his body wracked with violent convulsions before he finally lay still. By the end of the day, three more had followed, their bodies carried through the streets on hastily constructed carts, their faces covered with rough cloth.

The townsfolk were gripped by fear. Some barricaded themselves in their homes, nailing boards over their windows and doors in a desperate attempt to keep the rats out. Others gathered in the church, lighting candles and praying fervently for deliverance. But no prayer could stop the shadow that had fallen over Wisborg, and no wall could keep the sickness at bay.

Ellen sat by the window, her hands clasped tightly in her lap as she watched the street below. She had barely slept since the *Empusa* had arrived, her nights plagued by the same vivid dreams of Orlok and her days consumed by a growing sense of dread. Now, as the plague spread through the town like wildfire, her fear turned to grim certainty. The ship had brought more than rats—it had brought death itself.

She thought of Thomas, of the strange journey he had undertaken and the warnings he had tried to give her. She thought of the shadowy figure in her dreams, his hollow eyes and skeletal hands reaching for her, and she felt the chill of his presence settle over her like a shroud. He was here. She could feel it.

Outside, the cries of the townsfolk echoed through the streets, their desperation a constant hum beneath the relentless squealing of the rats. The air itself seemed heavier, thicker, as though the sickness that gripped Wisborg had infected the very atmosphere. Ellen pressed her forehead against the glass, her breath fogging the pane, and whispered a prayer—not for herself, but for Thomas.

Somewhere in the distance, the tolling of the church bell marked the hour, its mournful chime carrying through the fog. And beneath it, faint but unmistakable, came the sound of something else—a low, guttural whisper that sent a shiver down her spine.

Ellen turned from the window, her heart pounding in her chest. The shadow had arrived.

# Chapter 13
## Knock's Madness

The small office of Herr Knock was a world unto itself, a claustrophobic den of shadows and disorder. The air inside was stagnant, thick with the mingled odors of old paper, ink, and damp wood, but lately, another scent had begun to creep in—a faint, acrid tang that no one could identify. Dust motes hung suspended in the weak sunlight that filtered through the grime-streaked windows, but the light failed to pierce the oppressive gloom that seemed to emanate from the walls themselves.

Knock sat hunched at his desk, his gaunt frame shrouded in darkness despite the hour. His bony fingers clutched a quill, the nib scratching feverishly across a scrap of parchment. The ink smeared in places, the jagged lines and symbols he scrawled bearing no resemblance to any recognizable language. His muttering filled the room, a low, incoherent murmur that rose and fell like the tide.

It had been days—weeks, perhaps—since the master had first spoken to him. The voice had come suddenly, seeping into his mind like water through a crack in stone. It was soft at first, barely audible, a whisper that teased the edges of his thoughts. But it had grown stronger, more insistent, until it consumed him entirely. Now, the master's words were all he could hear, a relentless chorus that drowned out the mundane sounds of the world.

"The master is coming," Knock muttered, his voice a rasp that barely rose above the sound of the quill scratching against the parchment. His lips curled into a twisted smile, his eyes gleaming with an unnatural light. "He will bring the shadows. He will bring eternity."

The words were not his own. They were given to him, implanted in his mind like seeds that had taken root and begun to grow. He could hear the master now, clearer than ever before, his voice a low, guttural whisper that echoed in the hollow spaces of Knock's soul.

"You will prepare the way," the voice said, its tone like the rustle of dead leaves. "You will serve, and you will be rewarded."

Knock's hand trembled as he wrote, the quill carving deep grooves into the parchment. His writing had devolved into madness, the once-neat lines of his correspondence replaced by jagged spirals and indecipherable symbols. He no longer cared about his business or his reputation—those things were meaningless now. All that mattered was the master's will.

The door to the office creaked open, and Gustav, Knock's nervous young servant, stepped inside. He carried a tray with a mug of tea and a plate of bread, his movements hesitant as he approached the desk.

"Herr Knock," he began, his voice faltering as he took in the scene before him. "You haven't eaten all day. Perhaps you should—"

"Silence!" Knock barked, slamming his hand down on the desk. The sudden noise made Gustav flinch, nearly spilling the tea. Knock's eyes, bloodshot and wild, snapped up to meet the young man's. "Do you not hear it?" he demanded, his voice trembling with a mix of fury and exultation. "Do you not hear him?"

"Hear who, Herr Knock?" Gustav asked cautiously, his hands tightening around the tray.

"The master!" Knock hissed, leaning forward until his face was inches from Gustav's. His breath smelled sour, his thin lips stretched into a grimace. "He speaks to me. He speaks through me. He is coming, and he will remake this wretched world."

Gustav took a step back, his face pale.

"I don't understand," he stammered. "What master? What are you talking about?"

Knock let out a sharp, grating laugh that sent shivers down Gustav's spine.

"You will understand soon enough," he said, his tone eerily calm. "When he arrives, there will be no need for understanding. There will only be submission."

As the days passed, Knock's behavior grew increasingly erratic. He stopped attending to his business entirely, leaving contracts unsigned and correspondence unanswered. The townsfolk who came to his office seeking his services were met with locked doors or, worse, with glimpses of Knock through the window—his gaunt frame hunched over his desk, his hands moving feverishly as he muttered to himself.

Gustav, though loyal, began to grow fearful. He tried to reason with his employer, to convince him to rest or take a break from his work, but Knock would not listen. The master's voice consumed him, guiding his every thought and action. He would spend hours staring out the window, his dark eyes fixed on the horizon as though expecting to see the master materialize from the fog.

One evening, as the sun set behind a veil of clouds, Gustav found Knock sitting in the corner of the office, his knees drawn to his chest. His lips moved silently, his eyes unblinking as he stared at a spot on the wall. The air in the room felt heavy, oppressive, as though it carried the weight of something unseen.

"Herr Knock," Gustav said softly, stepping closer. "Please, you need help. Let me fetch the physician—"

"No physician can help me," Knock interrupted, his voice low but sharp. He turned his head slowly, his gaze locking onto Gustav's with a chilling intensity. "The master has claimed me. My fate is sealed."

"Claimed you?" Gustav repeated, his voice trembling. "What do you mean?"

Knock smiled, a thin, crooked smile that sent a shiver through Gustav.

"You'll see soon enough," he said. "The master is coming. He will bring the darkness, and I will stand at his side."

That night, Gustav fled the office, leaving Knock alone with his madness. As the hours dragged on, the harbormaster's lanterns outside flickered faintly in the mist, casting long shadows across the cobblestones. Inside, Knock's whispers continued unabated, a ceaseless murmur that filled the room like the droning of insects.

"The master is here," Knock whispered, his fingers tracing patterns in the air. "He watches. He waits."

He turned to the window, his hollow eyes fixed on the distant harbor. In the shadows of the room, something seemed to stir, an unseen presence that pressed against the edges of his perception. Knock felt it as a weight in his chest, a chill that seeped into his bones.

And then, faint and distant but unmistakable, he heard the master's voice again.

"Soon."

Knock smiled, his lips curling into a grin that bordered on ecstasy. He leaned back in his chair, his hands resting limply in his lap as he closed his eyes. The whispers in his mind grew louder, drowning out the sounds of the world outside. He was no longer afraid. He was ready.

Wisborg was a town teetering on the edge of chaos. The air was heavy with the smell of sickness and despair, and the once-vibrant streets were now littered with abandoned market stalls and hastily boarded windows. Death stalked the town like a shadow, and the whispers of the plague's origin had begun to take on a fevered tone. Fear had given birth to anger, and anger demanded a scapegoat.

It did not take long for the townsfolk to settle on Knock.

Knock's strange behavior had always been a source of gossip among the people of Wisborg. He was an outsider in every sense—a man whose eccentricities and reclusive tendencies had made him an object of ridicule and distrust. His peculiar mutterings and odd hours were easily dismissed when life in the town was steady, but now, in the grip of pestilence, those peculiarities became damning evidence.

"He's the one who brought that cursed ship here," muttered an old woman as she ladled water into her cracked clay pot. Her words carried easily in the stillness of the marketplace. "The *Empusa*. It's his doing."

Her neighbor nodded grimly, clutching her shawl tighter around her shoulders.

"And have you seen him lately? Muttering to himself, locked up in that office of his. He's not right in the head. He's in league with... with something."

The rumors spread like the sickness itself, growing darker and more exaggerated with each retelling. The coffins aboard the *Empusa*, the swarms of rats, the creeping plague—all of it was laid at Knock's feet. It didn't matter that no one had seen him near the ship since its arrival, or that no one truly understood what was happening. Fear needed a face, and Knock's wild-eyed madness made him an easy target.

The turning point came when one of the town's wealthier merchants collapsed in the market square, his face ashen and marked with dark lesions. He had been one of the first to handle cargo from the *Empusa*, and his sudden death fueled the growing hysteria. A crowd gathered around his body, their whispers growing louder, their accusations sharper.

"It's Knock," someone shouted, their voice cutting through the murmurs like a knife. "He's cursed us all!"

Others took up the cry, their voices rising in a crescendo of anger and fear.

"He's a devil! He's brought this plague to our town! He must pay for what he's done!"

The crowd swelled as more townsfolk joined, drawn by the commotion. Men armed themselves with crude weapons—clubs, pitchforks, and iron tools—and women carried torches, their flames flickering against the encroaching twilight. The mob moved as one, their collective rage fueling their steps as they marched toward Knock's office.

The narrow street leading to Knock's office was eerily quiet, the only sounds the muffled shuffle of boots on cobblestones and the occasional crackle of a torch. The mob came to a halt outside the building, their voices echoing off the walls as they shouted for Knock to show himself.

"Come out, you coward!" bellowed one man, his face red with fury. He slammed the butt of his pitchfork against the door, the wood rattling under the force. "Face us!"

Inside, Knock stood perfectly still, his head cocked to one side as though listening to something only he could hear. The cries of the mob reached his ears, but they were distant and unimportant, mere background noise to the whispers of the master. He smiled, his thin lips curling into a crooked grin as he turned toward the window.

"They're afraid," he murmured to himself, his voice soft and almost affectionate. "They should be."

The door shuddered under the blows of the mob, splinters flying as the wood began to crack. Knock moved to the center of the room, his hands clasped behind his back, and waited. He could feel the master's presence growing stronger, his whispers weaving through Knock's mind like a dark melody. The master had promised him safety, and Knock believed.

With a final, deafening crash, the door gave way, and the mob spilled into the office. Their torches cast jagged shadows on the walls, illuminating the chaos of papers and overturned furniture. At the center of it all stood Knock, his wiry frame hunched slightly, his eyes gleaming with manic energy.

"You've doomed us all!" shouted one of the men, stepping forward with his pitchfork raised. "You brought that cursed ship here! You're the cause of the plague!"

Knock laughed, a sharp, grating sound that silenced the mob. He spread his arms wide, his grin growing even wider.

"The plague?" he said, his voice filled with mockery. "You think this is my doing? Fools! The master is coming, and there is nothing you can do to stop him!"

His words only enraged the crowd further.

"Seize him!" someone shouted, and the mob surged forward, their torches and weapons raised.

But Knock was faster. With a sudden burst of energy, he darted toward the back of the office, shoving over a cabinet to block their path. The mob cursed and shouted, their movements slowed as they stumbled over the debris. By the time they reached the back door, Knock was already gone.

The mob spilled into the streets, their torches bobbing like fireflies as they searched for Knock. Some ran toward the harbor, hoping to cut off his escape, while others fanned out through the alleys and side streets. The anger that had united them began to splinter into frustration, their shouts growing disjointed as they failed to find their quarry.

But Knock was clever. He moved quickly and silently, slipping through the shadows like a wraith. His laughter echoed faintly through the narrow streets, a taunting sound that sent chills through the mob.

"He's heading for the forest!" someone cried, and the group turned as one, their torches casting flickering light on the gnarled trees that loomed at the edge of the town.

The gnarled trees of the Wisborg forest loomed ahead, their twisted branches stretching skyward like skeletal hands clawing at the darkening sky. The torches of the mob flickered and hissed in the cool evening air as the crowd surged toward the tree line, their anger and fear propelling them forward. Knock's laughter echoed faintly through the dense underbrush, rising and falling like a mocking specter just beyond their reach.

"He's in there!" shouted one man, gripping his pitchfork tightly. "He can't have gone far!"

The mob hesitated at the forest's edge, their confidence faltering as the shadows of the trees seemed to stretch outward, swallowing the last rays of sunlight. The forest had always been a place of whispered superstitions, its depths said to harbor wild animals and vagrants, but tonight it seemed alive with something far more sinister. The men glanced at one another, their expressions uncertain.

"He can't get away with this," said another, his voice trembling but resolute. He raised his torch higher, the flame casting jagged shadows over his face. "We have to find him."

One by one, the mob pressed into the forest, their footsteps crunching against the dry leaves that carpeted the ground. The air grew colder with each step, the thick canopy above blotting out the fading light of the evening sky. The once-ordered line of torches began to fragment as the men fanned out, their shouts growing softer and more scattered.

"Knock!" one man called, his voice echoing faintly. "You can't hide forever!"

But the only reply was the rustling of leaves and the faint, mocking echo of Knock's laughter.

Knock darted through the underbrush with a speed and agility that belied his gaunt frame. His bony hands clawed at the branches that snagged his coat, and his thin legs carried him deeper into the labyrinth of trees. The whispers of the master filled his mind, guiding his every step.

"Keep going," the voice urged, low and insistent. "They cannot touch you. You are chosen."

The mob's shouts grew fainter behind him, their torches flickering like dying stars in the distance. Knock's laughter bubbled up from his chest, spilling out in jagged bursts that echoed through the forest. It was a sound devoid of sanity, tinged with both triumph and hysteria.

As he ran, the forest seemed to shift around him. The trees grew denser, their trunks gnarled and blackened, their branches knitting together above to form a canopy that blotted out the sky. The air grew thick and cold, and the ground beneath his feet became soft and spongy, as though he were treading on a bed of moss and decay.

Knock slowed, his breath ragged, his wide eyes darting through the darkness. He could no longer hear the mob, but he could feel their presence—an angry, chaotic energy that lurked at the edges of his awareness. He pressed on, deeper and deeper into the forest, his laughter now a whisper in the still air.

The men of Wisborg, their anger giving way to frustration and fear, began to falter in their pursuit. The forest was a maze of shadows and tangled underbrush, and their torches seemed to cast more darkness than light. Every snapping twig and rustling leaf set their nerves on edge, and more than one man turned back, muttering about curses and devils.

"He's toying with us," one man said, his voice tight with fear. "He knows this forest better than we do."

Another man, his face pale in the torchlight, nodded grimly.

"This is madness. We should let him go. The plague will claim him soon enough."

But a few pressed on, their determination burning as brightly as their torches. They called Knock's name into the darkness, their voices hoarse with exertion, but no answer came. The forest seemed to swallow their cries, the silence growing heavier with each passing moment.

"He can't be far," one man muttered, though his grip on his pitchfork trembled. "We'll find him."

Deep within the forest, far beyond the reach of the mob, Knock finally stopped. He leaned against a tree, his chest heaving as he struggled to catch his breath. His coat was torn, his face streaked with dirt, but his eyes burned with a manic light.

"The master…" he murmured, his voice barely audible. "I have done as you asked."

The shadows around him seemed to shift, the air growing colder still. Knock tilted his head, his lips curling into a crooked grin as he listened to the voice that only he could hear.

"You are loyal," the master whispered, his tone soft and serpentine. "Your faith will be rewarded."

Knock fell to his knees, his laughter rising again, sharp and grating in the stillness of the forest. His hands clawed at the damp earth, his body trembling with the force of his exultation. He had escaped the mob, escaped their ignorance and fear, and now he was free—free to serve, free to fulfill the master's will.

Far above, the moon broke through the canopy, its pale light illuminating Knock's gaunt face. He looked upward, his eyes wide with rapture, his laughter fading into a low, guttural whisper.

"The master is here," he said, his voice filled with reverence. "And I am his."

# Chapter 14
## The Count's Lair

The abandoned manor by the river had stood for decades as a husk of its former self, a remnant of an era long past. Once the pride of a wealthy merchant family, the house had been left to decay after a string of tragedies drove its inhabitants to ruin. Now, its walls were weathered and cracked, its windows like hollow eyes staring out over the water, and its grounds a tangled mess of weeds and brambles. Locals avoided it instinctively, their whispers painting it as a place cursed by death and misery.

On the night Orlok arrived, the house seemed to awaken.

The *Empusa* had docked just before midnight, its coffins of soil quietly unloaded by unseen hands. The harbor had been deserted, the fog too thick and the air too heavy for anyone to linger. Orlok moved among the coffins with deliberate slowness, his towering frame obscured by his black cloak, his every step accompanied by the faint rasp of his breath. He guided the procession of coffins like a silent conductor, his hollow eyes fixed on the darkened path that led to the manor.

The journey to the manor was a slow, deliberate march. The heavy coffins, damp with the soil they carried, were hoisted onto wagons that groaned beneath their weight. The horses pulling them snorted and shivered, their breath visible in the chill air. The animals seemed uneasy, their ears twitching and their movements jerky, but Orlok's presence kept them subdued. He walked beside the lead wagon, his long, clawed fingers occasionally brushing against the reins, as though the mere touch of his hand could compel obedience.

The narrow path to the manor twisted through the outskirts of Wisborg, winding between fields of frost-covered grass and barren trees. The fog hung thick and low, muffling the sounds of the wagons and cloaking the procession in a shroud of gray. The river, dark and sluggish, mirrored the dim moonlight in patches where the fog thinned, its surface disturbed only by the occasional ripple of unseen movement.

As the manor came into view, its jagged silhouette rising against the horizon, the horses balked. They reared and whinnied, their hooves scraping against the frozen earth as if they sensed the malevolence that awaited them. Orlok paused, his gaunt frame motionless as he turned his head toward the animals. His eyes, gleaming faintly in the darkness, locked onto them, and the horses stilled almost instantly. Their breaths came in short, ragged bursts, but they obeyed, pulling the wagons forward with trembling steps.

The gates to the manor were rusted and overgrown, their iron bars twisted and jagged like the teeth of some great beast. Orlok pushed them open with ease, the hinges shrieking in protest as he stepped onto the overgrown path that led to the house. Weeds and thorns clawed at his cloak, but he moved without hesitation, his shadow stretching long and thin across the ground.

The manor loomed above him, its façade cracked and crumbling, its once-grand columns leaning at precarious angles. The windows were dark and empty, save for the faint reflections of the moon and fog. The front door, thick and warped with age, seemed to bow under the weight of the house's decay.

Orlok reached out with one pale, clawed hand, his touch almost reverent as his fingers traced the grain of the wood. Then, with a single push, the door creaked open, revealing the darkness within. The air that greeted him was cold and stale, heavy with the scent of mold and rot. It was a place long forgotten, a tomb that had been waiting for its new occupant.

The coffins were brought inside one by one, their weight pressing into the rotting floorboards. Orlok directed their placement with silent gestures, his bony hands moving like a conductor orchestrating a grim symphony. The wagons were unloaded quickly, their task completed in eerie silence, and the horses were led away, their trembling forms disappearing into the mist.

As the final coffin was lowered into place, Orlok descended into the basement. The steps groaned beneath his weight, the damp stone walls pressing close as he moved deeper into the earth. The basement was little more than a crude cellar, its low ceiling dripping with condensation and its corners choked with cobwebs. But to Orlok, it was a sanctuary.

The coffins were arranged in a precise pattern, their lids left slightly ajar to reveal the damp soil within. Orlok's long fingers trailed over the wood as he passed, his expression one of quiet satisfaction. This soil, taken from his homeland, was his lifeblood, the anchor that tied him to this new place. Without it, his strength would wane, his power diminished. But here, in this dark and forgotten corner of Wisborg, he would thrive.

Orlok's movements slowed as he reached the largest coffin, its dark wood polished to a dull sheen. He climbed inside with an almost mechanical grace, his elongated body folding into the narrow space. The lid lowered slowly, sealing him within. For a moment, the basement was silent, the only sound the faint drip of water from the ceiling.

Then the house began to change.

The manor groaned as if in protest, its ancient timbers creaking and shifting under an invisible weight. The walls seemed to darken, the shadows growing longer and more pronounced. The air grew colder still, a chill that seeped into the very bones of the house. It was as though the manor itself was awakening, responding to Orlok's presence like a slumbering beast stirred from its rest.

Above, the wind howled through the broken windows, carrying with it the faint cries of the river's inhabitants. The townsfolk, though miles away, felt the shift in the air, an unexplainable unease that gripped their hearts and sent shivers down their spines.

Orlok, sealed within his coffin, smiled in the darkness. The house was his now, its decay and despair the perfect vessel for his power. The shadows that clung to its walls, the silence that filled its halls—these were his allies, his tools. And through them, he would spread his influence across Wisborg, one death at a time.

The Count had found his lair, and Wisborg would never be the same.

The changes in Wisborg were subtle at first, almost imperceptible. The air grew heavier, the light dimmer, and the once-vibrant town seemed to lose its color as though a shadow had fallen over it. The birds that had filled the mornings with their songs vanished, leaving the town shrouded in a silence that was more oppressive than peaceful. The waters of the river, which had once sparkled under the sun, now seemed to ripple with unease, their surface dark and sluggish.

The townsfolk, already wearied by the plague, began to notice the shift but could not explain it. They whispered of strange dreams and an inexplicable sense of dread, their fears spreading as quickly as the sickness itself. Wisborg, once a town of bustling markets and cheerful gatherings, had become a place of silence and suspicion.

It began with the deaths.

Though the plague had already claimed many, these new deaths were different. The victims showed no signs of illness, no fever, no rashes—only an unnatural pallor and twin punctures on their necks. The physician, whose knowledge had been a source of comfort to the townsfolk, could offer no explanation.

"Perhaps it is the rats," he suggested weakly, though his voice lacked conviction. The people did not believe him.

The deaths came at night. A fisherman returning late from the river would be found lifeless in his boat come morning, his hands frozen in a final, desperate grip on the oars. A merchant working late in his shop would be discovered slumped over his counter, his eyes wide with terror. Entire families were found dead in their homes, the windows flung open as though they had tried to flee.

The graveyard, once a quiet place of solace, became a grim reminder of the town's suffering. The gravediggers worked tirelessly, their shovels cutting through the earth from dawn to dusk. Yet no matter how many were buried, the shadows seemed to deepen, as though the very ground was hungry for more.

The manor by the river had become the epicenter of the town's unease. Though none dared approach it, the people spoke of strange lights flickering in its windows at night, of whispers carried on the wind that seemed to emanate from its darkened halls. Some claimed to have seen a tall, gaunt figure moving through the overgrown grounds, his silhouette unnaturally long and thin.

Children, warned to stay away from the river, spoke of nightmares—visions of a pale man with hollow eyes and claw-like hands reaching for them from the darkness. Their parents dismissed these tales as the imaginings of frightened minds, but the fear in their voices lingered long after the stories were told.

The animals, too, were affected. Dogs refused to go near the river, their tails tucked and their ears flattened at the mere suggestion. The horses at the stables grew restless at night, their nervous whinnies filling the air until dawn. Even the rats, which had spread the plague through the town, seemed to avoid the manor, their scurrying forms steering clear of its shadow.

As the shadow of Orlok's influence spread, the town itself began to change. The cobblestone streets, once filled with the sounds of merchants hawking their wares and children laughing, now echoed with emptiness. The market stalls stood abandoned, their owners too afraid to venture out after dark. The church, once a sanctuary of hope, now held only the desperate prayers of the few who still believed they could be saved.

The people of Wisborg became prisoners of their own fear. Doors were bolted at sunset, and windows were shuttered tight. Candles burned through the night, their flickering flames casting long, jagged shadows on the walls. Sleep became a luxury few could afford, as every creak of wood and every rustle of wind set hearts racing.

The whispers began again, louder and more insistent than before. The town needed someone to blame, someone to hold accountable for the darkness that had consumed their lives. Though Knock had disappeared, his name was still spoken with venom, his madness tied to the curse that had befallen Wisborg. But as the bodies piled up and the shadow deepened, another name began to surface—Count Orlok.

Orlok moved through the town like a shadow, his presence felt but rarely seen. He was a master of subtlety, his influence spreading not through brute force but through fear and suggestion. The townsfolk, already weakened by sickness and despair, were easy prey. He needed only to watch and wait as their paranoia consumed them.

By night, he roamed the streets, his gaunt figure blending seamlessly into the darkness. He fed sparingly, choosing his victims with care to avoid drawing too much attention. Each death was a carefully placed piece in his growing web of control, a step closer to fully enveloping the town in his grasp.

And yet, Orlok's hunger was not only for blood. His shadow reached into the minds of the townsfolk, planting seeds of despair and mistrust. He reveled in their suffering, their slow unraveling, their descent into chaos. The town itself seemed to bend to his will, its very essence tainted by his presence.

Though Orlok rarely ventured near the Hutter home, Ellen could feel him. His presence pressed against her like a weight, a dark tide that ebbed and flowed but never truly receded. She would sit by the window for hours, staring out at the distant outline of the manor, her thoughts consumed by the shadow that had fallen over Wisborg.

The connection between them grew stronger with each passing day. It was no longer confined to her dreams—she could feel him even in the daylight, a faint but persistent pull that left her weak and trembling. She tried to push the thoughts away, to distract herself with small tasks, but the darkness always returned, creeping into the corners of her mind.

Ellen's health began to suffer. Her once-bright eyes grew dull, her skin pale and waxy. She moved through the house like a ghost, her energy drained by the relentless weight of Orlok's influence. And though she longed for Thomas's return, a part of her feared that it would be too late.

The shadow had taken root in Wisborg, and Orlok's grip tightened with every passing moment.

The nights had grown longer, the hours of daylight receding into a gray twilight that offered no solace. For Ellen, time had lost all meaning. Her days were spent in a haze of dread, her nights plagued by dreams so vivid they left her trembling and gasping for breath. She no longer felt like herself. It was as though her very soul had been tethered to something vast and incomprehensible, something that loomed just beyond the veil of the visible world.

She could feel him. Always. A presence that wrapped around her like an invisible fog, pressing against her skin and coiling in her mind. It was not the simple fear of an unknown danger, but an oppressive certainty. Count Orlok was near, and he was coming for her.

Ellen's dreams were no longer fleeting glimpses of unease—they were landscapes of horror that seemed as real as the waking world. She found herself walking through the shadowed halls of the manor, her bare feet silent against the cold stone. The walls seemed to pulse with a faint, otherworldly glow, the air heavy with the scent of damp earth and decay. She would hear the faint creak of wood, the whisper of something moving just beyond her sight.

And always, she would see him.

He would appear at the end of a long corridor, his gaunt figure silhouetted against the dim light. His hollow eyes would lock onto hers, unblinking, and she would feel his presence seep into her like poison. She could not move, could not scream, as he began to approach, his skeletal hands outstretched, his shadow stretching ahead of him like a living thing.

When she awoke, drenched in sweat and trembling, the sensation of his presence did not fade. She would sit upright in bed, her breath coming in ragged gasps, her eyes scanning the dark corners of the room as though expecting to see his figure materialize from the shadows.

During the day, Ellen tried to push the dreams from her mind, but they clung to her like cobwebs, their residue thick and inescapable. She felt an inexplicable pull toward the river, toward the manor that loomed like a dark sentinel on its overgrown grounds. She told herself she was only imagining it, that it was her grief for Thomas and the plague-ravaged town that made her thoughts wander to such dreadful places.

But her body betrayed her. She found herself standing by the river's edge, her hands clutching her shawl as the wind whipped through her hair. The water was still and black, its surface reflecting the gray sky in broken shards. The manor loomed on the opposite bank, its jagged outline cutting against the horizon. She could almost see the faint flicker of light in one of the upper windows, though no one had dared enter that house since Orlok's arrival.

## Nosferatu

Her legs felt rooted to the spot, her heart pounding in her chest as though it were struggling to escape. The pull was stronger here, almost physical, like an invisible hand reaching out to her. She could feel his gaze from across the river, his hollow eyes piercing the distance between them.

"Ellen?" a voice called behind her, and she turned sharply, startled. It was Frau Schröder, her neighbor, standing a few paces away with a basket of herbs clutched to her chest. "Are you all right, dear?"

Ellen forced a smile, though it felt like a lie stretched across her face.

"Yes," she said softly. "I was just... getting some air."

Frau Schröder glanced toward the manor, her expression darkening.

"You shouldn't linger here," she said, her voice low. "That place is cursed. Everyone knows it."

Ellen nodded and allowed herself to be led back to the village, but the pull of the manor lingered, a whisper in her mind that grew louder with each passing moment.

As the days wore on, Ellen began to notice the ways Orlok's presence affected her. She felt weaker, her body growing frail as though something was draining her vitality. Her appetite vanished, and her hands trembled when she tried to complete even the simplest of tasks. The townsfolk, already fearful of the plague, began to whisper about her.

"She looks like the dead," one woman said, her voice low but sharp as Ellen passed her in the market.

"She's been marked," another man muttered, his eyes narrowing. "Just like the others."

Ellen heard their whispers but paid them no mind. She could not explain it, but she knew that what afflicted her was not the plague. It was something far older, far darker. She felt it in her dreams, in the way the shadows seemed to move around her, in the low, guttural whispers that filled her ears when she was alone.

The connection between her and Orlok grew stronger, a thread that stretched across the distance and bound them together. She did not know how or why, but she felt as though she had been chosen—plucked from the world and drawn into his shadow.

Ellen began to spend her nights by the window, staring out into the darkness as though searching for something she could not name. She rarely slept, her nights broken by the same vivid dreams and her days haunted by the memory of them. Her health continued to decline, her cheeks hollowing and her skin taking on a pale, waxy hue.

One night, as she sat by the window, she saw a figure standing across the river. It was barely more than a silhouette, a tall, gaunt shape that seemed to blend with the shadows. But she knew who it was. Her breath caught in her throat, her heart pounding as she leaned closer to the glass.

The figure did not move, but she could feel his presence as clearly as if he were standing beside her. Her hand trembled as she reached for the window latch, her mind screaming at her to stop, to run, to hide. But her body would not obey. The connection between them was too strong, pulling her closer, binding her to him.

And then she heard his voice.

"Ellen."

It was a whisper, low and guttural, but it resonated in her mind like a thunderclap. She clutched her chest, her breath coming in short gasps as the darkness seemed to press in around her. The figure across the river remained motionless, but she could feel his shadow stretching toward her, reaching across the water, slipping through the cracks of her home.

Ellen collapsed into the chair, her trembling hand clutching the windowsill. She could feel him now, stronger than ever, his presence a suffocating weight that wrapped around her like a shroud. And in that moment, she knew there was no escape. He would come for her, and she would be powerless to stop him.

The master's shadow had fully claimed her.

# Chapter 15
## Revelations

The discovery of the book was an accident—or perhaps, Ellen thought later, it was fate. It had been another sleepless night, the shadows in her room seeming to stretch and breathe with a life of their own. Her dreams, when they came, were vivid nightmares of dark halls and skeletal hands reaching for her, of Orlok's hollow eyes pinning her in place. When she woke, the oppressive sense of his presence lingered, wrapping around her chest like an iron shroud.

She couldn't bear the suffocating stillness of her bedroom. The house felt too quiet, too empty without Thomas, and though she had lit candles in every room, the darkness always seemed to find her. She wandered the house aimlessly, her fingers trailing over the worn furniture and dusty shelves, searching for some distraction, some relic of comfort. It was in the old storage chest in the corner of her father's study that she found it.

The chest was a relic of another time, its wood scarred and its hinges rusted. She hadn't opened it in years, not since her father's passing, but tonight it seemed to call to her, its presence oddly magnetic. When she lifted the lid, the scent of age and decay wafted up to greet her. The contents were unremarkable—folded linens, a few yellowed papers, and an assortment of trinkets—but buried beneath them, she found the book.

It was bound in dark, cracked leather, the spine warped from years of neglect. There was no title on the cover, only an embossed symbol that looked vaguely like a crescent moon wrapped in thorns. Ellen hesitated, her hands trembling as she lifted it from the chest. Something about the book felt wrong, as though it were radiating a faint, invisible heat. But her curiosity outweighed her fear.

She carried the book to the study's desk and lit the oil lamp, its weak glow spilling across the aged surface. As she opened the cover, the faded ink on the first page seemed to pulse faintly in the light. The title, written in a cramped, spidery script, read: *On the Nature of Shadows: A Treatise on the Nosferatu.*

Ellen's fingers trembled as she turned the pages, the weight of the book seeming heavier with each passing moment. The text was dense, written in an archaic dialect that required her to read slowly, carefully, piecing the meaning together word by word. The language was dry and academic, but the subject matter was anything but.

The Nosferatu, the book explained, were not mere legends but a dark and ancient curse. These creatures were the living dead, cursed to roam the earth for eternity, feeding on the lifeblood of the living. They were bound to the soil of their homeland, carrying it with them wherever they went to sustain their unnatural existence. Their presence brought sickness and despair, their influence spreading like a shadow over all they touched.

Ellen's breath quickened as she read on. The text described their gaunt, skeletal forms, their elongated fingers and sharp teeth, their eyes that burned like hollow coals in the darkness. They were creatures of shadow, the book said, incapable of withstanding the purifying light of the sun. They moved with unnatural grace, their silence more terrifying than any scream, and their strength grew with each life they drained.

The book detailed their methods with chilling precision. They stalked their prey from the shadows, seducing them with a gaze that could bend even the strongest will. Once their victim was enthralled, the Nosferatu would feed, draining the life from their veins until nothing remained but an empty shell. The process was described clinically, but Ellen could feel the horror behind the words, the despair of those who had fallen victim to these creatures.

She paused, her hands shaking as she closed the book for a moment to steady herself. The room seemed colder now, the air heavy with the weight of what she had just read. She glanced at the flickering light of the oil lamp, the flame casting jagged shadows across the walls, and for a moment, she thought she saw movement—a faint ripple, as if something had stirred just beyond the edge of her vision. She shook her head, forcing herself to focus. There was more to read, and she could not stop now.

Ellen resumed reading, her heart pounding as she reached a section titled The Binding of the Nosferatu. This part of the text was written in a different hand, the script larger and more erratic, as though the author had written in a frenzy. The tone shifted from detached explanation to desperate warning, the words almost leaping off the page.

The Nosferatu were not invincible, the text claimed, though they were perilously close to it. They could not be harmed by ordinary weapons, and fire and water would not destroy them. They were creatures of the night, their power rooted in darkness. But there was one weakness—a single, fatal flaw woven into the curse that bound them.

"The Nosferatu," Ellen read aloud, her voice trembling, "are creatures of shadow, and shadows cannot endure the dawn."

The book explained that the Nosferatu could only be destroyed if exposed to the first light of the morning sun. Their bodies would dissolve into dust, their power shattered, and their curse lifted. But to

## Nosferatu

hold them in place until dawn required a terrible sacrifice.

Ellen's eyes widened as she read the final passage of the chapter, the words etched into her mind with terrible clarity: Only the pure of heart may bind the Nosferatu, offering their life as a distraction until the light of dawn consumes the shadow.

Her hands fell to her lap, the book slipping from her grasp and landing on the desk with a dull thud. The room was deathly silent, the only sound her own ragged breathing. The meaning was clear, and it struck her like a blade to the chest. The only way to stop Orlok was through a willing sacrifice—a life offered to hold him in place until the sun rose.

She sat frozen, her thoughts racing. The weight of the revelation was suffocating, pressing against her chest until it felt as though she couldn't breathe. She thought of Thomas, of the plague, of the people of Wisborg who had suffered and died under Orlok's shadow. She thought of the strange, terrible connection she felt to the creature, the way his presence had seeped into her very soul.

Ellen pressed her hands to her face, her fingers digging into her skin as though she could claw away the horror of what she had learned. But the truth remained, unyielding and inescapable. The book had been hidden for a reason, and now it had found her. She had been chosen.

Ellen sat for hours, staring at the book as the oil lamp flickered and the night deepened. The house was silent, but her mind was a cacophony of fear and doubt. She wanted to scream, to run, to hide, but she knew there was no escape. The Nosferatu had come for Wisborg, and it would not stop until everything she loved was consumed.

And yet, amidst the terror, a spark of resolve began to form. If the book spoke the truth, then there was a way to end this nightmare. The cost would be terrible, but it would mean saving Thomas, saving Wisborg, saving all the lives that Orlok had yet to claim.

Her trembling hands reached for the book once more, her eyes

scanning the faded text as she whispered a single word to herself:
"Why?"

But there was no answer, only the weight of the words on the page and the shadow that loomed ever closer.

The room seemed to close in around Ellen as she reread the passage in the ancient book. The words etched into the page were simple, yet their meaning was profound and devastating: Only the pure of heart may bind the Nosferatu, offering their life as a distraction until the light of dawn consumes the shadow.

Ellen's hands trembled as she traced the lines of text, her breath coming in shallow gasps. The weight of what she had uncovered settled over her like a burial shroud. The book had made its purpose clear—it was not simply a record of horrors but a manual for those brave or desperate enough to confront the creatures it described. Yet it read not as an instruction but as a death sentence, written for someone who would willingly give their life to end the curse.

She sat back in the wooden chair, her gaze unfocused as she stared into the flickering light of the oil lamp. The faint glow cast long shadows across the walls of the study, the shifting patterns making her feel as though she were being watched. Outside, the night pressed against the windows, thick and impenetrable, a mirror of the darkness creeping into her heart.

The book's description of the sacrifice was horrifying in its clarity. The Nosferatu, it explained, could not be confronted with brute force. These creatures were bound to the night, their power growing with the setting sun and peaking under the cover of darkness. They could evade any human weapon, their movements too swift, their forms too unnatural to be restrained.

But their flaw was also their curse. The rising sun was their undoing, the one force that could obliterate their shadowy existence. The Nosferatu's survival depended on remaining hidden during the dawn hours, retreating to the soil of their homeland that sustained their life in death. If exposed to the light, they would dissolve into ash, their power undone by the purifying rays.

However, to force such a confrontation required a terrible act of courage. The creature had to be kept in place, its attention captured long enough for the sun to rise. This could not be achieved by brute force, for the Nosferatu was too strong. It required a lure, an offering, something so irresistible that it would hold the creature's focus even as the first light of dawn crept across the horizon.

The book was explicit: the lure had to be a living soul, one untainted by darkness, one whose purity of heart would draw the Nosferatu's hunger to its zenith. The Nosferatu, it claimed, could not resist such a sacrifice. Their ravenous thirst for life and vitality would overpower their instinct to retreat, holding them in place until the sun's light claimed them.

Ellen closed the book and sat in silence, her thoughts churning like a storm-tossed sea. The room felt colder now, the faint warmth of the oil lamp unable to dispel the chill that seeped into her bones. The knowledge she now possessed was a heavy burden, one that pressed against her chest with suffocating weight.

She thought of Thomas, of his journey to meet the creature that now haunted Wisborg. He had gone with the hope of securing their future, of building a life together, but instead, he had unwittingly unleashed a nightmare. She thought of the townsfolk, their faces pale and gaunt as the plague swept through the streets, leaving death and despair in its wake. And she thought of the Nosferatu, of Orlok, whose shadow stretched over her like a noose tightening with every passing moment.

Her mind turned to the warnings she had ignored, the strange dreams she had dismissed as mere fancies. She could see now that she had been marked from the beginning, drawn into the creature's orbit by forces she could neither understand nor resist. The pull she felt toward him was not merely fear—it was a connection, a bond that defied explanation. She had been chosen, and the book's words confirmed what she had feared all along.

The sacrifice had to be hers.

Ellen pressed her hands to her face, her fingers digging into her temples as she tried to calm the rising panic in her chest. She did not want to die. The thought of surrendering herself to Orlok's grasp, of feeling his cold hands on her skin, of allowing him to drain the life from her veins—it filled her with a terror so profound it left her trembling. But the alternative was far worse.

She thought of the children playing in the square, of the families huddled together in their homes, of the town she had grown up in. She thought of Thomas, his warm smile and gentle hands, the way he had always looked at her as though she were his entire world. If she did nothing, all of that would be lost. Orlok would consume Wisborg, and the shadow would spread, leaving only death and despair in its wake.

Her life was a small price to pay to stop such horror.

As the hours passed, Ellen's fear began to give way to grim determination. She knew what had to be done, even if every fiber of her being rebelled against it. She would face Orlok. She would lure him to her and keep him there, her own life the bait that would bind him until the sun rose. She would not allow him to take any more lives—not Thomas's, not anyone's.

Her trembling hands returned to the book, flipping through its pages in search of anything that might help her prepare. The text offered little in the way of comfort, but it gave her the clarity she needed. The Nosferatu's hunger would be its undoing, and her purity of heart would hold it fast.

She closed the book and rose from the desk, her movements slow but deliberate. The room seemed darker now, the shadows pressing closer, but Ellen no longer flinched. She walked to the window and looked out at the distant silhouette of the manor, its jagged outline barely visible through the night's fog. She could feel Orlok's presence, a faint pressure on the edges of her mind, and she knew he was waiting.

Her breath fogged the glass as she whispered,

"You won't win."

The words felt hollow, but she repeated them until they steadied her trembling hands. She would not falter. She would not run. The shadow had come for Wisborg, but it would end with her.

Ellen turned from the window and extinguished the lamp, plunging the room into darkness. The weight of her decision settled over her like a shroud, but for the first time in weeks, she felt a glimmer of purpose. She would face Orlok, and she would stop him.

Even if it cost her everything.

The days after Ellen's discovery of the book passed in a haze of dread and clarity. The knowledge of what she must do had transformed her, though not in a way that the townsfolk could perceive. To them, she remained the frail, ghostly woman who wandered through the market with hollow eyes and a pallor that seemed to deepen with each passing day. But inside, Ellen felt a grim resolve hardening, a sense of inevitability that both terrified and steadied her.

She had chosen her path. Now, she had to see it through.

Ellen spent hours sitting by the window, staring out over the river toward the distant silhouette of the manor. Its jagged form loomed like a dark specter against the horizon, shrouded in mist and shadow. She felt its presence as though it were a living thing, its influence reaching across the water to wrap around her like a cold embrace. She no longer tried to deny the connection she felt to Orlok; it was undeniable, a thread that pulled at her soul with every passing moment.

At night, the dreams continued. She would see herself standing in her bedroom, the faint light of dawn filtering through the curtains. Orlok's shadow stretched toward her, long and grasping, until it enveloped her completely. She felt his presence, cold and oppressive, his hollow eyes fixed on her with a hunger that made her blood run cold. But the fear that had once consumed her was now tempered by resolve. She knew what she had to do, and the dreams, though terrifying, no longer left her paralyzed.

Instead, they felt like a rehearsal.

Ellen began to prepare herself in small, quiet ways. She spent hours in the solitude of her home, tidying the rooms and sorting through old belongings. She wrote letters to Thomas, each one filled with words she had never spoken aloud, confessions of love and regret and hope. She did not know if he would ever read them, but the act of writing felt like a way to leave a piece of herself behind.

She avoided the townsfolk as much as possible, their whispers and sidelong glances only serving to remind her of how isolated she had become. "Cursed," they called her, their voices low but sharp. "Touched by the plague." Ellen paid them no mind. Their opinions no longer mattered. Her world had narrowed to the shadow over Wisborg and the role she would play in ending it.

Still, there were moments when the enormity of her decision threatened to overwhelm her. She would find herself standing in the middle of the kitchen, her hands trembling as she clutched a dish or a broom, her mind spiraling with thoughts of what was to come. The fear was always there, a quiet, gnawing presence at the edges of her mind, but she forced herself to push through it.

"You must be strong," she whispered to herself, her voice trembling but determined. "You mustn't falter."

One evening, as the sun dipped below the horizon and the shadows deepened, Ellen ventured to the church. The building was nearly empty, the pews silent save for the faint creak of wood as she stepped inside. She knelt at the altar, her hands clasped tightly together, and closed her eyes.

"God," she whispered, her voice breaking. "If you are listening, please give me strength."

The words felt hollow, her faith a fragile thing that had withered under the weight of the darkness that had consumed Wisborg. But still, she prayed. She prayed for courage, for clarity, for the ability to face the shadow without succumbing to fear. And though the church remained silent, its air heavy with the weight of unanswered prayers, Ellen felt a faint spark of hope ignite within her.

When she rose, her knees aching and her heart heavy, she turned to see Frau Schröder watching her from the back of the church. The older woman's face was lined with worry, her hands clutching a rosary.

"You've been through so much," Frau Schröder said softly, stepping closer. "And yet you carry yourself with such strength. How do you manage it, child?"

Ellen hesitated, the weight of her secret pressing against her chest.

"I'm not as strong as I seem," she admitted, her voice barely above a whisper. "But sometimes, when you know what must be done, you find the strength to do it."

Frau Schröder nodded, her expression somber.

"Whatever it is you're facing, I will pray for you."

Ellen offered a faint smile, though it did not reach her eyes.

"Thank you."

As the days turned into nights and the nights back into days, Ellen felt the fear inside her begin to transform. It did not disappear—she still woke with her heart pounding and her skin slick with sweat from the nightmares—but it no longer consumed her. Instead, it became a part of her resolve, a reminder of the stakes and the urgency of her task.

She thought often of Thomas, of his journey to the castle and the horrors he must have faced. She wondered where he was now, if he was still alive, if he was making his way back to her. The thought of seeing him again filled her with both hope and dread. Hope, because she longed to hold him, to tell him everything she had left unsaid. Dread, because she knew that if he returned, it would be only to find her gone.

But Ellen did not allow herself to linger on those thoughts for long.

She had chosen her path, and there was no turning back. She would face Orlok, lure him to her, and hold him in place until the sun rose. She would give her life to end his reign of terror, to save Thomas and Wisborg and all the lives that would otherwise be lost.

On the eve of her final decision, Ellen sat by the window once more, her gaze fixed on the distant manor. The air was still, the sky heavy with clouds that obscured the stars. She could feel Orlok's presence as strongly as if he were standing in the room with her, his shadow pressing against her mind.

"I'm ready," she whispered, her voice steady despite the tears streaming down her face. "I won't let you win."

The shadow loomed, dark and impenetrable, but Ellen did not look away. She had accepted her role, and she would face it with courage.

# Chapter 16
## Thomas's Return

The road to Wisborg stretched endlessly before Thomas, winding through forests that seemed darker than he remembered and fields shrouded in an unnatural stillness. His legs ached, and his lungs burned from the cold air, but he pressed on, driven by desperation. Every step closer to the town filled him with a mix of dread and urgency. He had to warn them. He had to stop Orlok before it was too late.

The memory of the castle clung to him like a shadow, the grotesque image of Count Orlok burned into his mind. He could still see the gaunt figure looming over him, the hollow, penetrating eyes that seemed to reach into his very soul. Even now, far from the castle's walls, he felt the faint, oppressive weight of Orlok's presence, as though the creature's shadow had followed him on his journey.

When the spires of Wisborg's church finally appeared on the horizon, Thomas's knees nearly buckled with relief. The familiar sight of the town should have brought him comfort, but as he drew closer, the relief was replaced by unease. Something was wrong. The town lay silent beneath a heavy gray sky, its cobblestone streets deserted and its windows shuttered. Wisborg, once so vibrant, now seemed like a ghost town.

Thomas entered the outskirts of the town just as the sun began its slow descent behind a veil of clouds. The streets, usually bustling with life at this hour, were empty. The market stalls stood abandoned, their wares left to spoil in the damp air. The scent of rot and decay hung heavy, mingling with the acrid tang of burning wood from distant chimneys. A cold wind swept through the narrow alleyways, carrying with it a sense of foreboding.

"Hello?" Thomas called out, his voice echoing unnaturally in the stillness. There was no reply, only the faint rustle of leaves and the distant creak of a shutter swinging in the breeze.

His footsteps quickened, his boots clattering against the cobblestones as he made his way deeper into the town. The few faces he saw were pale and gaunt, their eyes hollow with exhaustion and fear. A woman hurried past him, clutching a small child to her chest, her gaze darting nervously toward the shadows. An elderly man sat slumped against a wall, his face hidden beneath a wide-brimmed hat, his breathing shallow and labored.

Thomas stopped a young man carrying a bundle of firewood, his voice urgent.

"Please," he said, gripping the man's arm. "What's happened here? Where is everyone?"

The man flinched at Thomas's touch, his eyes narrowing as he took in the disheveled state of his questioner.

"The plague," he muttered, his voice low and wary. "It's taken so many. The rest are hiding. You shouldn't be here."

Thomas shook his head, his grip tightening.

"It's not the plague," he said, his voice rising. "It's something worse. You have to listen to me. The man in the manor by the river—Count Orlok—he's not what he seems."

The man pulled his arm free, stumbling back as though Thomas's words carried a contagious madness.

"Stay away from me," he hissed, his voice trembling. "You're not right in the head." Without another word, he turned and fled, leaving Thomas standing alone in the empty street.

Thomas moved through the town like a man in a nightmare, his desperate warnings falling on deaf ears. Every door he knocked on was met with silence or the sound of hurried footsteps retreating from the other side. The faces he passed avoided his gaze, their expressions guarded and fearful. No one wanted to listen. No one wanted to believe.

At the market square, he stopped again, scanning the abandoned stalls and shuttered shops. A few townsfolk lingered at the edges of the square, their voices hushed, their movements cautious. Thomas approached them, his voice hoarse from shouting.

"Please," he begged, his hands outstretched. "You have to listen to me. The plague isn't what's killing us. It's him—Count Orlok. He's a monster, a creature of darkness. If we don't stop him, he'll destroy us all."

The group exchanged uneasy glances, their skepticism clear. One woman, her face gaunt and her eyes rimmed with red, stepped forward.

"We've had enough of this madness," she snapped. "Rats brought the sickness, not some fairytale monster. You're scaring people."

Thomas shook his head, his voice breaking.

"It's not madness. I've seen him. I've been to his castle. He's here, in the manor by the river. You have to believe me."

A grizzled man stepped forward, his expression grim.

"What we have to do is survive," he said flatly. "If you want to help, go bury the dead or tend to the sick. But don't stand here spreading fear and nonsense."

The others murmured in agreement, their gazes hardening. Thomas's shoulders sagged, the weight of their disbelief crushing him. He opened his mouth to argue further but stopped himself. What use were words to those who had already made up their minds? He felt like a drowning man, his cries for help swallowed by the uncaring sea.

As Thomas stood in the center of the square, his head bowed in defeat, he heard a familiar voice call his name. He turned to see Ellen hurrying toward him, her figure pale and fragile against the gray backdrop of the town. Her hands clutched the folds of her shawl, and her face was a mask of relief and fear.

"Thomas," she breathed, her voice trembling. "You're alive."

The sound of her voice was like a balm to his frayed nerves. He moved toward her, his legs weak with exhaustion, and pulled her into his arms.

"Ellen," he murmured, his voice breaking. "I thought—I thought I'd never see you again."

She pulled back slightly, her hands gripping his shoulders.

"What happened to you? Where have you been?"

He hesitated, glancing around at the watching townsfolk. Their stares burned into his back, their judgment and suspicion palpable.

"Not here," he said softly. "I'll tell you everything, but not here."

Ellen nodded, her fingers tightening around his arm. Together, they hurried away from the square, leaving behind the whispers and the shadows. For the first time since his journey began, Thomas felt a faint spark of hope. Ellen believed him—he could see it in her eyes. And with her by his side, he felt stronger, more certain.

But as they walked, his gaze drifted toward the distant river, where the manor loomed in the fog like a dark sentinel. The shadow was still there, waiting, and he knew their fight was far from over.

The air in Wisborg hung thick with fear and suspicion, a stifling weight that seemed to choke every word spoken aloud. Thomas could feel it as he moved through the streets, Ellen at his side, her hand gripping his arm as if to anchor him. He had returned home with a warning, a desperate plea to save the town from the shadow that had followed him from Orlok's castle, but the people of Wisborg were deaf to his words. Their fear had blinded them, narrowing their world to the immediate, tangible threat of the plague.

As Thomas and Ellen entered the town square, the few remaining villagers gathered there turned to stare. Their eyes were hollow, their faces pale and drawn, and their clothes hung loose on their gaunt frames. These were people already beaten down by loss, by sickness, by the slow unraveling of everything they had once held dear. Thomas could see it in their expressions: they were searching for something, anything, to make sense of their suffering. But he also saw something else—distrust.

Thomas stepped forward, raising his voice to address the small crowd.

"Listen to me," he began, his tone urgent but steady. "I've just come from the castle. I've seen the truth of what's happening here, and it's not the plague."

The murmurs began immediately, low and skeptical. Thomas pushed on, his hands outstretched as if to plead for their attention.

"The man in the manor by the river," he said, his voice carrying over the square. "Count Orlok—he's not what he seems. He's a creature of darkness, a Nosferatu. He's the one behind this sickness. He's draining the life from this town, one soul at a time."

A sharp laugh cut through the murmurs. Thomas turned to see a man step forward from the crowd, his weathered face twisted in disbelief.

"A Nosferatu?" the man repeated, his tone dripping with scorn. "What kind of nonsense is that? Have you lost your mind, Hutter?"

Thomas clenched his fists, frustration bubbling to the surface.

"You don't understand," he said, his voice rising. "I've seen him. I've seen what he is. He feeds on blood, on life itself. That ship—the *Empusa*—it wasn't carrying just cargo. It brought him here, along with his coffins of cursed soil."

The crowd stirred uneasily, but their faces remained skeptical. A woman clutching a small child to her chest shook her head.

"It's the rats," she said, her voice trembling. "Everyone knows it's the rats. They came off the ship and brought the plague with them. What you're saying—it's... it's madness."

"It's not madness," Thomas insisted, his voice growing hoarse. "You've seen the deaths—people pale as the dead, their necks marked. Do you think that's the work of rats?"

The crowd shifted, their discomfort growing, but the disbelief in their eyes did not waver. An older man, his beard flecked with gray, spat on the ground and pointed a gnarled finger at Thomas.

"We've lost enough to this plague," he growled. "Now you come here with your wild stories, stirring up fear and making things worse. What good are your words? Can they bring back the dead?"

Thomas felt the fight draining from him, the weight of their rejection pressing heavily on his chest. These were his neighbors, people he had known for years, yet they looked at him now as though he were a stranger—or worse, a madman. He turned to Ellen, searching her face for reassurance, and found her watching him with a quiet, steady gaze.

"They won't believe me," he murmured, his voice barely audible.

Ellen touched his arm gently.

"They're afraid," she said softly. "They've been through so much already. It's hard for them to believe in something they can't see."

But Thomas couldn't shake the frustration boiling inside him.

"They don't understand what's at stake," he said, his voice trembling with urgency. "If they don't act, if they don't fight back, Orlok will destroy everything. He'll take all of them."

A man in the crowd spoke up, his voice harsh and accusing. "If you've brought this monster here, Hutter, then it's on your head," he said. "Go back to your castle and leave us to bury our dead."

The crowd murmured in agreement, their fear and anger swirling together into a dangerous undercurrent. Thomas took a step back, his shoulders slumping as he realized the futility of his words. No matter how loudly he shouted the truth, they would not hear him. Their minds were closed, their hearts hardened by loss and despair.

Ellen stepped forward, her voice calm but firm.

"He's not mad," she said, her tone cutting through the noise like a blade. "I've felt it too—the darkness that's come over Wisborg. You all know it's more than just a plague. You can feel it, can't you?"

The crowd fell silent, their eyes fixed on her. There was something in her voice, a quiet conviction that seemed to hold them in place. She looked out at the gathering, her pale face illuminated by the fading light of day.

"Thomas isn't the enemy," she continued. "He's trying to save us. If you won't listen to him, then at least stay vigilant. Don't ignore the signs. Don't let the darkness consume you."

The villagers murmured among themselves, some nodding hesitantly, others still shaking their heads. But Ellen's words had planted a seed, a faint ripple of doubt that would linger in the back of their minds.

As the crowd began to disperse, Ellen turned to Thomas and took his hand.

"Come," she said softly. "Let's go home."

Thomas hesitated, his gaze lingering on the retreating villagers. He wanted to shout after them, to shake them out of their complacency, but he knew it would do no good. With a heavy heart, he allowed Ellen to lead him away.

As they walked through the quiet streets, Ellen squeezed his hand gently.

"They'll come around," she said, her voice steady. "They just need time."

Thomas shook his head.

"Time is the one thing we don't have," he said. "Orlok is already here. Every moment they refuse to act, he grows stronger."

Ellen stopped and turned to face him, her expression resolute.

"Then we'll find another way," she said. "If they won't fight, we will."

Her words sent a jolt through him, a flicker of hope sparking in the depths of his despair. He could see the determination in her eyes, the strength that had carried her through the weeks of his absence. She believed him, and for now, that was enough.

Together, they continued toward their home, the weight of the shadow looming over Wisborg pressing heavily on their shoulders. But for the first time since his return, Thomas felt a faint glimmer of hope. They were not alone in this fight, and though the road ahead was dark, they would face it together.

The house was quieter than Thomas remembered, its walls seeming to absorb every sound, every sigh. It was as though the home itself had been drained of life in his absence. Ellen moved ahead of him, her steps soft but deliberate as she lit a few candles, their flickering flames casting faint, golden light across the dim room. The faint smell of wax mixed with the cold, stale air, a reminder of how long it had been since warmth and laughter had filled this space.

Thomas collapsed into a chair by the hearth, his head in his hands. The weight of his journey, of the disbelief he had faced, bore down on him with crushing force. He felt as though he had run a race only to find the finish line erased, the townsfolk's dismissal of his warnings leaving him floundering in a sea of futility.

Ellen knelt beside him, her slender hand resting gently on his knee.

"Thomas," she said softly, her voice steady despite the worry in her eyes. "I believe you."

Her words pulled him from the depths of his despair. He lifted his head slowly, meeting her gaze. Her face was pale, her cheeks sunken, and her eyes bore the shadows of sleepless nights, yet there was a quiet strength in her expression. She wasn't doubting him, wasn't questioning his sanity like the others. She was listening.

### Nosferatu

"You do?" he asked, his voice hoarse with exhaustion and disbelief.

Ellen nodded, her fingers tightening around his knee.

"I've felt it too—the darkness, the way it clings to the town. It's like a shadow that won't lift, no matter how bright the day should be." She hesitated, her voice faltering slightly. "And the dreams…"

Thomas's brow furrowed.

"Dreams?"

She looked away, her hands knotting together in her lap.

"I didn't want to tell you before," she said, her voice barely above a whisper. "I didn't want to worry you. But since you left, I've been having these dreams—nightmares. I see him, Thomas. Orlok. I feel him watching me, even when I'm awake."

Thomas's heart sank, his stomach twisting into knots.

"Ellen, I—"

She cut him off, her voice firm despite the tremor in her hands.

"It's not your fault. You couldn't have known. But now that you're here, we have to stop him. We can't let him destroy Wisborg."

Ellen rose to her feet, her movements slow but deliberate. She paced the room, her hands clasped tightly in front of her.

"I've been reading," she said, glancing at the stack of books on the table. "There's a way to stop him. The Nosferatu—he can't survive the sunlight. If we can trap him, keep him here until dawn…"

Thomas's head shot up, his eyes widening.

"The sunlight," he echoed. "Of course. I read something about that in the castle—old texts, fragments. But how do we keep him in one place long enough?"

Ellen hesitated, her fingers brushing against the edge of the table. She couldn't tell him the full truth—not yet. The book she had found had been clear: only a pure-hearted sacrifice could hold the Nosferatu until dawn. She couldn't bear to lay that burden on him, not when he had already endured so much. For now, she would protect him from the weight of that knowledge.

"We'll find a way," she said, her voice steady. "We'll lure him out, trap him. Together."

Thomas rose from the chair, his exhaustion momentarily forgotten.

"Ellen, I don't know if we can do this alone," he said, his tone urgent. "The villagers—they won't listen. They think I'm mad. They're too afraid of the plague to see what's really happening."

Ellen stepped closer, her gaze unwavering.

"Then we'll do it without them," she said. "If they won't fight, we will."

The firelight danced between them, casting shadows across their faces as they stood in the silence of their home. For a moment, neither spoke, their shared determination filling the space between words. Thomas reached for her hand, his fingers brushing against hers, and she let him take it, her grip firm despite the trembling she could not quite hide.

"I don't deserve you," he said softly, his voice thick with emotion. "After everything I've put you through…"

Ellen shook her head, her expression resolute.

"This isn't about blame, Thomas. It's about what we have to do. You came back to warn us. That means something."

He nodded, though the guilt in his eyes remained.

"I just wish I could have stopped him before he came here."

"We can't change the past," she said gently. "But we can change what happens next."

Thomas pulled her into a tight embrace, his arms wrapping around her as though he could shield her from the horrors they faced. Ellen closed her eyes, allowing herself a brief moment of comfort before pulling back. She knew she couldn't let herself linger in his arms for too long. There was too much at stake, and the shadow was always watching.

As the night deepened, Ellen and Thomas sat together, speaking in hushed tones about what was to come. Thomas shared what he had

# Nosferatu

seen in the castle, the horrors that had driven him to flee, while Ellen revealed the strange and terrible pull she felt toward the manor. They spoke of Orlok, of his power and his presence, and of the growing darkness that had enveloped Wisborg.

"I feel like he's everywhere," Ellen admitted, her voice trembling. "Even when I'm alone, I can feel him. It's like his shadow is following me, waiting for the moment I let my guard down."

Thomas reached for her hand, his grip firm.

"We'll stop him," he said. "I won't let him take you. I swear it."

Ellen forced a faint smile, though her heart ached at his words. She wanted to believe they could face Orlok together, that their love and determination would be enough to defeat him. But deep down, she knew the truth. The book had made it clear: only a pure-hearted sacrifice could hold the Nosferatu until dawn. She could not tell Thomas, not yet, but she had already accepted her role.

"I believe you," she said softly, her voice steady despite the tears that threatened to fall. "We'll stop him. Together."

As the candlelight flickered and the shadows crept closer, Ellen felt the weight of her decision settle over her. She would do whatever it took to protect Thomas, to save Wisborg. And if that meant giving everything she had, then so be it.

The shadow might have claimed the town, but it would not claim her spirit.

## Chapter 17
### Chaos in Wisborg

The town of Wisborg was no stranger to hardship. Its streets had seen winters so cold that the river froze solid, summers so dry that the fields cracked under the sun's relentless glare. But this—this was something else. The plague had taken hold of Wisborg with a ferocity that defied understanding, its shadow spreading over the town like a living entity, choking the life out of everything it touched.

At first, it had been whispers. A man found dead in his bed, his face pale, his body untouched by signs of struggle. Then another, this time a merchant slumped over his counter, his lifeless eyes staring into the void. The townsfolk spoke in hushed tones, blaming the rats that had scurried off the *Empusa*, the ghost ship that had drifted into port laden with death. But as the days passed, the deaths became stranger, more sinister.

There were no rashes, no fevers, no coughing fits. The victims bore no signs of sickness, only an unnatural pallor and the same twin puncture wounds on their necks. The town physician, a weary man whose hands trembled as he worked, could find no explanation.

"Perhaps it's some new form of pestilence," he murmured, his voice heavy with exhaustion. But even he did not sound convinced.

The plague turned Wisborg into a tomb. The air grew heavy and stagnant, thick with the acrid scent of decay. The sound of life—the chatter of merchants in the square, the laughter of children playing in the alleys—was gone, replaced by the mournful tolling of the church bell. Each chime marked another death, another body to be buried in the overcrowded cemetery.

The streets, once bustling with activity, were now eerily silent. Shuttered windows and barred doors lined the cobblestone roads, the townsfolk barricading themselves inside their homes in a desperate attempt to ward off the unseen menace. Those brave or foolish enough to venture out moved quickly, their heads down, their steps hurried. They avoided eye contact, as if meeting another's gaze might invite death into their lives.

Rats scurried freely through the alleys, their beady eyes glinting in the dim light. They had become a symbol of the plague, their presence blamed for the town's suffering. Children's rhymes about the rats and their supposed curses echoed faintly in the minds of those who could still recall brighter days, now twisted into macabre reminders of the horrors that surrounded them.

The churchyard, once a place of solace, had become a grotesque spectacle. The graves, hastily dug by weary gravediggers, were shallow and crowded, the earth barely concealing the bodies beneath. The smell of rot hung thick in the air, a miasma that clung to the clothes and hair of those who passed by. The gravediggers worked tirelessly, their faces etched with fatigue and dread, but no matter how many bodies they buried, more seemed to appear.

"We're running out of space," one of them muttered, his voice hoarse from the effort of digging. He wiped his brow with a dirt-streaked hand and glanced at his companion, who merely shook his head and resumed his grim task.

The priest, Father Brandt, stood at the edge of the graveyard, his shoulders hunched under the weight of his cassock. He muttered prayers under his breath, his voice wavering as he performed rites for the dead. His faith, once a source of strength for the townsfolk, now seemed fragile, barely holding together under the strain of the plague's onslaught.

"Lord, deliver us from this darkness," he whispered, his trembling hands clutching the edges of his worn Bible. But the words felt hollow, their power lost in the face of the mounting deaths.

It was not just the deaths that terrified the people of Wisborg; it was the way the plague seemed to move, creeping from house to house with a malevolent will. Entire families were found dead in their beds, their faces frozen in expressions of terror. Livestock, too, began to perish, their lifeless forms discovered in the fields with no visible wounds. The town seemed cursed, its very soil tainted by whatever darkness had come with the *Empusa*.

The townsfolk tried to fight back in the only ways they knew how. They set traps for the rats, burning the creatures in great pyres that filled the air with the acrid stench of singed fur. They scrawled protective symbols on their doorframes, nailed crucifixes above their beds, and hung garlic in their windows. But none of it worked. The deaths continued, relentless and unyielding.

The whispers grew louder. People spoke of curses, of evil spirits, of sins that had brought divine punishment upon the town. Some began to point fingers, blaming their neighbors for harboring ill will or practicing witchcraft. Fear twisted into paranoia, and the fragile bonds of community began to unravel.

Ellen watched it all from the window of her home, her pale face framed by the curtains as she gazed out at the empty streets. She could feel the shadow pressing down on the town, a weight that seemed to grow heavier with each passing day. It wasn't just the plague—it was something deeper, something older, something that defied explanation.

She thought of Thomas, of the warnings he had brought back with him, and her heart ached with the knowledge of what lay ahead. The book she had found, with its grim descriptions of the Nosferatu, had confirmed her fears. Orlok was here, his shadow spreading like a stain over Wisborg, feeding on the town's fear and despair. And she knew it would not stop until he was destroyed.

The toll of the plague was not just measured in bodies. It was measured in the loss of hope, in the unraveling of trust, in the way the town itself seemed to shrink under the weight of its suffering. Wisborg was dying, piece by piece, and Ellen could feel the darkness pulling her closer to its heart.

But amidst the despair, a flicker of resolve burned within her. She could not stop the deaths, could not turn back the tide of fear that had engulfed the town. But she could face the shadow. She could confront the monster that had brought this plague upon them. And she would.

For now, though, she stood at the window, watching as the last rays of sunlight disappeared behind the horizon, plunging Wisborg into another night of darkness and fear. The shadow was growing, and she could feel it creeping closer, its cold tendrils brushing against the edges of her mind.

Ellen closed her eyes and whispered a silent prayer, her trembling hands clutching the edge of the windowsill. The plague had taken so much already, but it would not take everything. Not if she could help it.

The streets of Wisborg, once filled with warmth and familiarity, had become battlegrounds of mistrust and desperation. Fear was a potent poison, and it spread even faster than the plague. No one was immune to its effects, and its symptoms were subtle at first—averted gazes, hushed conversations—but soon, the disease of paranoia began to tear the town apart.

It began in whispers. People spoke behind closed doors, their voices trembling as they speculated about the source of the plague. The rats, the ship, the stranger in the manor—these were the obvious culprits. But as the deaths mounted and the despair deepened, the townsfolk began to turn their suspicions inward.

"I saw him out after dark," muttered one woman, her face pale and drawn. She sat at her kitchen table, her hands trembling as she clutched a cup of tea. "No good can come from a man who walks the streets when honest folk are asleep."

Her husband, a carpenter with tired eyes and rough hands, nodded grimly.

"I've seen him too," he said. "Always skulking near the river. He's hiding something, I'm sure of it."

It did not take long for these whispers to turn into accusations. A neighbor's unusual habits became evidence of guilt. A pale complexion or a lingering cough was enough to mark someone as cursed. The fear that had gripped Wisborg demanded a scapegoat, and the townsfolk were all too willing to provide one.

The accusations grew louder and more frequent, spilling into the streets and the marketplace. Shouting matches erupted between neighbors who had once shared meals and stories. A man accused his sister-in-law of bringing the plague into his home; a woman claimed her neighbor had cursed her crops. The bonds of trust that had held the community together began to unravel, replaced by suspicion and hostility.

"I know what you've done!" screamed a butcher, his voice raw with anger. He stood in the center of the marketplace, pointing a trembling finger at a fisherman whose face was pale with fear. "You brought this on us! You and your foul catches from the river!"

The fisherman stammered, his hands raised in protest.

"I've done nothing wrong," he said, his voice quavering. "I only fish to feed my family."

But the butcher would not be silenced.

"Liar!" he spat. "I've seen you muttering to yourself, casting your spells. You're in league with whatever evil has cursed this town!"

A crowd gathered, their faces dark with anger and fear. The fisherman backed away, his eyes darting frantically as the mob closed in around him. It was only the intervention of the priest, Father Brandt, that spared him from violence that day. But the damage was done. The seeds of division had been sown, and Wisborg was no longer a community. It was a collection of frightened individuals, each more concerned with self-preservation than with helping their neighbors.

As the days turned to weeks, the tension reached a breaking point. It began with small acts of cruelty—a shove in the marketplace, a door slammed in someone's face—but soon escalated to outright violence. A young boy was chased through the streets by a group of men who claimed he had stolen bread, though the boy's hands were empty. A woman was dragged from her home and accused of witchcraft, her cries of innocence drowned out by the jeers of the crowd.

The priest tried to maintain order, standing in the church square and pleading for calm.

"We must not let fear divide us," he said, his voice ringing out over the murmuring crowd. "We are stronger together. This plague is not the work of man, but of something greater. Turn to God, not against each other."

But his words fell on deaf ears. The crowd dispersed, muttering under their breath, and the priest was left alone in the square, his shoulders slumping with defeat.

That night, the woman accused of witchcraft was found dead in the river. No one spoke of it openly, but the fear in Wisborg deepened. The townsfolk locked their doors and barred their windows, not just against the plague but against each other.

From her window, Ellen watched the town descend into chaos. She saw the arguments in the streets, the fights that broke out in the marketplace, the accusatory glares that passed between neighbors. It was as though the shadow of Orlok had infected not just their bodies, but their minds and souls as well.

She thought of the book she had read, of the Nosferatu and the way their presence corrupted everything they touched. It was not enough for them to kill—they spread despair, turning communities into battlegrounds and families into enemies. Orlok had brought more than death to Wisborg. He had brought darkness.

Ellen's heart ached as she watched the people she had grown up with tear each other apart. She wanted to scream at them, to beg them to see the real enemy, but she knew it would do no good. They were blinded by fear, and fear was a weapon Orlok wielded with terrifying precision.

Her only solace was Thomas, who shared her growing horror at what was happening to their town. He tried to speak with the villagers, to warn them of the true danger, but they dismissed him as a madman. Ellen saw the pain in his eyes each time he returned home, defeated and frustrated, but she also saw his determination.

"They won't listen," he said one evening, his voice heavy with despair. "They're too consumed by their own fear."

Ellen placed a hand on his arm, her touch gentle but firm.

"Then we'll stop him ourselves," she said. "We can't wait for them to see the truth. We have to act."

Thomas looked at her, his eyes searching hers for a moment before he nodded.

"You're right," he said. "We'll face him together."

But as Ellen met his gaze, she felt the weight of her secret pressing down on her. She knew the truth—that it was not together they would face Orlok, but alone. The sacrifice would be hers to bear, and she could not let Thomas carry that burden.

As the sun set on Wisborg that night, the town lay shrouded in silence. But it was not the silence of peace. It was the silence of fear, of mistrust, of a community on the brink of collapse. Ellen stood by the window, her eyes fixed on the distant silhouette of the manor. She could feel Orlok's presence, the oppressive weight of his shadow pressing against her mind.

She knew the darkness would only grow stronger, that the town's descent into chaos was far from over. But she also knew that she could not allow herself to falter. The shadow could not be allowed to win. No matter the cost, she would confront it.

Wisborg was unraveling, but Ellen would hold herself together. For Thomas, for the town, for all the lives Orlok sought to claim—she would stand against the shadow.

Even if it meant stepping into the darkness alone.

The house was eerily still as Ellen sat at the small desk near the window, the glow of a single candle casting flickering shadows across the room. Outside, the town of Wisborg slumbered fitfully, its streets cloaked in darkness and fear. The muffled cries of grieving families and the occasional toll of the church bell drifted through the air, reminders of the plague's relentless grip on the town. But Ellen's thoughts were far from the despair outside. Her focus was fixed on what lay ahead, on the decision she had made and the role she would play.

She traced the edge of the leather-bound book in front of her, its pages open to the passage she had read countless times. The words describing the Nosferatu's weakness—the sunlight that could destroy it—were burned into her memory. So too were the warnings about the sacrifice required, the pure-hearted soul who must hold the creature in place until the dawn.

Ellen let out a trembling breath, her fingers tightening around the quill in her hand. She had begun writing letters earlier that day, letters meant for Thomas, though she doubted he would ever read them. They were confessions of love and regret, of the things she had left unsaid and the truths she would never share. The ink smudged as her tears fell onto the paper, but she continued writing, pouring her heart onto the page in a way she had never been able to speak aloud.

Ellen knew she didn't have much time. Orlok's presence in Wisborg was growing stronger with each passing night, his influence spreading like a shadow over the town. She could feel him, even now, as though his cold gaze were fixed on her from afar. The sensation was suffocating, but she refused to let it paralyze her. She had chosen her path, and there was no turning back.

Her preparations were small, methodical, and deliberate. She tidied the house as if she were preparing for guests, folding the linens and dusting the shelves with a care that bordered on obsessive. She wanted the space to feel orderly, even if chaos was all that awaited her. It was a futile gesture, but it gave her a sense of control in a situation that was spiraling beyond her grasp.

The book remained her constant companion. Its ancient pages, filled with warnings and grim truths, were both a comfort and a source of terror. She read and reread the passages on the Nosferatu, memorizing every detail about the creature's nature, its habits, and its weaknesses. She studied the ritual of the sacrifice, the method by which the Nosferatu could be held in place until the dawn. The text offered no reassurance, no promise of success—only cold, clinical descriptions of what needed to be done.

Ellen closed the book and pressed her hands to her face, her fingers trembling against her skin. She had never felt so alone. The weight of her decision pressed against her chest, suffocating in its finality. But there was no one she could turn to, no one who could share the burden. Thomas would try to stop her if he knew, and the townsfolk were too consumed by their own fears to understand. This was her fight, and hers alone.

As the night deepened, Ellen heard Thomas's footsteps approaching from the other room. He appeared in the doorway, his face lined with exhaustion, his eyes filled with worry.

"Ellen," he said softly, stepping into the candlelight. "You've been up all night. You need to rest."

She offered him a faint smile, though her heart ached at the sight of him. He looked so worn, so fragile, and she wanted nothing more than to ease his burden. But she couldn't—not in the way he wanted.

"I'm fine," she said, her voice gentle but firm. "There's too much to do."

Thomas frowned, crossing the room to stand beside her. He glanced at the letters on the desk, his expression darkening.

"What are these?" he asked, picking up one of the pages. "Why are you writing—"

"It's nothing," she interrupted quickly, her hand covering the page. "Just... thoughts. Things I wanted to say."

Thomas looked at her, his eyes searching hers for a moment before he nodded slowly. He didn't press further, but Ellen could see the questions lingering in his gaze. He reached out and placed a hand on her shoulder, his touch warm and steady.

"Whatever happens," he said quietly, "we'll face it together. You know that, don't you?"

Ellen nodded, swallowing the lump in her throat.

"I know," she said, her voice barely above a whisper.

But in her heart, she knew the truth. They would not face it together. When the time came, she would ensure that Thomas was safe, far from the shadow that sought to claim him. She would bear the weight of the sacrifice alone, no matter how much it tore her apart.

As the hours crept toward dawn, Ellen stood by the window, her gaze fixed on the manor by the river. Its dark silhouette loomed against the horizon, shrouded in mist and shadow. She could feel Orlok's presence there, a cold, malevolent force that seemed to seep into her very bones. The connection between them was undeniable, and it was growing stronger with each passing moment. He was watching, waiting.

Ellen pressed her hand to the glass, her breath fogging the window as she whispered a silent prayer. She wasn't sure if she believed in God, not anymore, but the act of praying brought her a small measure of comfort.

"Let this be enough," she murmured. "Let it end with me."

The first light of dawn began to creep over the horizon, its faint glow illuminating the streets of Wisborg. Ellen turned away from the window and extinguished the candle, plunging the room into darkness. She climbed into bed beside Thomas, her movements slow and deliberate, and laid her head against the pillow. For the first time in weeks, she closed her eyes and allowed herself to rest.

Tomorrow, the fight would begin.

# Chapter 18
## A Lure

Ellen sat motionless at the small table near the hearth, her fingers tracing the worn grooves etched into the wood. The flickering candlelight painted her face in sharp relief, casting deep shadows under her eyes that betrayed her sleepless nights. On the table before her lay the book, its ancient leather cover cracked and dry. The brittle pages seemed to hum with the weight of their secrets, the grim truths within pressing down on her like a leaden hand.

The words she had read over and over again echoed in her mind: "The Nosferatu cannot resist the pure-hearted. Their hunger binds them. A single soul must hold them fast until the light of dawn destroys their shadow." The meaning was clear, but Ellen had resisted its implications for days. Now, as the shadow over Wisborg grew heavier and the death toll mounted, she could resist no longer.

Her resolve solidified in the quiet of that dimly lit room. She would do it. She would lure Orlok to her, hold him until the first light of dawn pierced the darkness. It was the only way to end the plague, the only way to save Wisborg. And the only way to protect Thomas.

Ellen closed the book gently, as though it might shatter beneath her trembling hands. She stared at its cover, her lips pressed into a thin line, her mind racing. The plan had taken root during one of her many sleepless nights, growing slowly in the fertile ground of her desperation. Now it was fully formed, grim in its simplicity.

She would invite Orlok into their home. She would make herself the bait, the lure he could not resist. The creature's hunger would trap him, keep him focused on her while the sun rose and destroyed him. It was a plan fraught with danger, one that left no room for error, but Ellen knew it was her only choice.

Her movements were slow, deliberate, as she began to prepare. She fetched the broom from the corner of the room and swept the floor, her strokes measured and precise. She dusted the furniture, wiped the windows clean, and smoothed the wrinkles from the curtains. Each task was performed with an almost obsessive care, her focus narrowing to the details as if to stave off the growing tide of fear in her chest.

As she worked, she thought of Orlok, his gaunt frame and hollow eyes, the way he seemed to carry the weight of the grave with him wherever he went. She shuddered, her hands pausing on the edge of the table as a wave of nausea rolled over her. The idea of facing him alone was almost too much to bear, but she steadied herself. There was no one else who could do this. It had to be her.

The house was eerily quiet, the kind of silence that amplifies every creak of the floorboards and rustle of fabric. Ellen's footsteps seemed loud in the emptiness, a reminder of just how alone she was in this task. She paused by the window, gazing out at the streets of Wisborg. The town was a shadow of what it had once been, its vibrancy replaced by death and despair. She could see the faint outlines of houses in the distance, their windows dark, their inhabitants too afraid to venture outside.

Her chest tightened as she thought of the townsfolk, of the chaos that had gripped them. They were tearing each other apart with their paranoia, blinded to the true threat that loomed over them. She had tried to speak to them, tried to warn them, but her words had fallen on deaf ears. Now, she could only hope that her sacrifice would be enough to save them.

She turned away from the window and returned to her work. She polished the silver candlesticks on the mantle, arranged the flowers in the vase on the table, and folded the linens with careful precision. The house began to take on an air of calm, its orderliness a stark contrast to the chaos outside. It was a small comfort, a fragile illusion of control in a world that seemed to be unraveling.

As the afternoon light began to fade, Ellen sat down at the table once more, her hands folded in her lap. She stared at the candle in front of her, watching the flame dance and flicker. Her thoughts drifted to Thomas, to the way his face had lit up when he first returned home and saw her. She had seen the relief in his eyes, the love and desperation that had driven him back to her. And she had known, in that moment, that she would do whatever it took to protect him.

He didn't know about the book, about the plan she had devised. Ellen had kept it from him, not out of mistrust, but out of love. She couldn't burden him with the knowledge of what she intended to do. He had already endured so much, and she couldn't bear to see the pain in his eyes if he knew. It was better this way, better that he believed they would face the darkness together.

But Ellen knew the truth. She knew that the final confrontation would be hers alone. Orlok would come for her, drawn by her purity, by the light that still burned within her despite the shadow that had engulfed the town. And when he came, she would hold him, her life the price of Wisborg's salvation.

She reached out and touched the book, her fingers brushing over its cracked leather cover.

"I won't let you win," she whispered, her voice steady despite the tears that welled in her eyes. "I won't let you take him. Or this town."

As evening descended, Ellen lit the lanterns around the house, their soft glow pushing back the encroaching darkness. She laid out a simple dress, white and unadorned, on the bed in the next room. It was the dress she would wear when Orlok arrived, a stark symbol of the purity that would draw him to her. The sight of it made her stomach churn, but she forced herself to look at it, to accept the reality of what lay ahead.

She moved through the house one final time, checking the windows and doors, ensuring that everything was in its place. The air felt heavy, charged with a sense of anticipation that made her skin prickle. She could feel Orlok's presence, faint but unmistakable, a cold shadow pressing against the edges of her mind. He was coming. She knew it as surely as she knew her own name.

Ellen stood in the center of the room, her hands trembling as she clasped them together. She closed her eyes and took a deep breath, steadying herself. This was it. The moment she had been preparing for. The moment she would face the shadow that had consumed Wisborg.

She opened her eyes, her gaze hardening as she looked toward the window.

"I'm ready," she said softly, her voice resolute. "Come for me."

The shadows deepened, and the house fell silent. Ellen stood alone, her heart pounding, as she waited for the night to descend.

The light from the setting sun spilled faintly through the windows, casting long, golden rays across the quiet house. Thomas's footsteps echoed faintly from the adjoining room as he moved about, his restless energy betraying his unease. Ellen sat at the table, her hands folded tightly in her lap, her gaze fixed on the flickering flame of the lantern in front of her. Her thoughts were a whirlwind of fear and resolve, but her face betrayed none of it.

She had spent the day crafting a façade of normalcy, distracting Thomas with mundane tasks and small reassurances. The effort left her exhausted, each lie weighing heavier on her heart, but she had no choice. He couldn't know the truth—not yet.

"Ellen," Thomas called from the doorway, his voice soft but laced with concern. "You've been quiet all day. Are you all right?"

She looked up, startled out of her thoughts, and forced a small smile onto her face.

"I'm fine, Thomas," she said, her voice steady but devoid of its usual warmth. "Just... tired."

He frowned, stepping closer to her. The lines of exhaustion on his face mirrored her own, but his worry for her seemed to eclipse his own fatigue.

"You haven't been yourself since I came back," he said, sitting down across from her. "I can see it in your eyes. What's wrong?"

Ellen hesitated, her fingers twisting together in her lap. She had prepared for this moment, rehearsed the words in her mind, but now that he was looking at her with such open concern, the lies felt like lead in her throat.

"It's everything that's happening," she said finally, her voice barely above a whisper. "The plague, the deaths... I just feel so helpless."

Thomas reached out and took her hand, his grip firm but gentle.

"You're not helpless," he said. "We're in this together. We'll find a way to stop him."

Ellen's chest tightened at his words, the weight of her secret pressing against her ribs. She squeezed his hand, her smile faltering.

"I know," she said, though the words tasted bitter on her tongue. "I know we will."

As the evening wore on, Ellen busied herself with small tasks to avoid further questions. She moved through the house with purpose, her steps measured and deliberate. She adjusted the curtains, smoothed the linens on the bed, and refilled the oil lamps. Each movement was an excuse to avoid Thomas's gaze, to keep the truth hidden.

"Ellen," Thomas said from the doorway, his arms crossed over his chest. "You've been cleaning for hours. Why don't you sit down for a while?"

She paused, her hands gripping the edge of the table.

"I just want everything to be ready," she said, her voice carefully neutral. "In case—"

"In case what?" he interrupted, his brow furrowing. "Ellen, what are you preparing for?"

Her heart skipped a beat, panic flaring in her chest. She turned to face him, her expression carefully composed.

"In case we need to leave," she said quickly, the lie spilling out before she could stop it. "If things get worse... if the plague spreads..."

Thomas's expression softened, his shoulders relaxing slightly.

"We'll get through this," he said, stepping closer to her. "We just have to stay strong."

Ellen nodded, swallowing the lump in her throat. She hated lying to him, hated the way the lies built upon one another, forming a wall between them. But she couldn't let him know what she was planning. He would never let her go through with it if he did.

Later that night, as Thomas prepared for bed, Ellen lingered in the kitchen, her hands shaking as she wrote another letter. The words blurred before her eyes, her tears smudging the ink as she tried to put her thoughts into words. She wrote of her love for Thomas, of her regret for the things left unsaid, and of her hope that he would find peace once this was over.

She folded the letter carefully and placed it under the oil lamp on the table. Her hands lingered there for a moment before she withdrew them, her chest aching with the finality of the gesture. It was a goodbye, though Thomas didn't know it yet.

When she joined him in the bedroom, she found him sitting on the edge of the bed, his head in his hands. He looked up as she entered, his eyes dark with worry.

"Ellen," he said softly, reaching for her hand. "I'm scared."

She sat down beside him, her hand resting gently on his.

"I know," she whispered. "I am too."

He leaned into her, his head resting against her shoulder.

"Do you think we can stop him?" he asked, his voice trembling.

Ellen hesitated, her eyes fixed on the faint glow of the oil lamp in the corner of the room.

"I think we have to try," she said finally. "No matter what."

Thomas nodded, his grip on her hand tightening.

"I don't know what I'd do without you," he murmured.

Ellen closed her eyes, the tears slipping silently down her cheeks.

"You won't have to," she said, her voice barely audible. But even as she spoke, she knew it was a lie.

As Thomas drifted off to sleep, Ellen lay awake beside him, her gaze fixed on the ceiling. The quiet of the house felt oppressive, the weight of her secret pressing down on her like a physical force. She could hear the faint sounds of the night outside—the rustle of the wind, the distant creak of a shutter—but they did nothing to soothe her.

She turned to look at Thomas, his face soft in the dim light. He looked so peaceful in sleep, so vulnerable. The sight of him filled her with a fierce determination. She would protect him, no matter the cost. Even if it meant sacrificing herself.

Ellen reached out and brushed a strand of hair from his forehead, her touch feather-light.

"I love you," she whispered, though she knew he could not hear her. "More than anything."

As the hours stretched on, Ellen lay in the darkness, her mind racing. The plan was set, the pieces falling into place. All that remained was to wait for Orlok to come.

And she would be ready.

The house was unnaturally still, its silence broken only by the faint creak of the floorboards as Ellen moved through the dimly lit rooms.

Each step felt deliberate, heavy with purpose, as though every motion carried her closer to an unavoidable fate. The shadows stretched long across the walls, cast by the faint glow of the lanterns she had left burning low. Outside, the night pressed against the windows, dense and suffocating, carrying with it the oppressive weight of the thing she knew was coming.

Ellen stood by the window, her shawl wrapped tightly around her shoulders, and peered into the darkness. Her breath fogged the glass, her chest rising and falling with shallow, uneven breaths. She knew Orlok was out there, somewhere in the endless black, his gaunt figure moving through the night with inhuman patience. The thought of him—the hollow eyes, the claw-like hands, the grotesque hunger—made her stomach twist. But she forced herself to stay at the window, to look out into the shadows and wait.

Time dragged on, the minutes stretching into hours as the night deepened. The quiet of the house grew louder, every faint noise amplified against the backdrop of silence. The gentle creak of the old timbers, the soft rustle of fabric as Ellen adjusted her shawl—each sound felt like a thunderclap, breaking the oppressive stillness. And beneath it all was the sensation she could not escape: the sense of being watched.

She felt his presence long before she would see him, a creeping, insidious feeling that wormed its way into her mind and settled there like a cold hand gripping the back of her neck. It was not something tangible, not something she could pinpoint or explain, but it was undeniable. Orlok was coming, and she could feel the weight of his approach pressing down on her like a tide slowly rising.

Her fingers trembled as she reached for the lantern on the windowsill, turning the flame down to a faint glow. She didn't want him to see her yet, didn't want to draw his attention too soon. The plan required patience, and though her heart was racing, Ellen forced herself to remain still.

From the bedroom, the sound of Thomas's soft breathing drifted through the open doorway. He had fallen asleep hours ago, his exhaustion finally overtaking his worry. Ellen had sat by his side until he drifted off, brushing her fingers gently through his hair, whispering reassurances she knew she could not keep. Now, as she listened to the rhythm of his breathing, her heart ached with the knowledge that this might be the last night they would share.

She turned her head slightly, glancing toward the darkened doorway. She had left the room just as it was, the bed neatly made except for the corner where Thomas had pulled the blanket around himself. The sight of him, peaceful and unaware, had nearly broken her resolve. But she had steeled herself, kissed his forehead, and slipped away into the shadows.

Her actions tonight were as much for him as they were for the town. He would wake to a world without Orlok, without the shadow that had consumed their lives. He would live, and that was all that mattered.

Ellen moved through the house with quiet efficiency, her steps light despite the weight in her chest. She extinguished all but a single lamp in the sitting room, the faint glow casting long, flickering shadows across the walls. She straightened the chairs, adjusted the curtains, and set the small wooden table in the center of the room. It was a simple space, unremarkable in its furnishings, but it felt almost ceremonial now, as though it had been transformed into a stage for the final act.

On the table, she placed a single white lily, its petals stark against the worn wood. The flower was fragile and beautiful, a symbol of life in a house that felt consumed by death. Ellen touched the edge of one petal with her fingertip, her hand trembling. The gesture felt absurd, almost mocking in its simplicity, but it grounded her in the moment.

Finally, she positioned the chair she had chosen for herself near the window. She would sit there and wait, her figure illuminated faintly by the lantern's glow. She would be visible, her presence unmistakable, an invitation that Orlok would not be able to resist.

The hours crept by, the night deepening until it seemed to stretch endlessly. Ellen remained in her chair, her hands clasped tightly in her lap, her body rigid with tension. Her gaze was fixed on the window, the glass reflecting her pale, drawn face. Beyond it, the darkness seemed alive, shifting and moving as though it were a living thing.

And then, she saw him.

At first, it was just a shadow, a faint shape moving against the deeper blackness of the night. But as it drew closer, the figure became unmistakable. Orlok moved with an unnatural grace, his tall, skeletal frame cutting through the gloom. His head tilted slightly as he approached, his hollow eyes fixed on the house with a hunger that Ellen could feel even from a distance.

Her breath caught in her throat, her heart pounding so loudly she was certain he would hear it. She forced herself to remain still, her hands tightening in her lap as she watched him. He stopped just short of the house, his form partially obscured by the mist that clung to the ground. For a moment, he stood motionless, his head tilting as though listening for some silent signal.

Ellen could feel his gaze, cold and unrelenting, piercing through the walls and the glass and the very air itself. It was as though he could see into her, into the depths of her fear and resolve, and was savoring the moment. Her stomach churned, and her vision swam, but she refused to look away.

"Come," she whispered, her voice trembling but steady. "I'm waiting."

As if in response, Orlok began to move again, his long, spindly limbs carrying him closer to the house. Ellen's breath quickened, her body trembling as the shadow of his presence filled the room. The moment she had prepared for was here, and there was no turning back.

She sat upright in the chair, her hands gripping the edges of her shawl, and waited for the door to open.

# Chapter 19
## Face-to-Face with the Abyss

The house was deathly silent. The faint crackle of the lantern on the windowsill was the only sound, its flickering light casting wild, restless shadows across the walls. Ellen sat alone in the parlor, her body rigid in the straight-backed chair she had placed by the window. She had been waiting for this moment, but now that it had arrived, every fiber of her being screamed for her to run, to flee into the night and leave the horror behind. Yet, she stayed.

The weight of Orlok's presence was palpable. She could feel it even before she heard the first creak of the door. It was a cold, creeping sensation, like icy fingers trailing along her spine, wrapping around her throat. The air seemed to grow heavier, pressing against her chest, making it difficult to breathe. She gripped the edges of her shawl with trembling hands, her knuckles white, her nails biting into the fabric. This was no dream, no vision conjured by fear. He was here.

The doorknob turned slowly, the soft metallic groan reverberating through the quiet house like the toll of a distant bell. Ellen's breath caught in her throat as she watched the door swing open with agonizing slowness. The darkness beyond the threshold seemed to bleed into the room, thick and suffocating, a shadow more alive than inert. And then he appeared.

Orlok stepped into the room, his gaunt frame almost skeletal in the dim light. He was impossibly tall, his hunched shoulders brushing the edges of the doorway as he entered. His limbs were long and spindly, his movements unnervingly deliberate, as though he were a marionette pulled along by some unseen strings. His skin was pale, stretched taut over his angular bones, and his face—oh, his face—was a nightmare carved into flesh. Hollow, sunken eyes gleamed faintly in the flickering light, their gaze cold and unrelenting. His mouth, framed by thin, colorless lips, curled upward into a grotesque semblance of a smile, revealing teeth that were long, sharp, and yellowed with age.

The very air seemed to shift with his presence, growing colder, thinner, as though he carried the grave with him. His shadow stretched long across the room, distorted and jagged, moving independently of his form. It twisted and writhed on the walls like a living thing, a predator waiting to strike. Ellen's stomach churned as she forced herself to meet his gaze, her body frozen in place, her mind screaming for her to look away.

Orlok tilted his head to one side, his blackened nails curling as his claw-like hands rested at his sides. He regarded her with an intensity that was almost unbearable, his hollow eyes drinking her in like a feast laid bare.

"You have waited for me," he rasped, his voice low and grating, like dry leaves dragged across stone. "Why?"

Ellen swallowed hard, her throat dry, her heart pounding so loudly she thought it might burst. She willed herself to speak, to answer him, though her voice trembled with fear.

"I knew you would come," she said, her words barely above a whisper.

Orlok stepped forward, his movements slow and deliberate, each step accompanied by the faint creak of the floorboards. Ellen remained seated, her back rigid, her hands clenched tightly in her lap. She wanted to shrink away, to cower beneath his gaze, but she forced herself to hold her ground. If she faltered now, everything would be lost.

"You are not like the others," Orlok murmured, his head tilting further as he studied her. His voice was almost curious, though it carried a dark undercurrent that made her blood run cold. "They cower, they flee. But you… you invite me."

Ellen's lips parted, but no words came. Her mouth was dry, her body trembling, but she managed to lift her chin ever so slightly.

"I wanted to see you," she said, her voice stronger now, though still shaking. "I wanted to understand."

Orlok's smile widened, his teeth glinting in the dim light.

"Understand?" he repeated, his tone mocking. "There is nothing to understand. I am what I am, and you… are what I hunger for."

The words sent a shiver down her spine, but Ellen did not flinch. She watched as he moved closer, his shadow engulfing her, its edges clawing at the walls like dark tendrils. The air grew colder still, each breath a struggle as the oppressive weight of his presence pressed down on her. He was so close now that she could see the faint discoloration of his skin, the veins that ran like dark rivers beneath its surface. The stench of decay wafted from him, sickly and cloying, filling her nostrils and making her stomach churn.

Orlok stopped just inches away from her, his gaunt figure looming over her like a specter of death. His long fingers twitched at his sides, curling and uncurling as though restraining themselves from reaching for her. Ellen could feel the cold emanating from him, an unnatural chill that seemed to seep into her very bones.

"You are afraid," Orlok said softly, his voice almost a whisper. "I can feel it. It is exquisite."

Ellen's breath quickened, but she refused to let him see her falter.

"I am afraid," she admitted, her voice trembling but defiant. "But I will not run."

Orlok's expression shifted, his smile fading as he regarded her with something that almost resembled curiosity.

"Such resolve," he murmured. "And yet, such folly. Do you think your bravery will save you? Do you think it will save them?"

Ellen clenched her hands tightly in her lap, her nails digging into her palms.

"I don't care what happens to me," she said, her voice steady now. "But I will not let you take this town. I will not let you take him."

At her words, Orlok's smile returned, wider and more grotesque than before. He leaned closer, his face inches from hers, his hollow eyes boring into her.

"You are mine, little flower," he hissed. "Your light, your warmth—it will be mine."

Ellen's heart thundered in her chest, her pulse a deafening roar in her ears. She could feel his breath on her skin, cold and fetid, as he leaned closer still. She closed her eyes for a moment, drawing a deep, shuddering breath, and when she opened them again, her gaze was fierce.

"Then take me," she said, her voice firm and unyielding. "But know this—you will not leave this house alive."

Orlok stared at her for a long moment, his expression unreadable, before his lips curled back in a snarl.

"We shall see," he growled, his voice low and menacing.

As he straightened, his shadow shifted, spreading across the walls like a living thing. Ellen remained in her chair, her body trembling but her resolve unbroken. She had made her choice, and she would see it through to the end.

The predator had entered her den, and the hunt had begun.

The air in the room grew heavier with each passing moment, as if Orlok's presence alone was enough to draw every ounce of warmth and life from the space. Ellen sat still in her chair, her trembling hands hidden beneath the folds of her shawl. Though every fiber of her being screamed at her to flee, she held her ground, her gaze fixed on the monster before her. Orlok loomed over her, his shadow stretching across the walls like an invasive darkness that no light could dispel.

His hollow eyes studied her, unblinking and predatory. It was a gaze that seemed to pierce through her flesh and burrow into her soul, as though he could see the very essence of her being. The hunger in his expression was undeniable, a primal need that burned just beneath the surface of his grotesque, pallid features. His smile returned, slow and deliberate, a terrible mockery of humanity that exposed his yellowed, elongated teeth.

Ellen drew a deep, shuddering breath and forced herself to speak.

"You've taken so much from this town," she said, her voice wavering but audible. "The people are dying. Their lives mean nothing to you, do they?"

Orlok's lips twitched, his head tilting as though her question amused him.

"Their lives are fleeting, little one," he rasped, his voice low and grating, like the creak of an ancient coffin lid. "I merely hasten the inevitable. They are but grains of sand slipping through the hourglass."

"You feed on their fear," Ellen said, her tone sharper now. "You thrive on their suffering."

"Fear," Orlok repeated, his smile widening. "Yes, it is a fine seasoning, is it not? Their terror makes the blood sweeter, their despair more satisfying. You should taste it, little flower—it is divine."

Ellen's stomach churned, but she refused to look away.

"You think you're unstoppable," she said, her voice steadying despite the tremor in her limbs. "But even shadows can't escape the light."

At her words, Orlok's smile faltered, his expression darkening. He took a slow step closer, his elongated fingers twitching at his sides. The air grew colder, the shadows deepening around him as though in response to his rising anger.

"You speak boldly for one so fragile," he said, his tone laced with menace. "Do you think your words will save you?"

Ellen rose from her chair, her movements deliberate and controlled despite the fear that coursed through her. She stepped back, putting a few feet of space between herself and Orlok, though she knew the distance was meaningless.

"I don't expect you to understand," she said, her gaze unwavering. "You've lived so long in the dark, you've forgotten what it means to be human."

Orlok's head tilted further, his eyes narrowing.

"Humanity is a weakness," he hissed. "It binds you, limits you. I have transcended such frailty."

"Have you?" Ellen asked, her voice cutting through the silence like a blade. "You hide in the shadows, afraid of the dawn. You feed on the living because you can't create life of your own. You think you're powerful, but you're just… empty."

Orlok snarled, the sound low and guttural, and for a moment, Ellen thought he might strike her. His shadow writhed across the walls, its edges jagged and unnatural, as though it were alive and straining against its boundaries. But he did not move. Instead, he took a slow, deliberate breath, his claw-like hands curling and uncurling at his sides.

"You test my patience," he said, his voice a low growl. "I could end you now, snuff out your fragile little flame with a single breath."

Ellen's heart pounded in her chest, but she held her ground.

"Then why don't you?" she asked, her voice quiet but firm. "If you're so powerful, why do you hesitate?"

Orlok's lips curled back in a sneer, revealing his sharp teeth.

"Because," he said, stepping closer, "I savor the hunt. And you, little flower, are a prize worth savoring."

The minutes stretched into what felt like hours as Orlok circled the room, his movements slow and deliberate, like a predator stalking its prey. Ellen mirrored his steps, keeping a careful distance between them, her mind racing as she worked to maintain his focus. Every word, every gesture was calculated, designed to hold his attention and keep him from noticing the faint glow of dawn beginning to creep along the edges of the curtains.

"You've been watching me," Ellen said, her tone accusatory. "Even before you came to this town. Why?"

Orlok stopped, his hollow eyes fixed on her.

"Because you are different," he said simply. "Your light shines brighter than the others. It calls to me, a beacon in the darkness. You cannot hide from me, no matter how hard you try."

Ellen swallowed hard, her throat dry.

"You think you know me," she said. "But you don't."

Orlok smiled again, the expression cold and cruel.

"I know enough," he said. "I know your fear, your resolve. I know your warmth, your light. And I know that it will soon be mine."

Ellen's fingers tightened around the edges of her shawl, her knuckles white with tension. She took another step back, her movements drawing him closer to the window.

"You won't win," she said, her voice trembling but defiant. "No matter what you take, you'll never have what you truly want."

"And what is that?" Orlok asked, his tone mocking.

"Life," Ellen said, her voice sharp. "You'll never have life."

Orlok paused, his expression unreadable, as though her words had struck some deep, buried chord. But the moment passed quickly, and his smile returned, more menacing than ever.

"Perhaps not," he said, his voice low and chilling. "But I will have yours."

Ellen's breath quickened as he stepped closer, his shadow enveloping her, but she did not back away. The faintest sliver of light was beginning to seep through the curtains, the first sign of dawn breaking over the horizon. She could feel its warmth even as Orlok's cold presence pressed against her.

"Then take it," she whispered, her voice steady despite the terror that gripped her. "Take it, and see what it brings you."

Orlok's eyes gleamed with hunger as he reached for her, his clawed hands moving with a deliberate slowness that made her skin crawl. Ellen stood her ground, her heart pounding, her hands trembling at her sides. She could feel the heat of the rising sun behind her, could see the faint glow beginning to touch the edges of the room.

The trap was closing, and Ellen knew she had only moments left. She prayed silently, her lips moving without sound, as the light crept closer and closer.

The room seemed to constrict as Orlok's shadow stretched across the walls, its edges twisting and writhing like living tendrils. The air grew colder, heavy with an oppressive energy that pressed against Ellen's chest, stealing her breath. She could feel his hunger, palpable and insatiable, as though it radiated from him in waves. Orlok loomed over her, his gaunt frame casting a darkness that seemed to swallow the faint glow of the lantern on the table.

"You cannot escape me," Orlok rasped, his voice low and guttural, reverberating through the room like the scrape of stone on stone. His clawed hand hovered just inches from her face, his elongated nails sharp and stained. "You are mine."

Ellen's body trembled, her instincts screaming for her to recoil, to flee. But she forced herself to stand still, her back pressed against the far wall. She could feel the faint warmth of the approaching dawn at her back, its fragile glow creeping through the edges of the drawn curtains. It was so close now, the light she had prayed for, but it wasn't here yet. She had to keep him distracted—keep him focused on her—until it was too late for him to escape.

"You're afraid of the light," she said, her voice trembling but defiant. "You hide from it because you know it will destroy you."

Orlok's head tilted, his hollow eyes narrowing as he studied her. For a moment, his expression was unreadable, but then his lips curled back into a cruel smile.

"The light," he sneered, his voice dripping with contempt. "It is nothing but a fleeting illusion. It cannot save you."

"Maybe not," Ellen said, her gaze steady despite the tears welling in her eyes. "But it will end you."

Orlok snarled, the sound deep and inhuman, his shadow seeming to swell and darken in response to his rising anger. He took a step closer, his long, spindly fingers reaching for her with a deliberate slowness that made her stomach churn. Ellen pressed herself tighter against the wall, her heart pounding as his cold presence enveloped her.

"You are brave, little flower," Orlok said, his tone mockingly tender. "But bravery will not save you. It only makes the feast sweeter."

Ellen swallowed hard, her fingers clutching the edges of her shawl.

"You'll never have what you want," she said, her voice steadier now. "You'll never take my soul."

Orlok paused, his head tilting further, his expression darkening.

"Your soul?" he repeated, his voice low and venomous. "Your soul means nothing to me. It is your light, your life, that I will consume."

He reached for her again, his clawed hand brushing against her shoulder. The touch was ice-cold, seeping through the fabric of her shawl and into her skin. Ellen gasped, her body stiffening as fear surged through her, but she forced herself to hold his gaze. She couldn't falter—not now, not when the dawn was so close.

A faint golden glow began to seep through the edges of the curtains, its warmth cutting through the suffocating chill of the room. Ellen felt it before she saw it, a fragile heat brushing against her back, filling her with a flicker of hope. The sun was rising.

Orlok froze, his body stiffening as the first rays of light touched the edges of the room. His head snapped toward the window, his hollow eyes narrowing in alarm.

"No," he hissed, his voice sharp and frantic. "It cannot be."

# Chapter 20

## The Writhing Horror

The air in the room seemed to still as the first ray of sunlight pierced through the heavy curtains. It was a narrow beam, golden and fragile, yet its mere touch upon the darkened space carried an undeniable power. The light stretched forward like a blade, cutting through the dense shadows that clung to the walls and floor. Ellen, trembling and exhausted, remained pressed against the far wall, her wide eyes locked on the grotesque figure of Count Orlok standing in the center of the room.

Orlok's hollow eyes darted toward the invading light, his expression freezing in a grotesque mixture of rage and fear. The predator, so composed in his unnatural confidence, faltered for the first time. His gaunt frame stiffened, his clawed hands twitching as though uncertain whether to flee or strike. The light crept closer, spilling across the wooden floor and licking at the edges of his shadow. The moment the beam grazed his foot, Orlok recoiled violently, his body convulsing as a deep, guttural roar escaped his throat.

Ellen took a shaky breath, her hands trembling as she reached up to grasp the edge of the curtain.

"You've taken so much," she said, her voice steady despite the tears streaming down her face. "But you won't take me. And you won't take this town."

With a swift, decisive motion, she pulled the curtain back, flooding the room with the full light of dawn. The golden rays spilled across the floor, illuminating the room in a brilliance that seemed almost otherworldly. Orlok recoiled violently, his shadow shrinking and twisting as the light engulfed him.

The sound was inhuman, a dreadful cacophony of agony and rage that shook the very air. It was not merely a scream—it was the death rattle of something that should never have existed. Orlok staggered back, his spindly arms flailing as if to push the light away. The beam widened, growing stronger as the sun rose higher, illuminating the room inch by inch. Ellen could feel the warmth of it on her skin, but it was a warmth that Orlok could not abide. The light clung to him like fire, and his form began to unravel.

"No!" he roared, his voice a guttural, inhuman cry that echoed through the house. His body convulsed, his limbs contorting in unnatural angles as the sunlight burned into him. Smoke began to rise from his skin, curling into the air in wisps that smelled of decay and sulfur.

Where the sunlight touched Orlok's flesh, his skin blackened and split, curling back like burnt paper to reveal a gray, desiccated underlayer. Thin cracks spiderwebbed across his face, his hollow cheeks collapsing inward as though the very essence of his being was crumbling. Smoke began to rise from his body in thin, acrid tendrils, carrying with it the stench of decay and burnt flesh. The odor was overwhelming, a nauseating mix of rot and sulfur that made Ellen gag, though she forced herself to remain still.

Orlok's movements became frantic, his tall, skeletal frame lurching from side to side as though seeking an escape. His clawed hands clawed at the air, at the walls, at the very light that burned him, but there was no refuge. His shadow, once vast and commanding, twisted and shrank, writhing against the walls like a dying serpent. It seemed to fight against the light as though it had a will of its own, but the sunlight consumed it piece by piece, leaving nothing behind.

Orlok hissed, his voice a rasping, guttural snarl. It was no longer the composed voice of the hunter but the desperate cry of the hunted.

"This cannot be… this cannot be!"

His words dissolved into another terrible scream as the light found his chest, tearing through the thin fabric of his coat and exposing the sunken cavity beneath. His ribs were visible, their jagged edges splitting apart like dry twigs as the sunlight burned deeper into him. The cracks in his skin widened, black veins spreading outward like poison through the pale landscape of his flesh.

Ellen watched, frozen in both terror and awe, as Orlok fell to his knees. His movements were no longer deliberate or predatory; they were frantic, chaotic, the thrashing of a cornered animal. His long fingers clawed at the floorboards, leaving deep gouges in the wood as smoke continued to rise from his body. His shadow, now reduced to a flickering fragment on the far wall, shrank and twisted until it disappeared entirely.

The room filled with the sound of his agony—the creak and snap of his bones splintering under the relentless assault of the light, the wet hiss of his flesh melting away, the guttural roars that reverberated like the echoes of a dying beast. Ellen felt her chest tighten as she witnessed the monstrous form before her collapse in on itself, his once-imposing stature reduced to a crumpled, writhing mass.

Orlok turned his face toward her, his once-hollow eyes now black pits that oozed a foul, dark liquid. His mouth opened, and though his teeth were still sharp and jagged, they seemed to crumble as he tried to speak.

"You…" he rasped, his voice barely audible above the sound of his own disintegration. "You did this…"

Ellen's lips parted, but no words came. She could only stare, her heart pounding as the sunlight continued its relentless assault, reducing the Count to something unrecognizable. His skin peeled away in strips, revealing the gray, crumbling bones beneath. His once-terrifying claws were now brittle stumps, cracking and breaking apart as he writhed in the growing pool of ash that was all that remained of his body.

Orlok's body convulsed one final time, his head snapping back as he let out a piercing, keening wail that seemed to reverberate through the very foundation of the house. His gaunt frame shuddered, collapsing inward as though some unseen force was pulling him into himself. The blackened remains of his skin flaked away, carried on an invisible wind, dissolving into nothingness.

The last rays of sunlight struck his chest, and with a deafening crack, his entire body crumbled. A cloud of ash erupted into the air, the fine particles hanging for a moment before settling onto the floor. The room fell silent. The oppressive weight of Orlok's presence was gone, replaced by an almost unbearable stillness.

Ellen sank to her knees, her trembling hands clutching at the edge of the windowsill for support. Her chest heaved as she struggled to catch her breath, her mind reeling from the horror she had just witnessed. The pile of ash on the floor was all that remained of the nightmare that had plagued Wisborg, a grim testament to the monster that had once stood there.

The sunlight filled the room now, warm and golden, its radiance washing over Ellen like a balm. It illuminated the ash, the gouges in the floor, the overturned chair. The house felt lighter, as though a great shadow had been lifted. But Ellen felt no relief, no triumph. She had won, yes—but at what cost?

She pressed a trembling hand to her chest, her heart aching with the weight of what had just transpired. Orlok was gone, but his presence lingered, an echo in the stillness of the house. Ellen closed her eyes, her tears falling silently as she whispered, "It's over."

But even as she said the words, she knew she would never be the same.

The morning sun bathed the town of Wisborg in a warm, golden light, a stark contrast to the heavy shadows that had plagued its streets for weeks. The oppressive darkness, once so suffocating, seemed to dissolve in the brightness of the new day. Yet, even as the light crept through the alleys and glinted off the rooftops, the silence in the town was deafening—a quiet so profound it seemed to hold its breath in anticipation.

Ellen remained on her knees in the room where Orlok had met his end, her body trembling with exhaustion. The pile of ash at the center of the floor was all that remained of him, the nightmare that had haunted her and her town. The scent of decay still lingered faintly in the air, but it was fading, replaced by the crisp, clean scent of the morning breeze wafting through the open window. She pressed her hand to her chest, feeling the unsteady rhythm of her heartbeat, and whispered to herself,

"It's over."

Outside, the light revealed a town that had been brought to its knees. The once-bustling streets were now empty, save for the remnants of the chaos that had unfolded there. Discarded belongings lay strewn across the cobblestones, doors hung ajar, and windows were shuttered tightly as though trying to keep out the specter of death. But something had changed—an almost imperceptible shift in the air that hinted at hope.

The rats, those filthy harbingers of plague, had vanished. Their chittering, which had once filled the night like a discordant symphony, was no more. The alleys that had been alive with their scurrying were now silent, their absence both eerie and relieving. It was as though the light of the sun had driven them away, purging the town of their disease-ridden presence.

In the homes where families huddled in fear, the first signs of recovery began to emerge. The sick, who had been pale and delirious with fever, stirred weakly from their beds, their breathing steadier and their eyes clearer. The plague's grip on their bodies was loosening, its relentless hold faltering in the face of whatever invisible force had been unleashed with the dawn. Mothers wept as they cradled their children, fathers fell to their knees in silent prayers of gratitude, and neighbors exchanged wary but hopeful glances.

From her vantage point at the window, Ellen watched the sunlight creep further into the town, its warm glow spilling over rooftops and bathing the marketplace in golden hues. She could see figures beginning to emerge cautiously from their homes, their faces pale and weary, their movements hesitant. They stepped into the light as though unsure if it was safe, their eyes scanning the streets for any lingering signs of the terror that had gripped them.

Ellen's lips trembled as she watched the people begin to gather, their voices low and uncertain. She could hear snippets of their conversation, fragments of disbelief and hope.

"The rats are gone," one man said, his voice thick with emotion. "Do you think it's over?"

"It has to be," a woman replied, clutching a small child to her chest. "The air feels different. Cleaner."

Ellen's hand pressed against the windowpane, her fingers trembling. She wanted to call out to them, to tell them that it truly was over, that the shadow had been banished. But her voice caught in her throat, and she could only watch as the townsfolk began to rebuild their courage, their tentative hope growing stronger with each passing moment.

The church bell, silent for so long, rang out suddenly, its deep, resonant tones carrying through the air. The sound startled Ellen, making her flinch, but it was a sound of life—a declaration that Wisborg was still standing. The bell's toll seemed to awaken something in the townsfolk, and more people emerged from their homes, their cautious steps growing bolder.

Ellen saw a young boy run into the square, his laughter bright and startling against the quiet. A group of women followed, their faces streaked with tears but their expressions filled with relief. Even the air seemed lighter, as though the town itself was breathing freely for the first time in weeks.

But not everything was as it had been. The scars of the plague remained etched into the town like an open wound. Empty homes stood as silent reminders of those who had been lost, their doors marked with black crosses. The marketplace, once so vibrant, was subdued, its stalls empty and its cobblestones stained with the remnants of chaos. Yet, amid the sorrow, there was a flicker of determination—a collective understanding that life would go on.

Ellen leaned heavily against the windowsill, her body weak and trembling. The sunlight that bathed the town felt warm against her skin, but it also seemed to sap the last remnants of her strength. She closed her eyes, her breaths shallow, and let the sounds of the town wash over her—the low hum of conversation, the tolling of the bell, the distant cries of children.

She had done it. She had faced the darkness and emerged victorious. But the weight of her sacrifice was heavy, and she could feel it pressing down on her with every passing moment. Her limbs felt leaden, her chest tight, and her vision blurred as exhaustion overtook her.

As she sank to her knees, her hand slipping from the windowsill, Ellen whispered a silent prayer. It wasn't for herself but for the town she had saved, for the people who would carry on. Her sacrifice had been worth it. The plague was lifting, the rats were gone, and Wisborg would heal.

But deep within her heart, Ellen knew that she would not be part of that healing. Her role was done, her light spent. And as the golden glow of the morning filled the room, she let herself drift into the stillness, a faint smile on her lips.

The sunlight filled the room now, golden and warm, banishing every shadow that had once lingered within its walls. The house, so long cloaked in fear and dread, felt lighter, as if it were breathing again for the first time. Ellen knelt by the window, her pale hands resting on the floorboards, trembling from exhaustion. She could feel the warmth of the sun on her face, soft and comforting, but it was a distant thing, a fading ember in the growing chill that overtook her body.

Her breaths came shallow and uneven, each one a labor as her strength ebbed away. She had given everything to stop the shadow that had consumed Wisborg, everything to banish the darkness that had taken root in her town. And now, as she gazed out at the streets bathed in sunlight, she knew her sacrifice had not been in vain.

Ellen's body felt heavy, as though the very act of holding herself upright required all the strength she had left. Her limbs were weak, her hands trembling as she tried to push herself up. But the effort was too much. Her knees buckled, and she slumped to the floor, her head resting against the cool wood. She closed her eyes for a moment, letting the sounds of the town wash over her—the distant tolling of the church bell, the faint murmur of voices, the hesitant laughter of children.

A faint smile touched her lips. She had done it. Orlok was gone, his shadow destroyed by the dawn. The plague was lifting, the rats had disappeared, and the people of Wisborg would rebuild. They would heal. She had given them that chance, and it was enough.

But as her body grew colder, her breaths slower, Ellen knew she would not be there to see it.

From the bedroom, Thomas stirred, the warmth of the morning sun coaxing him awake. His body ached with exhaustion, but his heart was lighter than it had been in weeks. Something had changed—he could feel it. The suffocating weight of the shadow that had loomed over Wisborg was gone, replaced by a sense of peace that felt almost foreign.

He sat up, rubbing his eyes, and called out,

"Ellen?" His voice carried through the quiet house, but no reply came. A prickle of unease crept over him, and he swung his legs over the side of the bed, standing on unsteady feet. "Ellen?" he called again, louder this time, as he made his way toward the parlor.

When he reached the doorway, he froze.

Ellen lay on the floor near the window, her body bathed in the soft light of the morning. Her face was pale, her eyes closed, and her chest rose and fell with shallow, labored breaths. The sight of her there, so still and fragile, sent a bolt of fear through Thomas's heart.

"Ellen!" he cried, rushing to her side. He dropped to his knees, his hands shaking as he touched her shoulder. "Ellen, what happened? Speak to me!"

Her eyes fluttered open at the sound of his voice, her gaze unfocused but filled with a quiet peace.

"Thomas," she whispered, her voice barely audible. "You're here."

"I'm here," he said, his voice breaking. He cradled her head in his hands, his tears falling onto her pale cheeks. "Ellen, what's wrong? What's happening?"

She reached up with trembling fingers, brushing them lightly against his face.

"It's over," she murmured. "The shadow is gone. Wisborg is safe."

Thomas stared at her, his heart pounding in his chest.

"What do you mean? What shadow? Ellen, you're not making sense."

But Ellen only smiled faintly, her hand falling back to her side.

"I had to do it," she said, her voice growing weaker. "I had to stop him. For you. For everyone."

Thomas shook his head, his tears falling freely.

"No," he said, his voice cracking. "You didn't have to do this. We could have faced it together."

"You weren't meant to face this," Ellen said softly. "It had to be me. Only me."

Her breathing grew more labored, her chest rising and falling with effort. Thomas held her closer, his arms wrapped around her as though he could keep her with him through sheer will alone.

"Don't leave me," he whispered, his voice broken. "Please, Ellen. Don't leave me."

Ellen's lips trembled, her eyes closing briefly before she forced them open again.

"You have to live," she said. "You have to rebuild. Promise me, Thomas."

"I promise," he said, his voice barely above a whisper. "But I need you. I can't do this without you."

Ellen's gaze softened, a single tear slipping down her cheek.

"You're stronger than you know," she said. "And you'll carry me with you. Always."

Her eyes fluttered closed, her body growing still in his arms. Thomas felt the moment her breathing stopped, the light in her fading as the first true peace she had known in weeks claimed her. He clung to her, his sobs shaking his body, as the sunlight continued to pour into the room, warm and unyielding.

Outside, the people of Wisborg began to gather in the streets, their voices rising in cautious hope. They spoke of the disappearing rats, the easing of the plague, the sudden lightness in the air. They did not know what had happened, did not know the sacrifice that had been made to save them, but they felt its effects nonetheless.

The church bell rang again, its tolling a signal that life would go on. The villagers embraced one another, their faces streaked with tears but their eyes filled with determination. Wisborg would rebuild. It would heal. And though they did not yet understand the cost of their salvation, they would soon learn the name of the woman who had given everything for them.

Thomas sat by the window, holding Ellen's lifeless body in his arms as the sunlight bathed them both. His tears fell silently now, his grief a deep, unrelenting ache. But amid the sorrow, there was a glimmer of something else—something that Ellen had left behind. It was her love, her courage, her unyielding resolve to protect the people she cared for. It was the light that had saved Wisborg.

Thomas closed his eyes, his forehead resting against Ellen's, and whispered,

"Thank you."

The sun rose higher, its golden rays spilling across the town and chasing away the last remnants of the shadow. And though Ellen was gone, her sacrifice would never be forgotten.

# Chapter 21
## Mourning

The sunlight blanketed Wisborg in a warm embrace, a stark contrast to the oppressive gloom that had gripped the town for what felt like an eternity. The golden light seeped into every corner of the streets, illuminating the broken shutters, the blackened crosses painted on doorways, and the pale, weary faces of those who had survived. Yet, even in its brilliance, the light could not erase the grief that now settled over the town like a veil.

Ellen's death had become the whispered truth that spread through the streets with quiet urgency. At first, there was disbelief. How could someone so full of life, so steadfast and brave, be gone? But as neighbors spoke in hushed tones of her final sacrifice, the reality of her passing settled heavily in their hearts. Those who had glimpsed the horror that had taken root in Wisborg understood that Ellen had faced it alone, offering herself to the shadow so that the rest of them might live.

The church bell tolled late that morning, its deep, mournful notes reverberating through the town. It was a sound that once would have signaled the death of another victim of the plague, but today it carried a different weight—a call to gather, to remember, and to grieve. The villagers emerged from their homes slowly, their faces pale and drawn, their steps hesitant. Though the rats were gone and the air felt lighter, the scars of the plague were etched into their expressions.

They gathered in the square, a small, somber crowd standing in the shadow of the church steeple. Children clung to their mothers' skirts, their eyes wide with confusion, while the adults spoke in low voices, their words tinged with sorrow and reverence.

"She was a brave soul," one man murmured, his voice breaking. "She gave herself so we could see this day."

"Ellen Hutter," said another, wiping her tears with a corner of her apron. "She's the reason we're still here. The reason we're alive."

A young boy, no older than eight, held his mother's hand tightly and asked,

"Will the shadow come back?" His voice trembled with fear, his gaze darting toward the empty windows of the abandoned manor by the river.

His mother knelt down, cupping his face in her hands.

"No," she said firmly, though tears filled her eyes. "The shadow is gone. Ellen made sure of it."

While the townsfolk gathered in the square, Thomas remained at Ellen's grave, unable to leave her side. Her resting place was simple—a patch of freshly turned earth on a quiet rise overlooking the river. A single white lily, plucked from the small garden she had tended, rested atop the soil. The wind whispered through the trees, carrying with it the faintest scent of wildflowers and the murmur of the river below.

Thomas knelt by the grave, his hands resting on the cool earth. His body trembled, his shoulders hunched as though the weight of his grief were too much to bear. He had barely spoken since that morning, when he had found her lifeless body bathed in sunlight, her face serene, her sacrifice complete. The sight of her like that—so still, so final—had torn something irreparable from him.

He traced his fingers along the edge of the grave, his mind replaying the events of the past days in vivid, unbearable detail. He saw her smile, the quiet resolve in her eyes when she told him she loved him. He heard her voice, trembling but steady, as she reassured him that everything would be all right. And he felt the hollow ache in his chest as he realized she had known all along what she would do.

"You saved them," Thomas whispered, his voice hoarse and broken. "You saved me. But at what cost?"

He closed his eyes, his forehead resting against the earth. The tears came slowly at first, then in a torrent, shaking his body as he wept for the woman who had been his light in the darkness. He thought of all the moments they would never share, the life they had dreamed of but would never have. And yet, amid the anguish, there was a faint glimmer of pride—pride in the courage she had shown, in the love she had poured into her final act.

"I'll make sure they remember you," Thomas murmured, his voice barely audible. "I'll make sure they know what you did. You'll never be forgotten."

The days that followed were quiet but determined. The people of Wisborg, though battered and broken, began the slow, arduous process of rebuilding their lives. The black crosses that marked so many doorways were scrubbed away, though the memories of the lives lost would remain etched into the hearts of the survivors. Families buried their dead, their grief tempered by the knowledge that the plague had finally loosened its grip on the town.

The marketplace reopened, though its once-bustling stalls were sparse and subdued. Farmers and merchants returned cautiously, their wagons laden with the bare necessities of food and supplies. The townsfolk, pale and weary, traded their meager goods with quiet words and cautious smiles. It was a tentative step toward normalcy, a fragile hope that life would go on.

The children, who had been kept indoors for weeks, began to

venture outside once more. Their laughter, hesitant at first, grew stronger with each passing day. They played in the square and chased one another through the alleys, their joy a balm to the wounds of the town. The sound of their laughter brought tears to the eyes of many, a reminder that even in the darkest times, life would find a way.

But the scars of the plague were not easily forgotten. Empty homes stood as silent reminders of those who had been lost, their windows dark and their doors locked. The townsfolk moved through the streets with a quiet solemnity, their joy tempered by the weight of their grief. They spoke often of Ellen, her name whispered with reverence and gratitude.

"She faced the shadow alone," an old woman said one morning, her voice trembling with emotion. "She gave herself so we could live."

"And we must honor her," replied the village priest, his hands clasped in prayer. "Not just with words, but with our lives. We must rebuild. We must remember."

For Thomas, the days passed in a haze of grief and determination. He threw himself into the work of rebuilding, repairing homes and clearing debris from the streets. It was hard, grueling labor, but it kept his mind occupied, giving him purpose in a world that felt emptier without Ellen by his side.

"I see you everywhere," he whispered one morning, his gaze fixed on the horizon. "In the sunlight, in the laughter of the children. You're still here, Ellen. I can feel you."

And though the ache in his chest never truly lessened, Thomas found strength in the legacy she had left behind. Ellen had been the light in the darkness, the spark that had banished the shadow. And though she was gone, her sacrifice would live on in the hearts of Wisborg's people, a testament to the power of love, courage, and hope.

The days following Ellen's death passed in a blur for Thomas. Time seemed to stretch and fold in on itself, the hours bleeding together in an endless cycle of grief and hollow routine. He woke each morning to the warmth of the sun streaming through the window, a cruel reminder of the light Ellen had given her life to summon. The golden glow that had once brought him comfort now felt like a blade twisting in his chest, cutting deeper with each sunrise.

Each day, Thomas made his pilgrimage to her grave. The path to the hill was well-trodden now, the grass worn thin by his frequent visits. He carried with him small tokens—a flower from their garden, a stone he'd found near the river, a book she used to love—and left them at her resting place as though they might bridge the chasm between life and death.

Kneeling by the mound of earth, Thomas would trace the edges of the single white lily that lay atop it, his fingers trembling as he spoke to her. His voice was raw, his words fractured by the weight of his sorrow.

"I don't know how to do this without you," he confessed one morning, his tears falling freely. "Every corner of this house, every street in this town—it all feels empty now."

He paused, his gaze drifting to the horizon where the river glinted in the sunlight.

"You saved us," he whispered. "You saved me. But I don't know how to keep going without you."

The silence that followed his words was unbearable, a void that seemed to stretch endlessly. The wind whispered through the trees, carrying with it the faintest echoes of laughter, of joy, of life. But to Thomas, it felt distant and unreachable.

Though the plague had lifted and life in Wisborg was slowly returning to normal, a heaviness remained in the hearts of its people. The townsfolk spoke often of Ellen's bravery, her selfless act that had saved them from the shadow. Her name was woven into their prayers, her story retold around hearths and in the quiet of the marketplace. Yet, for all their reverence, there was an undercurrent of unease that no amount of sunlight could dispel.

Some villagers claimed to feel a presence in the dead of night, a coldness that seeped into their homes even as the days grew warmer. Others spoke of dreams—strange, unsettling visions of hollow eyes watching from the darkness, of long, clawed hands reaching out from the shadows. The children, so quick to find joy again, would occasionally fall silent, their laughter cut short by an inexplicable fear.

One night, Thomas sat alone in the house he and Ellen had shared, the quiet pressing against him like a physical weight. The faint creak of the floorboards, the rustle of the curtains in the breeze—it all felt amplified, as though the house itself were holding its breath. He lit a candle and carried it to the window, gazing out at the town bathed in moonlight.

The streets were empty, the windows dark, but Thomas couldn't shake the feeling that something lingered just beyond his sight. It wasn't Orlok—of that, he was certain. The Count was gone, destroyed by the dawn. But the shadow he had cast, the darkness he had brought to Wisborg, seemed to have left an indelible mark.

As Thomas stared into the night, the flame of his candle flickered, casting jagged shadows on the walls. For a brief moment, one shadow seemed to stretch further than it should, its edges twisting unnaturally. Thomas blinked, his breath catching in his throat, and the shadow was gone. He told himself it was his imagination, a trick of the light. But the unease settled deep in his chest, refusing to be dismissed.

The people of Wisborg continued to rebuild, their determination a testament to their resilience. The marketplace began to thrive again, the church bell rang regularly, and the fields surrounding the town turned green with new life. Yet, the shadow of what had transpired lingered, a specter that could not be entirely banished by the sunlight.

At night, the villagers still barred their windows and lit candles to chase away the darkness. The abandoned manor by the river remained untouched, its windows broken and its walls draped in ivy. No one dared to approach it, and even the children, with all their curiosity, gave it a wide berth. It stood as a silent reminder of the nightmare they had endured, its empty halls echoing with the memory of the shadow.

Thomas, too, felt the weight of the past pressing down on him. He continued his work in the town, helping to rebuild homes and mend broken lives, but his own heart remained fractured. He could feel Ellen's absence in every breath he took, every step he walked. Her sacrifice had saved them all, but it had left him hollow.

One evening, as the sun dipped below the horizon and the first stars began to appear, Thomas returned to her grave. He sat beside it in the fading light, his hands resting on the earth. The world around him grew quiet, the stillness of the night settling over the town like a blanket.

"I'll carry you with me," he said softly, his voice breaking. "Every day, in everything I do. I'll make sure they remember you. I'll make sure they remember what you gave for them."

As he spoke, the wind stirred, rustling the leaves of the trees and carrying with it the faintest whisper of her name. It was a fleeting sound, almost imperceptible, but Thomas heard it. He looked up, his heart pounding, but there was no one there. Only the night, vast and unyielding.

For a moment, he thought he saw a shadow move at the edge of the graveyard, a flicker of darkness against the silver light of the moon. But when he blinked, it was gone. He stared into the distance, his mind racing, and then forced himself to turn away.

The shadow was gone, he told himself. Ellen had destroyed it. But deep down, a part of him wondered if some fragments of it had remained, buried deep in the cracks of the world. A memory. An echo. A reminder that the darkness, though banished, was never truly gone.

As Thomas rose to leave, the wind stirred again, colder this time, carrying with it a faint unease. He shivered, pulling his coat tighter around him, and began the walk back to the house. Behind him, the graveyard fell silent once more, bathed in the pale glow of the moon.

And somewhere, far beyond the reach of Wisborg's light, the

shadows stretched long, waiting for their time to rise again.

# About The Author

Jonathan Miller is an accomplished media scholar, educator, and storyteller with decades of experience in communication and media studies. Born and raised in the Midwest, Jonathan's fascination with storytelling and visual media began in childhood, inspired by classic films, television shows, and the rich tradition of gothic literature. This early passion evolved into a lifelong dedication to exploring the intersections of culture, technology, and narrative.

*Nosferatu: A Symphony of Horror* marks Jonathan's debut as a novelist, blending his academic expertise with his love for atmospheric, gothic storytelling. This novel reimagines the haunting tale of Nosferatu for modern readers while preserving the eerie tone and timeless themes of the original 1922 silent film. Jonathan's approach to writing is deeply influenced by his background in media studies, as well as his fascination with the psychological and cultural impact of classic horror stories.

When not writing or teaching, Jonathan enjoys exploring cinematic history, mentoring aspiring creators, and traveling to places rich with narrative inspiration. He lives in the United States with his family, where he continues to combine his academic pursuits with his passion for storytelling.

Printed in Dunstable, United Kingdom